EVERYWHERE IN CHAINS

EVERYWHERE IN CHAINS

A Novel

By

James Casper

IGNATIUS PRESS   SAN FRANCISCO

Cover photographs © iStockphoto.com

Cover design by John Herreid

© 2013 by Ignatius Press, San Francisco
All rights reserved
ISBN 978-1-58617-821-5
Library of Congress Control Number 2013941178
Printed in the United States of America ∞

In loving memory of my parents,
Holly Joseph Casper and Marion Valerie Casper

Contents

Part One
The Severed Hand

How good was proved the heart that is in blameless Penelope.
—Homer, *The Odyssey*

The Mouse in the Wall

Lake Superior is the largest, deepest, and coldest of the five Great Lakes. The other four emptied into its basin would leave room and then some for the ten thousand and more lakes Minnesota claims within its borders. Lake Superior's water could cover North and South America with a wading pool nine inches deep. Agates of exceptional beauty are strewn along its beaches, with pebbles worn smooth by the action of its waves. Its rock is the oldest on the face of the earth. From most points on its shoreline of over two thousand miles, its opposite shore cannot be seen.

Like any ocean, this vast lake encourages speculation and wonderment. It has its own folklore and mysteries; its ghosts and ghost ships; its own *Flying Dutchman*; and its pirates, sea shanties, and even a few mermaids. Its depths, darker than the darkest nights, are littered with shipwrecks and human remains preserved in water too cold to support bacterial decay. Here science and superstition agree: This lake truly never gives up its dead. Its drowned mariners have no graves but the lake. Their names can be found inscribed on plaques, like the one destroyed in a Bell Harbor church fire fifteen years ago. St. John Vianney Church was soon rebuilt in a modern design. The plaque bearing names no one alive could remember, from two shipwrecks nearly a century ago, was never replaced.

Not all of Lake Superior's well-kept secrets lie inscrutably in its cold, dark depths, the stuff of speculation, legend, and sea song. Some are within easier reach on shore in the light of day but equally unknown. One is to be found in the cheery company of Sister Hilaria and her third graders at St. John Vianney School adjacent the new church. Almost a generation of eight-year-olds have stowed their snow boots and hung their coats and scarves beneath the high shelf holding a brown cardboard box among three others of the same color, size, and shape, one to its right and two to its left.

The names of school subjects written on the boxes suggest they contain old textbooks and outdated teaching materials. Three of them do. Sister Hilaria is tall enough to reach them without aid of stool or stepladder, but she has been busy with her students, happy with the textbooks in hand, and till now has never bothered. After eight years at St. John Vianney School, she is being transferred. She intends to do some spring cleaning and straightening up before handing over her classroom to her replacement. She has her eyes on the boxes, layered with the dust of many school years, and a few odds and ends her pupils have tossed up there and forgotten.

Sister Hilaria soon discovers that the box second to the right marked "Geography" contains no textbooks, but instead what appear to be the broken pieces of an elaborate, hand-forged weather vane. Underneath this jumble is a white envelope bearing a blackened scorch mark on one corner as if meant to be burned, or perhaps it had been pulled from a fire by someone who reconsidered, or perhaps it is one of those inexplicable survivors of an inferno. How such things came to be stored in her classroom is beyond imagining.

The envelope holds a letter torn in two. Sister trembles as she holds its two sides together and attempts to read it. She herself thinks of burning it, for it describes what only two men could know for certain. One, the father of a former student, is in prison. The other is dead. Just two Sundays ago, the second Sunday of Lent, his passing was announced in church. What she holds in hand is too late to change anything. It might not have mattered regardless, but perhaps here is the spark that ignited the match that set fire to the church. The inexplicable at last has been explained.

As Sister Hilaria so often says, *Not everything we will never know is unknowable. Some things are just never discovered.* But some secrets gnaw like the mouse she hears from time to time in a wall of the convent visitor's parlor. What is it doing in there day by day? Is it trying to find its way out?

Perhaps it knows a time has come to awaken and explore. Migrations will soon begin. A voice seems to urge: *Repair the net and the line! Restore the broken connection! Find the lost mitten in the melting snow and bring it home to the other!*

Along the north shore of Lake Superior, ice still extends out as far as the eye can see, but not much farther. From her classroom windows Sister Hilaria sees the ice and mist as a thick gray line hugging the horizon over open water beyond the ice. It might be mistaken for a cloud, but the day is bright with sunshine.

She knows what she must do.

Easter is little more than a week away. Inland, snowdrifts are becoming puddles, rain has already pattered on roofs, shirtfronts appear from unzipped jackets, and the Bell Harbor *Sentinel's* front page reports a first robin sighting. Beyond the horizon in waters frozen only in the coldest winters, the Great Lakes shipping season has already begun, with taconite boats toiling northeast toward Sault Ste. Marie, meeting freighters on their way to Duluth-Superior Harbor to be loaded with last year's harvest. Icebreakers have created a pathway. Sunlight has done the rest.

At Lighthouse Consolidated High School, perched on a hillside above the lake, the day ends with yet another surprise, a question out of nowhere and an answer having nowhere from which to come. Words seem to echo and reverberate as words do in hollow places and empty spaces, some words in particular.

"So, where is your *real* dad?"

"At the sawmill."

"No, not Marvin, the *other* one!"

It seems like forever before Penelope can think of much of an answer. Never in her life had she been asked this most natural of questions. The world till now has been keeping her father, *the other one*, a secret.

The mouse gnaws. Another time is at hand.

"I ... I don't remember", Penelope says, turning away.

Ninth grader Jackie Rae clicks her tongue, gives Penelope a knowing look, then hoists a book bag over her shoulder, almost brushing Penelope's face with it. Jackie darts away to catch her bus, fortunately not the same bus as Penelope's.

Penelope's father, her *real* father, is never discussed when Penelope is near. He has to be an old story by now, the kind found in a yellowed newspaper stuffed between cracks to keep the chill out. She cannot believe anybody ever talks about him, even when she isn't in the next room and close enough to hear. Yet if nobody ever talks about him, what made Jackie ask? Who had been talking, and what had Jackie overheard?

One question leads to another and then to another and soon becomes a cascade of springtime melting. Penelope's father is still alive as far as she knows, but even had he died, nobody would have told her. He is in prison somewhere, but she doesn't know where. *Why is he there? What had he done? Would he ever get out? Did he ever think of her?* Once she started thinking about him, where would it lead? It's true she doesn't remember him, but she feels as if she *does*, making it even stranger. Whenever Penelope thinks about her father, she seems to be in two places at the same time, but more aware of one of them. The one of which she is least aware scares her more with its strange, magnetic attraction.

2

The Black Mask

Staring out a school bus window on her way home, Penelope tried to think of something else. This had the usual effect of being able to think of *nothing* else. The world had become a blur, with her father the center of it. The bus was speeding more quickly than any bus can go, traveling like a spaceship through time to a destination behind her somewhere. Whatever was out there stayed a blur even when the bus stopped to let someone off. Twenty voices talking at once and the low, floor-shaking roar of the bus could not drown out the echoes of questions she was unable to answer. Out there somewhere was a man beyond imagining except for his severed hand.

In one of Penelope's baby pictures, cut in half, there remained a hand resting on the railing of her crib. It had to be her father's hand, pointing to her upturned face aglow in a swath of sunlight.

The bus rumbled past thick stands of jack pines and water-filled ditches along both sides of the road. In another mile or so it would turn off this road onto another leading to Penelope's home on Star Island. Penelope straightened the pile of school books in her lap and balanced on top of it a coat button that had come loose when she pulled on a thread. She ought to have known pulling on loose ends almost always leads to stray buttons.

The only time Penelope had asked about her prison father, her mother had said, "Forget about him. It never happened."

But if "it" never happened, what was there to forget? Being told to forget about something that never happened had twisted into a knot winding back on itself.

The bus stopped at a railroad crossing where these days there were never any trains. If there never had been trains, why was it there, and why did the bus stop? With most of the snow gone, Penelope could

see last summer's dead grass folded over and flattened against blackened timbers between rusty rails that *had* to lead somewhere. Yet like
thoughts of her father, they seemed never to lead anywhere.

To Penelope's left beyond a line of brush and piles of blue-gray
boulders was a lake the color of her eyes and, like her thoughts this
afternoon, invisible under a dark layer of thawing ice and gathering
mist. After crossing the railroad tracks, the bus stopped a dozen times,
and now it was quieter around her. Penelope knew without looking
back that a line of cars would be following. Weekdays, the bus rides
to and from school were almost always the same. They were like something memorized and stuck in her mind. She knew what was next
before it happened. This day, though, was unlike any other. Inserted
between things known by heart, under the skin, was something
unknown yet painful like a sliver bound to throb and fester.

At last, where houses were farther apart, the highway straighter,
and where there were but few resorts, cars would be able to pass. By
the time Penelope's bus got to the Star Island turnoff, she would be
the last one on it. Home was on the end of the school route beyond
a narrow causeway of boulders, rocky rubble, and an old board bridge
joining Star Island to its Minnesota mainland.

A long time ago Star Island had been a real island, but over time it
had become a peninsula and was no more a real island than Marvin
was her real father. The difference was that people still called the place
Star Island, and nobody ever asked if it was real or not.

In the beginning she had been Penelope Hall, daughter of Warren
Hall. Now she was Penelope Lister, ever since her mother's second
husband had adopted her long ago. At least as far as school records
were concerned, Marvin had always been her father. She had been
Penelope Lister on every one of her report cards, ten of them, including this year and kindergarten.

She might have said to anyone, "It's okay. Really, it's okay."

Penelope said that about many things other than the main thing,
and much of the time she meant it.

Somehow Penelope's mother had ignored, forgotten, or despaired
of the fact that her prison dad had also named her Penelope. Back
further in the blur, this had been his grandmother's name. Back much
further Penelope was the name of a woman in a story by a blind poet
named Homer. A portion of *The Odyssey* had been assigned reading

in an English class, and when Penelope's name came up in a teacher's lecture, everyone turned to look at her.

Homer's Penelope had waited many years for her husband to return from a war. She had been faithful to him, strong, and patient until he did return at last. Penelope had yet to read all of *The Odyssey*, but hearing this much reinforced a sort of obstinate pride she took in her name. She absolutely rejected occasional attempts to call her Penny. She would never be Penny. Even when some people pronounced Penelope wrong and grinned as if the mistake were hers for having a name that looked like it rhymed with antelope, better that than Penny.

Penelope could not explain why she guarded her name so fiercely. She thought it important to be faithful, strong, and patient, but long before the day she first heard of *The Odyssey*, she wore her name like a badge of honor and a duty without knowing for what or for whom she was waiting.

Whatever happened to her father had *really* happened and could not be erased by simply saying, "Forget about it." Everywhere she could see reminders and gaps left by what had been.

Over a garage door, the bolt holes in a rectangular patch marked the location of her father's welding shop sign. After all these years the patch was still noticeably less weathered than the wood around it. Down a trail behind the house, in an abandoned family dump, the sign with paint flaking off it leaned against a tree. A pile of old tires hid it from view on one side, and a set of rusty bed springs blocked her way from the other. She could read her father's name through bed spring coils. Above all that, in a crotch of the tree, her father's black welding mask had been wedged. It faced her each time she came down the path, as if her father himself stood there facing her, waiting for her to say something and keeping quiet till she remembered him one day.

How could her mother say, "Forget about it"? How could she cut her baby picture in half and not notice the severed hand? How could she change her last name and leave her first? More surprising than the things her mother thought of were the things she did not think of, such as disguising her birthday present in a box three times the size of it so she would be surprised while leaving the credit card slip in full view on the washing machine downstairs.

Penelope would say, "It's okay. Really, it's okay."

Was it possible her mother really did want her to notice little details such as receipts, and that is why she left certain things around? Some of these items could be clues to a mystery she was supposed to solve.

One clue perhaps was the Listers' mailbox, with its two bullet holes. Otherwise it could look like any other mailbox when it leaned in the usual manner from snow heaved against it by plows clearing the Star Island Road. With its squeaking hinge, it could sound like any other. It was the same mailbox from the very beginning, when she had lived here with her father and her mother and then alone with her mother, not remembering any of those years. Her first memories included Marvin, as if he too had been with them from the very beginning, and the severed hand in the picture was supposed to be his.

Marvin built his pole barn and redesigned the turnaround so that it met the island road at a different spot. Still the mailbox stayed where it had always been, with "Lister" painted over the name she was supposed to forget, which showed through more and more as the years went by till it was almost easy to read. Wouldn't her mother get another mailbox if she were really supposed to forget her other father, the real one?

In older parts of the family photo album, fasteners marked the corners where snapshots of him had been removed. Why remove the pictures and leave the empty spaces for her to imagine what had been there? Aunt Charlotte, her father's sister, remained in what was left of the picture cut in half. Her hand, extended over the crib railing, nearly touched his. She was all he had for family unless Penelope could still be counted. How could *his own daughter* not be counted, along with Aunt Charlotte, who lived in Bell Harbor no more than three blocks from Penelope's school?

Penelope was never supposed to visit Charlotte. She was supposed to avoid Charlotte as if she carried around a deadly disease, and yet here Charlotte was in the family photo album, smiling at Penelope while spreading germs. If Charlotte ever wrote her dad, Penelope wondered, did he write back? Did she sometimes visit him in his prison?

Forget Aunt Charlotte, but there she was one afternoon on a Bell Harbor sidewalk as Penelope's school bus crept by her in a row of cars. The woman carrying a guitar case was unmistakably Penelope's aunt. Her carrot red hair was the same as in the picture and the same as Penelope's hair. With her fingertips out of sight below the window ledge, Penelope had even waved. How could Penelope be told she should never see someone whose hair was the same odd color as hers? How could she ignore Aunt Charlotte, who maybe played a guitar?

Searching on a school computer, Penelope had learned that prisoners could write letters and have visitors. This privilege was not available to her dad where his daughter was concerned; there was not supposed to be any communication between them, ever. Was he supposed to forget her, just as she was supposed to forget him? If it were so important for them to forget each other, why was the court order preventing their communication left in the drawer of a china cabinet for Penelope to read any time? Why did it say that such communication would be too disturbing and confusing for her in her formative years?

Here Penelope was in her formative years, and instead what had become disturbing and confusing was that she was supposed to forget him because an attorney had argued it might impair her in forming a loving relationship with her stepfather, Marvin Lister.

Having a loving relationship with Marvin was the easy part, and it did not require pretending her father had never existed. Marvin wasn't what people might expect, given all the horror stories about stepparents. He seemed more like an uncle. She would have been happy to call him Uncle Marvin instead of Dad as her mother insisted, and he would have been happy to be called that.

Marvin never shooed her away the minute the telephone rang for him. When he answered, he would say, "Hang on a minute", and while he held his hand over the speaker, he finished what he was saying or finished listening to what she was saying. Marvin was as easygoing as chewing gum, the pink stuff he not only tolerated but seemed to enjoy watching her soften up and work into a glorious, sweet bubble with the patience of a glassblower.

Marvin's face kept its easy, absentminded grin even while she peeled the gummy explosion off hers. He never glared at her across the dinner table when a pea rolled off her fork. He knew he had a lapful of his own peas. He was the all-time sloppiest eater, this coming from sheer awkwardness, not piggish tendencies. Marvin was as lean, straight up and down, and disproportionate as a giraffe. He reached for things out of reach as if, tall as he was and long as his arms were, he had yet to figure out his true dimensions.

Marvin never bothered Penelope about homework or anything else. He was all grins and no frowns. Most of the time he was every bit as cheerful and hopeful as he looked, though if he had a bad day at work, she could always tell. He wasn't a very good actor.

If she seemed bored, he might even point to the door and say, "Should we go for a walk? It will help you pass the time."

Marvin loved to hike along the lake and repeat tales of superstition, shipwreck, and logjams passed along by old-timers he knew from working at the sawmill. With arms too long for his jacket and legs too long for his jeans, he seemed constructed for scrambling over driftwood and boulders. He brushed his hair every morning, gray streaks and all, and ten minutes later, a straight hank of it would already be down on his forehead, dancing over his nose. By noon his part had disappeared.

Marvin was a year or two from fifty, making him about six years older than Penelope's mother, whose name was June. Yet much of the time June seemed to treat him like an older child of hers. She pulled him left when he was trying to go right and urged him to sit up straight when he wanted to slouch. Marvin didn't mind or at least never showed that he did.

He could laugh at himself when he looked in a mirror or at a picture someone had just taken. His close-set blue eyes were forever squinting, whether on bright days or in gray evenings at their kitchen table, where he liked to sit long after supper, leafing through his antique car magazines. Sometimes he gave out a short whistle when he found something he particularly liked in the want ads.

Old cars were Marvin's passion. He owned fifteen, some of them jalopies, but in his eyes all were antiques and classics. He treated each like a prize won in a raffle on a lucky day or like a trophy won in a contest where his persistence had paid off. Every car in his collection came with a story about how he came by it. Repeating the story, he would lick his lips as if living the adventure all over again. This in turn would remind him of related tales involving the near misses, mischances, instances of blind luck, and ironies of car collecting. Sometimes he seemed to relish these stories even more than the cars themselves. He might look at a calendar page near the kitchen table first thing in the morning and say, "It was five years ago I picked up the Desoto at an estate auction."

Marvin, who said things like "by gosh" and "yup", had always been good to Penelope. At table, he passed things to her first without exception, even when his nephews were visiting. He let her go into the pole barn and sit in any of his antique cars, whether he was around or not.

He bought her a rabbit, and when it got out of its cage one night and was killed by an owl, he helped her bury it and bought her another one. Everything was fine between her and Marvin. It just struck her as strange to have his name. It was like wearing shoes on the wrong feet. It felt more natural to be growing up with Marvin as her father, even if he wasn't her real father, than to have his last name.

The only time she and her mother ever talked about it was by accident when Penelope answered the phone one afternoon and someone using an old mailing list asked for Mrs. Hall.

"Get used to it. It's what happens to women", her mother said. "Someday your name will probably change again." This sounded like a warning.

June Lister worked long days in Bell Harbor, more or less managing an insurance agency without ever being given that position. Everyone doing insurance business there knew that if you had an important question or wanted something done right, you should ask for June when you called or came in, even if the owner himself answered the phone or was sitting alone in his office. June was a quiet, terse, and methodical sort who always changed her clothes when she got home from work. Anything not going into the wash was hung precisely where it had been in the morning. Then she would often turn to insurance matters left over from her day at work. When it came to much else at home, she seemed to lose a firm grip on the efficient ways that made her a mainstay in the Bell Harbor insurance business and its owner the envy of other agents in town.

She might have smiled her professional smile while churning through a ten-hour day when anything and everything came up, but at home she seemed to struggle with details. Spontaneity, affection, and even notes under refrigerator magnets were beyond her. Sometimes when her eyes fell on her daughter and her husband sitting off to the side, giggling over something ridiculous Marvin had just said, June seemed to look at them as if they were strangers with policies expired for nonpayment.

Whenever Penelope thought about it, it struck her as strange that among these two parents, the one real and the other pretend, the pretend one had so much more to say to her. She had ten conversations with Marvin for every one with her mother. Though he left for work later, he would be home first, and her mother another hour after that. Most mornings, June would leave for work before Penelope's bus arrived on the island.

About a half hour before he had to leave for the sawmill, Marvin seemed to make a special point of visiting with Penelope. It was all easygoing Marvin stuff: About the weather, somebody he saw at work yesterday, some antique car parts he had heard about, or what she would be doing in school today. They would walk together down the path to his pole barn, where the bus usually arrived while he was inside picking out a car to drive to work that day.

Star Island could be a lonely place, for Penelope's family were the only ones living there, but as Marvin often said, without elaborating, "It sure has its charms."

He must have meant the lake fogs and mists, which could move in suddenly, blotting out the brightest day and turning the nearest things Penelope could see from her bedroom window into ghostly apparitions. Add to this the lake sounds, which were particularly keen at night; the rolling rumble of its cracking ice; winds in the shoreline treetops; the various clucks and toots of summer's restless shorebirds; and especially the bells and whistles of ships far out beyond the bay. Here were sounds lonely enough to put your heart in your throat.

"It's okay", Penelope would say. "It really is."

She could not imagine living anywhere else, away from these black boulder outcrops festooned with pines, from which she could look down on the rock-strewn shore and across Lake Superior as far as any eye could see. She didn't have to imagine what an ocean was like. Nor, thanks to Marvin, need she imagine what a father might be like, even if the very sound of the word *stepfather*—no matter how good the man was—had loneliness enough in it.

Star Island was full of trees, wildlife, and Great Lakes history. Marvin was full of contentment and good suggestions. It was his idea that she advertise for a pen pal in a life insurance company magazine he received a couple of times each year.

The bridge thumped now as the bus drove over it and continued down the causeway. Soon Marvin's pole barn lurched into view beyond a bend, with a driveway turnaround in front of it. She would be let out there and walk the rest of the way to her house, out of sight behind a further bend in their road and screened from view by an aspen grove whose leaves clacked in the summertime whenever gusts blew in from the lake.

Larry, the bus driver, waved as he always did when he had turned the bus around and was driving away, leaving Penelope alone by the mailbox. She was usually the first one home. She would pick up the mail before she walked on to the house, but she never opened the mailbox till Larry had waved and driven away. This was her habit: First Larry and then the mail, even when she was expecting something.

The bus was out of sight thumping back over the bridge as she pulled the mail from the box, closing it with the back of her hand. Once in a while Larry would honk *goodbye* when he got that far. Today he honked. People were just so kind to her: Sometimes it could make her feel like crying. How did Larry know she had been asked a question that she might be the one kid in Bell Harbor unable to answer? Jackie probably even knew the answer and had asked it just to see if Penelope did.

Questions were like mail waiting in a box, and mail was like French fries. One led to another. She could not just take them from the counter back to her table, sit down, and then start eating. She had to pick one or two and have them on the way. Since her feet knew the way to the house, she could flip through the mail before she got there, even with her school books tucked under her arm.

An envelope slipped from her hand as her fingers shuffled through the stack folded within one of Marvin's car magazines. A gust of wind caught it and sent it cartwheeling. It landed face up on the first of thirty-seven flat stones she knew by heart lining the last fifty feet of a path to their door. Stooping to retrieve it, she saw it was addressed to her in an odd handwriting she would never forget. Her last name looked like *listen*: *Penelope Listen*. That too would prove memorable.

"Oh, my God, it's from my pen pal!" Penelope exclaimed and ran the rest of the way to the house.

3

Secret Societies

When it arrived every six months, Marvin usually put his insurance policy magazine on the bottom of a pile of antique car magazines, where it surfaced from time to time before he threw it away unread. His most recent issue had lasted much longer than most because its cover story featured an antique car, a 1913 Model T Roadster, still being driven by a policy holder somewhere in Nebraska. Because Marvin owned a 1921 Model T Roadster, he set this magazine aside for reading. When he finally got around to it, the last two pages forced him deeper into the magazine than he had ever gone, so far that he discovered between him and its last words on the Tin Lizzie a page devoted to youth activities.

This feature, like everything else in the magazine, had been there from volume one, issue number one, unchanged over half a century, as if adolescents continued to be interested in activities now relegated to the Tin Lizzie era. Among other things behind the times was an advertisement for pen pals. Hardly anyone under the age of twenty would have known what the word meant, let alone recognize the fountain pen illustration introducing it.

Ignored were the perverts pen pal ads might have attracted these days and the fact that it made little sense to be advertising for a pen pal when practically every young person had a computer and a cell phone and could be in touch with people all over the world instantly, even simultaneously. Once, this feature had contained dozens of names and addresses from coast to coast. The current issue had three, all of whom seemed to be from the same family.

Marvin knew enough about kids and the world to know that the pen pal concept was old-fashioned, but he also knew that Penelope was not like most children her age. Thus, one evening while they were doing dishes and he was thinking about her isolation on Star Island, he asked if she had ever considered having a pen pal. When he was about sixteen, he himself had had a pen pal, a German girl named Christa. As mail flew back and forth, Marvin fell in love with Christa, and she, on that account thinking he must be crazy, broke it off—whatever *it* was—by simply not answering any more of his letters.

Marvin didn't mind telling Penelope the story so many years later, when it no longer embarrassed him to think about it. In fact, it now made him laugh. Somewhere he still had a pack of unused, remarkably sensational airmail envelopes, blue with red-and-blue-striped piping along their edges. Marvin was neither still in love with Christa nor sentimental, but only something of a packrat who kept things he thought might come in handy someday.

Marvin had not lived with Penelope most of her life without seeing her as happy with her own company, creative, independent, and a bit of a dreamer. She wrote little poems on scraps of paper he would sometimes find between sofa cushions, kept a diary, had conversations with her rabbit, liked to go for walks, and assembled a rock collection she exhibited at a school science fair. These, among other things, set her apart from children as normal and up-to-date as his nephews, who sometimes visited.

The contrast was too obvious when they brought along their computer games and their cell phones and shrugged off their uncle's suggestions about activities he had enjoyed as a boy. Fishing, exploring the lakeshore for agates, whizzing downhill on a toboggan, and reading *Tom Sawyer* had no appeal. They did not even care about his car collection. Lake Superior might as well have been a pothole and *Tom Sawyer* an algebra book. Fishing and whizzing in all seasons they could do on a computer, along with hide-and-seek, monkey in the middle, snowball fights, and anything else he could think of.

Forget aesthetics. By their standards, Marvin should have been teaching art appreciation at the local community college. Why would they want to stop staring at a flashing computer screen to notice a freighter on the lake just then positioned beneath a rainbow arch? Uncle Marvin was out of touch and weird, Penelope along with him.

Marvin found himself dreading more and more the weekend visits of his nephews. He was almost grateful when they filled their hours chatting with friends, each on his own cell phone, and otherwise ignoring everyone and everything around them while wrapped in cocoons of self-absorption. Two could play at that game: Marvin buried himself in his car magazines out in the pole barn and pretended not to care. When his sister would return and ask her sons—as she always did—what they had been doing and whether they had a good time, they gave Marvin an incriminating glance suggesting they were afraid to say how bored they were.

Penelope never seemed bored. She didn't want a cell phone. Had they gotten her one regardless, she would have left it in her bedroom, in a drawer of the writing desk where she would sit with her diary, her poems, and her daydreams.

She had a way of gazing off in the distance as people do when they come to Lake Superior on a clear, sunny day when its blue waters seem almost to bend approaching the horizon, when its half-submerged boulders are like the backs of gigantic turtles, and its ore boats like water beetles crawling along its distant surface. She need not be near the lake to hold and maintain such a gaze. She could do it anywhere, as if for her, all life was a blending of seascape and dream.

Some of her teachers and a school counselor suggested Penelope was "introverted" and "socially disadvantaged". Her mother described her as "withdrawn" and "maladjusted", terms no longer used by school professionals, who these days favor soothing observations as less likely to alarm parents. Not so with June, who ascribed her daughter's personality to a circumstance best forgotten and a parent who otherwise never existed. *He* was responsible, and the more abnormal Penelope seemed, the heavier his load.

Marvin would pretend to ponder this possibility if he had to go that far to keep the peace, but he would do his best to change the subject. He kept to himself the thought that Penelope seemed more like his family than his sister and her three boys. If her real father were somehow the reason, he ought to shake the man's hand for producing such a daughter. His wife's stern opinions did not prevent him from recasting other versions of Penelope, skipping over jargon sometimes used to describe her in favor of his own.

"Penelope sure is a good kid", Marvin would say again and again.

He would say it a hundred times and leave it at that, as if defying anyone—even June—to say otherwise. If he suggested anything to

Penelope—like starting a butterfly collection or identifying those shore-birds, or having a pen pal—it was his way of encouraging her to be herself, which in his opinion was much better than most children her age.

I was almost an only child myself. My sister was so much younger, he might say as if this settled it; others were wrong.

He might even retrieve a scrap of a poem and attempt reading it to June. He knew little about poetry, but it seemed like pretty good stuff, as he put it. He would often take refuge in old sayings that did not quite apply.

"You can lead a horse to water, but you can't make him drink."

June had laughed a not very agreeable laugh and remarked sardoni-cally that she would bring news of this to Penelope's next teacher's conference. Despite having adopted her, Marvin was never encour-aged to be at these. Where Penelope was concerned, June could be simultaneously dismissive and possessive.

The Lister family had evolved into something resembling two secret societies, or perhaps three if Marvin alone with his Labrador in the pole barn counted for another. The first two had their own pass-words, rituals, and inner sanctum deliberations. One Lister was a mem-ber of both. Marvin chafed under the burden of this, for depending on the circumstances it turned him into go-between, tattletale, secret confidant, or reluctant referee, none of which suited him and all of which he did his best to avoid. He shrugged a lot, pretended not to hear a lot, played dumb a lot, and changed the subject a lot. How this had come about was hard to explain beyond the obvious that he and June could talk, he and Penelope could talk, but June, burying herself in her work, had few words for her daughter. In addition to his other out-of-character functions, Marvin had become a sort of daily news-paper they both read for news of the other. He seemed to be living simultaneously in two worlds.

4

Penelope, Listen

Unbeknown to June, Penelope had advertised her name, age, and address in Marvin's life insurance magazine. Several months passed before this was published, and now, three weeks later, a boy named Felix had written.

It mattered little that he was *only* thirteen and a grade behind Penelope in school. He had a name as uncommon as hers and the oddest handwriting she had ever seen, printing with curlicues. He might have been writing from a foreign country using a foreign script. It seemed like the beginning of an adventure. So it would prove, but in ways far more amazing than Penelope could envision.

Felix' lines wove close together and then far apart, with letters sometimes distinct and sometimes as light as if his pencil barely touched the paper. It was the writing of someone in the backseat of a car lurching over a winding, bumpy road or perhaps someone on a ship at sea in a storm. An odder feature yet was that his r's were made to look like little n's with flags on them, and so her last name on the envelope looked like Listen. She finally deciphered this when Felix began talking about the "noosten cnowing eveny monning on his uncle's fanm".

The day had yet another surprise: Her mother for once arrived home before Marvin. Much that followed might have been different had June noticed the tablet pages her daughter held in plain view, unfolded at her side. Much that followed might never have happened. June had only to ask, "What do you have there?" Instead she swept by on her way to her home office with an armload of insurance work and her usual two questions trailing behind, not waiting for answers.

"How was school? Do you have any homework?"

There stood Penelope with Felix' letter, close enough to hand it to her and then an instant later out of reach. She could now save her news until after supper, when she and Marvin were doing dishes and, as they often did, sharing the day's events at sawmill and school. Marvin would be the first to hear. She kept it for last in her account of the day, which usually consisted of what happened at school, an answer to the question her mother had left hanging in the air. Regardless, the worst of this particular day couldn't have been shared with her.

Marvin would at least listen. Truly his name should have been Listen, because that is what he always did. He was expert at it. He might even ask her to repeat something or ask her a question to make sure he understood. This time he only shook his head, told her not to worry about what other kids thought, and reached for another old saying that seemed not quite to fit.

"People living in glass houses shouldn't throw stones", he said.

His evident sadness made her regret even bringing it up, but he was not unhappy only because of what she had said. It was what he *could not* say: They had reached the boundary of talk about her father.

"It's okay. Really, it is."

"I am sure of it," said Marvin with a soapy spatula in hand, even though he wasn't sure, "and now, what's that surprise you're saving for last?"

She pulled Felix' letter out of a pocket and waved it in his face while pointing to her name.

"Listen, Marvin Listen!" she said.

"What do you have there?"

Marvin had not forgotten his pen pal suggestion from six months ago, but it was far enough away to leave him perplexed for the few seconds it took to notice something even more perplexing. It was enough to stifle Felix' mysterious *cnowing noosten* and banish the mystery of his name becoming *Listen* in the day's mail. Penelope chattered on about all this and then waited for a laugh that didn't come.

"What's the return address on that envelope?"

She waved it in his face again: PO Box 45, Clay Corners. "Do you know where it is?"

Not a man to linger over dishes, Marvin took an exceptionally long time with a plate. Moments before it had seemed clean by his standards, but he went over it front and back again. Then he glanced over his shoulder to see if June happened to be anywhere near. She had gone upstairs for the moment.

"Clay Corners is just about smack dab in the middle of the state", he said, lowering his voice between throat clearings of the sort secrets require.

Thanks to many expeditions in search of antique cars, he knew Minnesota and much of the Midwest firsthand. He could see it like a map on another plate he was washing with unusual care. He had even been through the village a time or two. Had he been given a choice of any place on the map to have Penelope's pen pal living, Clay Corners would have been his last choice for reasons he must keep to himself.

"If you blink even going the speed limit," he said, "you might miss it, not that there is much to miss."

This was about as close as Marvin could come to a lie, although almost anyone but Penelope would have agreed with him.

Clay Corners was a dreary little rural village of the sort described as having seen better days. Even in the best of its better days, village scenes had never been on postcards. It had not been the sort of place people included in their vacation plans. They had never stopped there to take pictures. They drove through it on their way to somewhere else and never mentioned it when they got home.

Ironically, only in the era of its decline had the town become a destination of sorts: For the most thoroughly reluctant and disheartened of travelers, convicted criminals escorted to Shade Creek Penitentiary. It had been built a decade ago in a nearby farmland valley. Penelope's father was imprisoned there. Were she ever to pass through Clay Corners, there would be much for her to miss, too much.

Of all the people on earth who could have answered Penelope's request for a pen pal, why Felix from Clay Corners? A secret seemed to be unraveling, with Penelope groping her way toward it, blindfolded and unaware. Marvin was tempted to shout, "Warmer! Warmer!", as he would in a game of blind man's bluff. The last person he would want to hear it was Penelope; the next last was June.

Penelope blinked and pictured Clay Corners as a little village far away whose name belied a hidden beauty like an agate buried in the sand. Nearby lived a boy named Felix on a farm where a crowing rooster awoke him every morning. "Listen, Penelope Listen", the rooster seemed to say. It knew what Penelope did not yet know, the answer to the question Jackie Rae had asked today. "Awaken, Penelope, awaken! Your father lives nearby", the rooster might have been saying. Her daydreams could not yet reach so far.

Marvin had no need to dream. Feeling more uncomfortable by the second, he said something completely out of character using an uncharacteristic whisper.

"Don't mention this to your mom for the time being. I'll explain one of these days. Promise? And keep that letter out of sight for now."

"Promise!" she whispered, puzzled yet enjoying the secrecy, whatever lay behind it.

Secrecy, if that is what Marvin wanted, added yet more to this adventure. June's footsteps could be heard on the floor above them. Penelope looked at him and merrily pointed toward the ceiling.

Eventually, with only a jangling tangle of knives, forks, and spoons in the bottom of a sink where dish soap had all but given up, they returned to Felix' letter. Penelope approached it the way she approached her bubble gum, chewing to get it just right before attempting bubbles. Marvin approached it as he might have followed a dangerous animal: From behind, at a safe distance, and prepared to run.

"Are you going to write him back?"

It had not occurred to her that she wouldn't.

"I was just wondering about that PO box", said Marvin rinsing a fistful of forks and spoons. "A lot of farmers still collect their mail in town. Felix might not live anywhere near Clay Corners", or anywhere near Shade Creek.

Marvin could hope. More than once he had made a beeline for a spot given in a magazine want ad, only to discover the car he sought parked in a barn or shed ten miles away. Doing his best to appear nonchalant, he recalled that his old pen pal Christa's handwriting in some ways resembled what he had seen on the envelope.

"Is Felix a German name?" she asked.

Marvin wasn't sure. He peered out a window over the sink as if German names might be found out there in the aspen grove. He had only to look hard enough. He sloshed a sponge around the edges of a pot. He brushed hair out of his eyes, leaving a streak of dishwater across his forehead where his hair had been. At the point where he was close to an opinion, June came in and took the dish towel from her daughter.

"I'll take over", she said. "Have you done your homework? Have you fed the rabbit? It's getting dark outside."

The rabbit, being a pet, of course had a name, but June was not the sort to refer to pets by name, so the rabbit was "the rabbit"; Marvin's Labrador was "the dog"; and the cat, if they had had one, would have been "the cat". Felix, new on the scene and for the time being a secret, had not yet become "that strange boy who writes you". June always said such things through her teeth with a minimum of lip movement, a skill developed in high school and perfected in her first job, at a Bell Harbor bank where chattiness between tellers' stations was as discouraged as chattiness between girls in study hall.

Her Star Island home, in fact her childhood home, was the same as her insurance office. She was equally inclined in both places to say things without appearing to be speaking. No ventriloquist could have done it better, and whether at home or work, she had no time for the idle chitchat of her study hall days. It was the hallmark of efficiency to stay focused. Focus had become June's way. Upon graduating from high school, she would have been voted most efficient instead of most fun to be with, which, in days long past and no longer easily imagined, had once been her accolade. She would have gladly exchanged the latter for the former. Given the chance to speak at a class reunion, she would have said, "I grew up in the insurance office. That's where I finally learned what life was about."

Night had come to the island. Outside behind the house near a honeysuckle bush, in a shaft of light from the kitchen window, Penelope stared through the wire mesh of the hutch at her French lop, whose distinctive feature was one floppy ear at least an inch longer than the other. Her rabbit, Marvin said, was a lopsided lop and the rarest of the rare in his opinion, although he admitted to not knowing much about rabbits.

Penelope could see through the hutch into the kitchen where Marvin and her mother stood with their backs to the window. At that moment June turned and glanced her way. They were talking about her.

"So what's my daughter up to? I heard you both laughing."

"Actually it's not very funny", said Marvin. "One of her classmates asked about her father today."

"You?"

"No, Warren."

"Please don't say his name."

"Well, anyway, that's who she was asked about, and I think it really troubled her."

"I'll talk to the principal about this. I'll speak with her counselor."

"Nobody can control what kids say, June. I think it best to leave it alone. Sometimes things only get worse if you don't leave them alone."

June was not the sort to leave things alone, least of all this.

5

Inscriptions

Penelope answered, Felix replied, and this continued back and forth through five or so letters and what remained of the school year. Where June was concerned, Penelope's pen pal remained a secret. Marvin had yet to explain why.

Meanwhile Lighthouse Consolidated School behaved like the old-fashioned wind-up toy Felix described owning in one of his letters. Fully wound at the beginning of the year, school days at Lighthouse Consolidated slowed month by month; first from a hop, skip, and jump to a determined stride, then from an aimless ramble to a trudge, and finally to a beleaguered slog across some wasteland toward a mirage. Teachers meeting school buses and smiling at classroom entrances in early September seemed by late April to be rehearsing for parts in plays about martyrdom; either that or they appeared to be passing through the so-called stages of grief in reverse, beginning with a sense of reconciliation, eager to put last year behind them, and ending with angry outbursts blaming everyone for this year being as wretched as the last.

Time dragged, and students watched clocks and stared out windows even on foggy days, when nothing much could be seen. Teachers puttered aimlessly. At the very end, only a Salvador Dali painting with clocks resembling pancakes draped over the edges of tabletops could express how school life seemed to be. Throw in a wilted potted fern on a stand just inside the principal's office, throw in the principal's wrinkled suit and the several goldfish found floating belly up in a reception area aquarium, and the picture needs no more detail.

Like everyone else, Penelope dreamed of summer whether the fog drifted overhead or the sun broke through. At this time of year she could seem just as normal as other children, or rather other children could seem more like her. Daydreaming and introversion had become an epidemic. Even teachers had the disease.

Few witnessing this would change their opinion of Penelope. She *was* who she was year in and year out. The various frets, clichés, and stereotypes twirling around her had been spun along like gossip to classroom teachers up ahead. Impressions might as well have been inscriptions on gravestones. Next year, reinvigorated teachers would glance up from their new class rosters and see the girl they had heard about from others last year, the one who did not fit in, daydreamed a lot, did not like cell phones, and kept to herself. Her father was in prison, a detail they should *never* mention to her. At her mother's insistence, this rubric appeared everywhere in her school records.

Written in margins, scrawled across page corners, underlined and asterisked, "Father in prison" could also be found throughout her records at St. John Vianney, the Catholic school she had attended for all of its six grades. There too everyone had been informed and cautioned. Sister Hilaria's subtle response was tucked between the earliest pages of Penelope's diary. It had taken the form of a holy card given her without explanation, a depiction of the Curé d'Ars. Across the back of it she had written, "For you, a very special saint!!" It was just like Sister Hilaria to have underlined *you* twice and used two exclamation marks. Subtlety she had to work at.

Sister Hilaria herself was all exclamation marks and underlines, as if no words could ever suffice on their own to convey how she felt. Her classroom whiteboard, with its colorful arching arrows, its circles, lines, and *x*'s, with now and then a spiral, might have been mistaken for a football coach's play diagrams for next week's big game.

But even at St. John Vianney, springtime days could sometimes drag and stop in the middle of a handspring or somersault. If anyone could, Sister Hilaria should have been able to make days whiz past. Clearly no one could, not even hilarious Sister Hilaria, who would fly a kite at recess on the right sort of day, or serene Sister Serena, as pleasant as a duck no matter what the weather. These two from Penelope's days were still there. Scientific labels could not have described them better than their own religious names.

Sister Serena's classroom board, as her name suggested, was all perfectly formed cursive letters of the same size. Sister Hilaria's lines, when she actually used words, might curve off anywhere. She had once told the class, "If your lines head up as you write, it means you're happy and full of hope." Her lines went that direction much of the time.

Last Sunday after church Sister Serena had waved to Penelope from across a swatch of parish lawn between them, a tentative little wave from the hip where her rosary hung. A subdued Sister Hilaria seemed not to have noticed her. At the end of Mass Father Ulrich had announced her departure. This school year, her eighth, would be her last. The following Sunday afternoon the parish would hold a reception to thank her for her years of service and wish her well in her new assignment.

Penelope had wanted to run to them both. It seemed like part of her own life was going away with Sister Hilaria. She might have told her about a pen pal whose lines went all over the place, but Marvin and her mother were already getting into his 1955 Chevrolet Bel Air. Penelope threw herself into the rear seat and lay face down with her legs doubled. Jackie Rae was walking past, and behind her came Mr. Stiller, the school librarian, who had been dusting books on Friday during study hall. In his happy detachment he resembled a turtle just having stuck its head out for a look around. Mr. Stiller directed the church choir with the same motions he used for dusting books.

"Buckle up!" June said through lips already buckled. "Penelope, sit up. What's wrong with you?"

"Gentlemen, start your engines!" said Marvin.

He always said this when Penelope was in the car. It was the way races began, but Marvin's old cars were too precious for racing. They were forever being passed and honked at by people who knew and liked Marvin. In one such car this Sunday morning Jackie Rae cruised by with her face pressed against a window.

Sundays especially, Marvin had to choose his vehicle carefully because June hated being late for Mass or anything else. If they left home a little late, he would bring the Bel Air around from his pole barn. Of the whole collection it was his best-tuned, had the newest tires, and could be counted on to get them there on time without overheating, stalling, sputtering in front of the church as its engine coughed to a halt, or worst of all where June was concerned—even worse than being late and sputtering—backfiring. Backfiring could ruin her day.

6

Cheers and Jeers

Now here it was another Sunday, this year Pentecost Sunday, and Father Luke Ulrich was robed in Pentecostal red, in this case the faded, rather dusty red of an old sofa. This befitted a man who had evolved into a rather odd piece of priestly furniture. His was an earlier era when chair backs were higher, upholstered chair seats were narrower, wooden arms and legs had scrolled ends, every fabric seemed dusty, brass nails seemed tarnished, and all of it had been that way from the day it left a now defunct furniture factory, whose discolored labels still clung to undersides not upended in living memory.

Father Ulrich, as if in a dream, had sleepwalked out of that world into a conspicuously modern St. John Vianney Church. In his old clerical black he might have looked more at home among conductors in the passenger train era.

St. John Vianney was the second church by that name, built on the same site fifteen years ago after the first burned to its foundation. Father Ulrich would have found a congenial setting there had the fire never occurred. In the old church he would have seemed as well placed as an old horse under a half-dead oak in an overgrown meadow among sagging fences and gates hanging by a single rusty hinge. You would barely have noticed him had you strolled into the old St. John Vianney a half hour before Sunday Mass and caught him fumbling about in semidarkness among rows of brass candlesticks along its ivory-colored altar beneath a crucifix suspended from black chains like a piece of dungeon equipment. You would have had to squint in the low light to find Father Ulrich moving about, still in his black shirtsleeves, among pastel-colored statues in shadowy alcoves where vigil lights flickered in ascending trays, among pews with creaky kneelers and wood nearly onyx beneath coats of old varnish. Scattered about were the glints and glimmers of stray sunbeams flashing through painted glass panes, catching as if by chance a saintly statue nose, a brass knob, or a single blossom among many in a vase placed there the evening before by one of the local women's guilds.

Minutes later, with the lights on and parishioners filing in, you would finally see him in his robes arranging papers in a pulpit resembling the lower half of a Victorian era bird cage. Head down with many eyes on him, he would seem unaware. Then he would retreat to the sacristy until minutes later a jangling bell would signal his reappearance behind maybe four servers. So it had been at the old St. John Vianney for many rickety priests before him, but it was not to be for Father Ulrich, who had come after them and after the church had burned.

And so also it was not to be for Penelope, born when the old St. John Vianney perched on the verge of catastrophe. She had only pictures of it to judge for herself, one for a time in the new church vestibule and then removed, and another in the principal's office at the school a hundred yards away across the parish lawn. Like Father Ulrich, she would have been more at home there, in the old church infused with all things romantic. In the new St. John Vianney, with its hexagonal playhouse design, there was almost no place for either of them to hide, no matter how early the hour and how dim the lighting. Whatever Father Ulrich thought of the church he kept to himself. He would have seen this as his priestly duty. Perhaps the building made him speechless. No matter. It was not for him to complain it had all the gleam and glister of a shopping mall theater. In fact, a screen could be lowered in front of the altar and pulpit for a meeting or a picture show there. Raked seating three-quarters around ensured everyone could see the picture or—with the screen raised—see Father Ulrich in the middle of Mass prayers, sometimes unaware his microphone was off.

No parishioner on hand will ever forget the day a church usher attempting to let the Word of the Lord be heard pushed the wrong button, lowering the theater screen over the amiable priest in the middle of the Gospel reading. When it came up again, Father said, "I always knew I was behind the times." Among his congregation, some laughed affectionately, for they liked him that way. Those who thought him a fuddy-duddy sniggered.

A sense of intimacy has its drawbacks, and equally so good hearing. Architects had trumpeted the church's design for its intimacy. Father

Ulrich, in what might be described as the entrance hall of that dilapidated mansion called old age, could nonetheless hear very well. Without difficulty he could distinguish the cheers from the jeers. Had he bothered to look, he could have identified their sources and named them one by one. Instead he lowered his eyes to the Gospel page and resumed reading.

Everyone could see and hear everyone in this place, so evenly lit and acoustically pure. Everyone was on display, and June's choice of seating Sunday after Sunday was from her daughter's viewpoint the worst of all places, midway down in the center of this display.

Pentecost found them in their usual spot. To their right, in a front row off to one side but directly in front of the organ, sat the school's teaching sisters, who always filed in together and were always among the first to be there. Almost always, someone approached Marvin from behind, laid a hand on his shoulder, and whispered something to set them both grinning. And so it happened at Pentecost, as almost always, that June reminded Marvin in her best ventriloquist fashion that Mass was about to begin.

Then a cluster of bells rang out, and Father Ulrich wandered in looking surprised to find himself there, as if he had just gotten off a bus in an unfamiliar neighborhood. Meanwhile, between Marvin and June sat Penelope pretending to be on the shore of Lake Superior, where a seagull hovering above the waves resembled a stained glass dove high above the altar.

At the end of Mass, Father reminded the assembly of Sister Hilaria's farewell reception later in the day, and then, because he knew not everyone could be there, he invited her to stand. During the brief pause that followed, he let his glasses slide down his nose and seemed to be looking over their dark rims at Penelope and her parents. To her right, she felt her mother shift positions ever so slightly. She glanced at Marvin, who some might have thought wore a sheepish grin. She couldn't see behind her, where from various quarters eyes were settling on the three of them. The church had become suddenly empty, with Sister Hilaria and Penelope gazing at each other.

At the end of general applause, which an entranced Penelope could but faintly hear, Sister Hilaria said, "I will miss you."

Someone shouted, "We will miss you, Sister!" More applause followed.

"I will leave St. John Vianney with so many happy memories to take along to my new school in St. Cloud." She pronounced St. Cloud as the French would say it. "*Au revoir!*" she said and sat down.

Penelope thought Sister Hilaria's French more beautiful than her own language. She felt herself rushing out to meet her words suspended somewhere in the sunlight streaming from the church's cupola. All around applause exploded in a church full of people again.

As sometimes happens at the end, when people who came in together are sitting in the middle of a row, one leaves by one aisle, thinking the other is following, and the other leaves the other way, thinking the same. At the end of the applause for Sister Hilaria, Marvin went left, and June went right, each preoccupied and thinking Penelope was behind them.

By the time they learned otherwise, as they came together near the church entrance, Penelope was at a side door talking to Sister Hilaria. She could only have gotten there using acrobatics of a sort seldom seen in churches. Marvin grinned and June frowned while the exiting crowd pushed them both into the vestibule just as Penelope and Sister Hilaria stepped outside into the grassy churchyard.

"I came to say goodbye", said Penelope, more out of breath from the internal acrobatics these words required than from her flight through rows of pews and a current of people heading the other way. "We won't be coming to your party this afternoon."

After eight years in St. John Vianney parish, where the eighth commandment was about as neglected as it is in most places these days, Sister Hilaria would have been surprised to hear otherwise. She knew Charlotte Hall was the reason the Listers would not be there, but she did not have to *act* surprised, because in front of her was a real surprise. Here was "little" Penelope no longer little and doing something truly amazing for a quiet girl who had grown several inches during her time at the school.

"God bless you!" said Sister Hilaria.

Beyond them a few yards, Sister Serena was bent over with her hands on her hips, examining a spiderweb spun across flowery branches of a honeysuckle. Spiders were one of many interests Sister shared with her students.

"I will always remember you, Penelope, and pray for you; and you pray for me, will you?" said Sister Hilaria.

There was something especially ominous in her tone, something fretful and genuinely concerned, seldom heard from this flyer of kites and creator of swirls and curlicues. A storm might have been approaching. In the convent wall a mouse might have been gnawing.

It struck Penelope as strange that Sister Hilaria might need prayers. Sister, sensing this, said sisters need prayers too, which she repeated in her wonderful native French that Penelope so much loved to hear: *"Les religieuses ont besoin de prières aussi."*

Penelope spread out her arms, hesitating as if poised to dive at the deep end of a pool that in this instance rose up to meet her. Sister wrapped her in the draped arms of her habit.

"Au revoir", she said, just as June came running from around a corner of the hexagon where Marvin stood waiting in the shadows.

Penelope had barely time to shout goodbye to Sister Serena before being whisked away. Neither Sister understood why June felt the need to apologize for her daughter's behavior.

7

Stuck in Circles

Among those unable to be at Sister Hilaria's sendoff, the Listers alone were unwilling. This had nothing to do with Sister Hilaria and little more with Marvin and Penelope. Marvin could not be blamed for what is described as seeing the handwriting on the wall, even as he kept his nose in the *Sentinel*'s comics section, reading what he called the "funny papers". Penelope could not be blamed for her carrot-colored hair. As it was, after a Sunday nap on the living room couch, Marvin planned to wash his cars, weather permitting, and Penelope would have her hair trimmed no matter what the weather.

June applied herself to hair shears with almost Pentecostal fervor, while Marvin parked all fifteen of his vehicles along the turnaround in front of his pole barn. Penelope, perched on the edge of a picnic table, watched him heedless of the hair clippings fluttering to earth all around her, each one doing nothing to obliterate reminders of her aunt. Nothing short of shaving her head would have achieved that. Even then a telltale highlight might have remained, as indelible as a mark on the soul.

Others who missed the reception could be asked why, but no one would ever ask the Listers. They already knew the Listers would never be seen in the same room or even on the same patch of grass with Charlotte Hall, the organist for St. John Vianney at the Saturday Vigil and eleven o'clock Sunday Masses. The Listers avoided church at those times. They avoided Charlotte at all times. The most cynical of those observing this ongoing drama would have been surprised to discover June and Charlotte even buried in the same cemetery.

Local gossip and conjecture had long ago begun to bore itself with the old story behind this, save among a few sorts who enjoyed feuds and hoarded grudges like pennies in a jar, never finding anything new to interest or anger them.

In common with so much else in Bell Harbor, these incidental remains had long ago found a home among things outliving their reasons: Picnic pavilions in a park where no one had picnics anymore, an abandoned railroad siding where iron ore cars were once parked, bells in a harbor where ships no longer docked, and flags in a community cemetery fluttering for a forgotten war. The town's senior citizens might tell their stories about all this, readers of yellowed newsprint might take note, tourists might puzzle, but most people just let it go.

Whatever anyone thought, it was not a case of June and Charlotte either hating or blaming each other for what had happened long ago. June didn't want reminders; Charlotte needed to avoid them. The distinction, while appearing to be slight, was in fact astronomical.

Around Bell Harbor the drama had evolved into theater whose well-understood staging the whole town knew. Of course missteps were inevitable in a world as compact as a swallow's nest hanging from a cliff. At such moments both parties could seem to be on stage at the Bell Harbor Community Theater, pretending not to see each other, while the whole town watched a scene as exciting as fireworks in a rainstorm.

Charlotte would never have risked mentioning Penelope to her imprisoned brother. To do so would cause too much pain. When Warren asked about his daughter, Charlotte claimed to know nothing, and the less she knew, the easier this was. She had admitted as much to Father Ulrich. Being a practical theologian, he reassured her by shaking his head and asking rhetorically, "My gracious Lord, what else can you do?"

More than once he had told the story of his navy chaplain uncle saying Masses every hour for beleaguered sailors while battles raged overhead in an era when the Vatican had prescribed no more than three Masses each day. "What else could I do?" he would ask as a question already answered. "What else would the Lord have done? Men were dying at my feet."

Of course no strategy for remembering works better than insisting people forget. "Forget Aunt Charlotte, forget June, forget Penelope, and forget everything" had become its opposite for those most concerned. They were unable to forget anything. No one else had hair quite the color of Penelope and Charlotte's. Put them in the same place, and no matter how far apart they were, everyone there would

pair them. Once people paired them, even in a black-haired mob they
would think of something else. This is where June was mistaken. Once
people had become used to seeing them together, they would have
quit noticing. Only June could never have gotten used to it.

Everyone seemed stuck in a circle. June's was a small orbit in which
the planets Home, Work, and School all rotated in predictable rhythm.
More distant than the remotest planets, but fixed there nonetheless,
Penelope's father lurked in the depths and darkness of unexplored space.
June could no more escape him than could her daughter, who of
course thought about him all the more because she *wasn't* supposed to
think about him and who had all the more questions because she
lacked any answers. Warren Hall was out there somewhere, in an orbit
of his own, locked away for almost all of Penelope's life, but circling
around her and her mother.

No wonder June clipped and snipped Penelope's hair at the end of
every month without fail. No wonder by evening of this Pentecost
Sunday strands of carrot red might be seen in the beaks and bills of
nesting birds. No matter her daughter's hair was unfashionably shorter
than that of any other girl in her class, and no matter Penelope might
be teased in those early teen years when girls can be merciless. June
would have dyed it any other color, even blue or green, had her reason not been so obvious.

As June snipped and Marvin chamoised, Charlotte was holding an
ice cream cup at Sister Hilaria's reception. High overhead a late spring
sun projected cloud shadows upon the St. John Vianney lawn. Tree
buds were bursting. A leafing border of Russian olive had already con-
cealed a custodian's storage shed in plain view just last week. The
growth of a new spring season was ascending as always from the ground
up. Robins clucked at safe distances, and dandelions winked beneath
feet. Balloons bobbed from low-hanging tree branches. Loudspeakers
hung from parish lampposts.

With his microphone switch turned on, Father Ulrich sang a German song he had learned as a child from hearing his mother sing it so
often. Sister Hilaria followed with one of her own in French. Hardly
anyone understood either song, but those who were not crying laughed,
till at the end all were laughing till they cried again. Sister Hilaria's
reception had become a party, with people lingering as they do in the
warm glow of good times. Many parishioners stayed much longer than

they had planned, and many attempted to leave several times without success. A couple with children in hand, walking toward the church parking lot, would find themselves in the thick of things again, while one of the children chased a squirrel around a tree. No one could have said for sure when it quite ended, the surest sign no one wanted it to end.

8

Eureka!

Marvin's black Labrador bounded from the pole barn to meet Penelope as she pulled a bundle of mail from the mailbox. She wasn't usually home this time of day. The dog knew something was up, and with the mail waiting on a front step, he was soon up as well. On his hind legs with his paws in Penelope's hands, the dog danced with the girl in the grassy middle of the turnaround. They waltzed and whirled in awkward circles because canines are not designed to be dancing partners. What the dancers lacked in grace was more than made up for by enthusiasm, for here was the Friday after Pentecost, the first day of June, and the last of the school year.

Lighthouse Consolidated had dismissed its students at 12:30. Forty-four minutes later Penelope had stepped out of her school bus and turned around to say goodbye to Larry, the driver. She knew the exact time because he checked his watch and made a point of telling her this was the end for both of them. Hers being by far the longest bus route, and Star Island being the most remote stop at the end of that route, she had the distinction of being his last student of the school year. Larry had the distinction of being the school's last working bus driver. "We ought to be given a prize for having the shortest summer vacation", said Larry. Checking his watch again, he added, "By a few minutes anyway. Have a great summer!"

Larry had no problem with what some at the school saw as Penelope's introversion. Introversion behaved. Introversion was courteous, respectful, and quiet. Give him a busload of introversion any day. As far as he was concerned, kids like Penelope were normal, healthy sorts. The truly maladjusted ones were forever roaring in the back of his bus, pulling hair, spitting soda pop across aisles, kicking rubbish under the seats, swearing, stealing cell phones, and yelling from windows

46

that were supposed to stay closed. Anybody who looked upon those kids as normal, Larry surmised, needed a new pair of glasses and a few rides on his route at the end of the day. He honked three times as the bus rumbled back over the wooden bridge.

Penelope's dancing partner was named Osgood, a Marvin inspiration, because when Osgood first arrived six years ago as a pup, June was well into her first decade at Osgoode Insurance Agency. While she failed to see the humor in this, Marvin protested in his good-natured manner that Osgood, the puppy, spelled his name differently. This was met with silence, the best June could manage when up against Marvin's formidable smiles.

For her, his lab remained "the dog" regardless of the name. Between Marvin and Penelope the name became a joke worth repeating in the safety of the pole barn or on their Star Island walks, when their banter came around to Mom working late for Osgoode, how it was that other Labradors equally as smart as their Osgood had never managed to set up such a successful business for themselves, how kind it was of Osgoode to give Mom a two-week vacation and to call her only five times a day every day of it with questions any dog as smart as Osgood should be able to manage by himself, and so on.

When she returned to the front step, Penelope found Felix' fifth letter between two of the many specialty car parts catalogues sent Marvin's way. Deeper in the pile of such things was a small packet she took to be his without looking at it, since something was always coming for Marvin. It might be a chrome interior door handle for one of his several dozen doors or a custom light bulb for a headlamp that once shined the way home along dirt roads after a Christmas party ten thousand nights ago.

She couldn't be out there in Marvin's vast pole barn reading Felix' letters without wondering where these cars had been and who had sat in the seats, looking at scenes from long ago or perhaps at other times reading letters. With no one home for much that remained of the afternoon, she sat on a front step this time and read aloud to Osgood, who cocked his head now and then and seemed to appreciate being involved in a secret.

Felix' latest brought word of a spider he had been watching day by day in the doorway of an old barn, the biggest spider he had ever seen. He said its body was almost as big and as round as a ball of chewing gum foil he had been growing for more than a year, now the size of a plum. Penelope thought this a very strange thing to be saving. Neither she nor Osgood had heard of pressing gum foil into a ball. Felix, in the wavering lines of his five letters with all those little flags topping his *r*'s, had mentioned many things she had never heard of and struggled to imagine. She tried to picture a spider with a body as big as a plum. As far away as Felix was, it still made her shiver with fear and excitement mixed.

Sister Serena would want to be told. She would be stationed at St. John Vianney for much of the summer and all next year, playing the organ for eight o'clock Sunday Mass, with Mr. Stiller directing the choir on its every-other-week summer schedule.

As the time neared for Marvin's arrival from the sawmill, she ran to the pole barn as rain began to patter on its metal roof. Felix' latest letter was destined to join the others, tucked away in the glove box of a 1952 Frazer, where never in the remaining history of the world June would have looked. Marvin had chosen the hiding place, but he had yet to provide an explanation for keeping Felix a secret; but with so much else like that in their lives for so many years, this didn't seem all that strange. With all the tippy-toeing around that had been going on long before Felix first appeared in their mailbox, keeping him secret in the old Frazer seemed almost less strange than telling June about him.

Penelope settled into the red leather front seat of Marvin's 1960 Desoto and set his mail in its passenger seat. Not by far the oldest of his collection, the Desoto was in many ways the most exotic and surprising, and perhaps because of its amazing tail-finned profile, he called it his White Whale. Anyone about to open its front doors for the first time would never have guessed its seats swiveled out. In place of any sort of gearshift lever on the floor or by the steering wheel was a cluster of buttons. Its wraparound windshield seemed designed for space travel and let in plenty of light by which to read as she sat there with a book propped against its steering wheel, or in this case with Felix' letter. The Desoto's red leather upholstered seats were as comfortable as Marvin's favorite living room chair.

Osgood, as was his habit at such times, had divided himself between the floor of the Desoto under Penelope's legs and the pole barn floor, a compromise as far as Marvin would permit when it came to pets in

his cars. Otherwise for Osgood the pole barn was one enormous ken-
nel, just as for Penelope it could seem to be a tree house, notwithstanding its hard-packed earthen floor. Osgood paid for his room and
board by serving as a car-thief alarm, which given his gentle disposition would have involved a bit of barking and a lot of tail wagging as
someone drove a stolen car away.

High overhead as they immersed themselves in sudden summer contentment, rain continued drumming on the pole barn's corrugated
roof, a repetitive sound making Penelope almost as sleepy as Osgood
seemed to be. In open sectors of exposed rafters, spiders of much less
note than Felix' had been assembling their webs. Along the building's
perimeter, water sloshed as puddles formed from runoff, and tiny streams
seeped in beneath its timber frame. Now and again thunder rolled
between there and the lake, where warm air and cold collided.

Felix had moved on from his hair-raising description of the spider
to write about school, which he somehow got to each day by way of
his Uncle Milton and not a school bus. He said his uncle normally
drove him there in their Ford, but because the car had a flat tire this
day, he instead used a Cord 810 set aside for Sunday church and special family occasions. Since in all of Marvin's talk about cars she had
never heard of one called a Cord, Penelope thought it possibly an
airplane, a far-fetched assumption when it came to church attendance,
but less so when it came to Uncle Milton, who in Felix' letters had
taken on the features of a larger-than-life hero. It was clear the boy
worshipped him.

Not your ordinary Minnesota farmer, Milton actually owned two
airplanes kept in a machinery shed he had adapted for use as a hangar.
Felix had occasional rides in both those planes and had even done
some local "barnstorming" with his uncle, on one occasion landing at
an airstrip when Charles Lindbergh was just taking off.

Much of this, which might have been taken as bragging, had flown
right over Penelope's head as if she had been in the barn being stormed,
until she asked Marvin about it. Barnstorming, he said, was something like antique car rallies going from town to town but up in the
sky instead of over highways. Lindbergh had seemed to puzzle him.
As far as he knew, the retired aviator hero died some years ago in
Hawaii.

"I think Felix is stretching things a bit", he had suggested.

Osgood bolted up and ran for the pole barn double doors as Marvin arrived in one of his three pickups. Minutes later he was rifling through his mail at his workbench while Penelope was on her way to the Frazer's glove box with Felix' letter.

"Hey!" he shouted over the cab of his Studebaker. "This package is for you!"

What Penelope had thought was a car part turned out to be a small book and a folded note from Sister Hilaria. The note thanked her for her greeting after Mass on Pentecost Sunday. Penelope had made one of the most exciting days of the Church year, if possible, even more exciting, as befitted an occasion when Christ's closest friends found their tongues at last. Sister ended the note by saying she had left something too big to mail with Sister Serena. The enclosed book was a paperback life of St. John Vianney, whose cover bore the same picture of him with his pointed nose that she had first seen on the holy card Sister had given her years before.

Penelope returned from the Frazer empty-handed. Somehow even Sister Hilaria had become a secret. Marvin opened the door to the rain pouring down outside. Osgood barked.

"We will have to run for it!" he shouted.

The pole barn became once again Osgood's domain.

June had arrived from the other Osgoode domain, and Penelope made a point of greeting her at the garage entrance. June made her usual motherly fuss, asking her how her day had gone, unable to suppress the same wary tone people might use when reporting a mysterious package to the police. The package might have looked ordinary and innocent enough, and Penelope, except for her carrot hair, looked ordinary and innocent enough, but that was reason enough to be suspicious. Standing there, holding open her mother's car door while June gathered a pile of work to do over the weekend, Penelope could not have looked more innocent and more capable of concealing something.

After supper June withdrew to what had become her home office, once Marvin's den in the days before he constructed the pole barn and moved his desk, desk lamp, and even magazine shelves to join his workbenches and his arsenal of tools.

"So what did Felix have to say this time?" He spoke into something resembling a sculpted head of dish soap bubbles rising toward them both from beneath a gushing faucet.

Penelope mentioned the spider, which for Marvin seemed easier to account for than Lindbergh in that earlier letter.

"They can get pretty fat and happy on all those farm flies", he said.

"But what kind of an airplane is a Cord 810? Could Felix' uncle fly him to school in one of those and maybe land it in a play yard?"

"That baby can fly," said Marvin swept into a daydream all of a sudden, "but it's not an airplane. The Cord 810 is just about the most beautiful car ever made. Back in the thirties it was a design wonder, with features nobody making cars had ever dreamed of. I've only seen pictures of them, only a few left. Nobody would take one out unless the president or somebody as important came to town."

Marvin stopped right there in the middle of his dream, in the middle of a casserole dish, and in the middle of Felix' fifth letter.

"Did you say Uncle Milton drives a Cord 810/812?"

"No, it was just a Cord 810." Penelope practically knew by heart all of Felix' letters.

"Just?"

"Just."

Marvin scooped out a large heap of bubbles, which as a piece of it clung to his nose in passing he put on top of Penelope's head.

"Eureka!" he exclaimed. He had just seen a vision.

Not for almost anything in the world would he go near Clay Corners. Not for anything would he mention that rural village to June. Not for even more than that would he take Penelope there. Yet Marvin, the next morning after a fitful night's sleep, spun the closest he could come to subterfuge.

Not to Penelope quite yet, and certainly not ever to June, but to Osgood, out in the pole barn with his head in his bowl of dog chow, he said, "I've gotta see that car!"

Part Two

The Jig Is Up

You can fool all of the people some of the time, and some of the people all of the time, but you cannot fool all of the people all of the time.

—Abraham Lincoln (attributed)

9

A Crazy Idea

Meanwhile, more than two hundred miles away, Felix was sitting on the edge of his bed on the second floor of the rooming house where he lived. He was tying his shoes while deep in thought, so tugging at various eyelets was taking longer than usual.

The rooming house was Ed's Hotel, though it rarely served as a hotel and for most of its existence had been inhabited by village bachelors and widowers, with an occasional traveling salesman showing up for a night or two in days gone by. Clay Corners bachelors could be regarded as predestined for Ed's, their arrival one day being inevitable once their mothers died or became incapacitated or their sisters tired of looking after them. They could only hope a room would be available when the fated day dawned. Ed's widowers were mostly retired farmers who had come in off the land, but wanted to live close to its corn tassels, bean rows, and gossip.

Felix was an exception to this, for though he had grown up on a farm and for a time actually owned a farm, he had never thought of himself as a farmer. He had been a rural mail carrier, and this, combined with a keen memory connecting names and faces, meant he knew everyone who had ever lived within twenty miles of Clay Corners for the forty years he delivered countryside mail.

If a farmer informed him his mother-in-law was moving in for two weeks in July and might be getting a letter, Felix would remember; no need to put "in care of" on the address. If she returned for another two-week visit the following July, he needn't be reminded. His mail route having changed several times over those many years, he had been everywhere, over every road with a rural mailbox, and had become friends with every farmer and farm dog. Even milk cows gazing up from their pasture grass as he drove by seemed to know him.

His boss, the Clay Corners postmaster, had been deliberate about changing Felix' delivery route. Over time, not very much time, Felix would turn his rural rounds into a chain of social engagements, holding conversations from his car window with farmers mending fences or idling their tractors at the ends of corn rows. He turned ordinary mail into special delivery by driving right up to a kitchen door, where coffee and fresh doughnuts would be waiting. As the months went by, all this socializing meant that mail came later and later in the day. Felix, parched from talking, swollen with maybe ten cups of coffee, bloated with cookies and pastries of all sorts, could barely cover his delivery route before the day had to end.

All this began anew when his route was changed. The mail on his previous route in the hands of a less sociable sort arrived hours earlier, and for the interlude it took Felix to rebuild his acquaintances, even Felix' deliveries came sooner.

So well-known was Felix that he might have run for public office and had even been encouraged to do so. To get elected as a county commissioner or a state representative would have been no challenge at all, but he disliked the ways of politics and politicians. Better to be rural Clay County's newspaper on wheels, hobnobbing and carrying tales of births and illness from farm to farm, along with crop and weather reports. Doors were always open when he was near, and people glad to see him and hating to see him go. Theirs were the votes that mattered.

He put off retirement and his postal service pension until failing eyesight made him both a road hazard and haphazard. Even then, ten years ago, as he approached seventy-five with a new postmaster on the scene, he resisted retiring until practically being forced out. Folks who had discovered in their mailboxes more mail for their neighbors than for themselves nevertheless mourned his absence. If a man did not have to be dead to have his face on a commemorative stamp, they would have started a campaign for Felix.

Felix still had a full head of boyish brown hair and was alert as a jack rabbit, though he wore glasses as thick as the bottoms of goldfish bowls and even so could not see much. The extent of his experience beyond Clay County was three years in the army, two spent in a Nazi prisoner-of-war camp.

His best friend, Ralph Corrigan, was waiting across the street in a booth at the Depot Café, formerly the village train depot. Ralph too had been deep in thought.

"It's a crazy idea", he said when Felix had settled into a seat across from him and was stirring sugar in his coffee. "Do you realize the trouble you could get into writing letters to little girls, a man your age?"

Felix' age as of last week was eighty-five.

"It's only one girl", said Felix, "singular, not plural, and the fellow writing her is a year younger than she is, depending on when her birthday is, of course."

Ralph, the not-quite-retired village druggist, snorted his disgust. Though twenty years Felix' junior, Ralph had infirmities not yet apparent in Felix. He had a tremor in his left hand, which he normally controlled by keeping it tucked under his thigh or pressed against a convenient wall. When he became sufficiently excited to lose track, the hand would come out and its fingers tap insistently as if to make a point much like a telegrapher sending Morse code. His fingers appeared and began tapping, in this circumstance an SOS.

"Besides, Ralph, she will never know how old I really am."

"Oh, you think so, do you? Well, the unforeseen—I long ago learned—has a way of happening, and by this time you should have learned it, too."

Felix had a policy from the same life insurance company insuring Marvin Lister and thus received twice a year the same boring magazine whose format had not changed in either's memory. The difference was that Felix' memory stretched back decades further, and he actually read his copy because he got so little mail in his post office box. The arrival of anything other than a grocery store flier or a hearing-aid ad was an occasion demanding his full attention. With a large magnifying glass in hand, he pored over every word, applying the concentration of a detective or a stamp collector.

"So what the hell did you say to her?" his friend Ralph asked with his restless hand now once more tucked under his thigh.

"Well, I talked about the weather, my uncle's farm, and how I was doing in school, for starters."

"Let's see", said the other. "Seventy or so years ago that would be. Did you tell her your school was painted white and had only one room?"

"Not yet. I told her about our playground on the lake—"

"Where all those million-dollar houses are now."

"No, that's where my uncle used to run his turkeys during the thir-ties' drought years."

Ralph snorted. "And about your school's five-holer outhouse?"

"Would you believe that's still being used as a storage shed on one of my old mail route farms? Wouldn't mention that. Do you think I'm stupid?"

Ralph smiled at him over his raised coffee cup. Among the many words describing Felix, all of them growing more inadequate every year he had a birthday—and all of them adding up to the same word at the bottom of a column, that word being *amazing*—would never be found the word *stupid*.

Nor would anyone attempting to explain his reasons for writing Penelope and pretending to be a boy about her age find the word *lonely* there. Felix, for whom a single adjective did not seem to exist, was the very opposite of lonely. He had a village and its countryside all around full of friends. Felix would not have written Penelope from loneliness but from its very opposite condition, from being full of friendliness bursting its seams everywhere. He lived beyond bound-aries and borders; beyond stereotypes, clichés, and convictions; and well beyond any words trotted out to describe him.

Felix' old schoolhouse had been the one-room sort, and like so many things in both his life and Ralph's, it no longer existed. After it had gone through a second life as a rural town hall, with its old stu-dent desks piled out back in a brush patch before antique hunters carted them away, it had been abandoned and finally torn down. In alternating years corn and soybeans grew where it used to be. In the haphazard way a long buried past will occasionally surface, a farmer's plow might turn up an old inkwell, a broken hinge, a shingle, or the brass hook belonging to a pole used to raise and lower windows too high to reach. These in turn would be buried again until they sur-faced like cicadas a few years later.

Felix' memories never underwent this fate. His past and present overlaid each other as semitransparent pages in an atlas and gazetteer displaying subsequent eras of history. It was all there at once, even in fields overturned and laid bare. He could not look at any of it without seeing it all in a single panorama. His Uncle Milton's airplanes still soared and swooped overhead, with Felix up there beside him at times. The giant spider still hung in an open doorway of a barn bulldozed to make way for a perimeter of stone walls. Nothing ever vanished simply because something, even something ugly, took its place. It was all there at once, held in place by the vision of a man who needed a magnifying glass to read and write letters to Penelope in those wavering lines.

Nearby, in the same township as the school house, surrounded by more corn and soybeans in alternating years, at the end of a winding road on the edge of a Reed canary grass marsh, was a cemetery all but surrounded by spruce trees. Among its graves could be found that of Felix' wife, gone now some twenty-five years, and that of "Penelope, beloved daughter". Felix' only child had died of rheumatic fever when little more than twelve years old.

Thus Felix picked Penelope for his pen pal from the list of those advertising in the magazine. It was not a very long list, but had it been a hundred times longer, hers of all names would have caught his squinting eyes. Had Penelope not been there, he would not have written anyone.

Now that he had begun, no word of caution Ralph threw in his path and nothing anyone else might say would keep him from writing her again. Ralph knew Felix well enough to know he might as well caution a duck about swimming in a pond. That the unforeseen had a way of happening would not have stopped the duck either, so he kept further advice to himself as he walked Felix back to Ed's before crossing the street to his Corner Drug, where a CLOSED sign hanging askew indicated a customer had come in anyway. Felix was not the only duck in Clay Corners.

10

Weather, School, Farm, and Ed's

Letters between Felix and Penelope resembled tennis, a game neither of them had ever played: Felix served and controlled the game, while Penelope raced this way and that to return his successive volleys. Awkwardness and unfamiliarity dominated Penelope's side, while Felix, becoming ever more comfortable, let down his guard—weak as it was to begin with—and said things that could hardly have come from a boy of thirteen, unless he had been thirteen for the past seventy or so years.

His habit of sincerity got in the way of pretense. He would never have succeeded as an actor. He could not for long be something he wasn't. His successive letters to Penelope sounded less and less like the thoughts of a thirteen-year-old boy and more and more like the ramblings of an old man with a keen memory. Having had no experience writing old-fashioned letters on paper to pen pals or anyone else, Penelope knew nothing about starting a subject of her own. If Felix talked about weather, school, and life on his uncle's farm, she felt obliged to reply about *his* weather, *his* school, and *his* life on his uncle's farm. It was always Felix' tennis ball. This sense of obligation collided with another, somewhat like the ball hitting the net on its way back to Felix: She felt that her letters ought to be interesting even while she did her best to be interested in his. Many a rumpled sheet of the notebook paper on which she wrote found its way into a rubbish bucket under the kitchen sink before something made its way to Felix' Clay Corners post office box.

Marvin, who emptied the trash every day, noticed this and reminded her to be more careful. Still he didn't explain.

Felix never had to start over, never rumpled a page of his writing tablet, and was never at a loss for something to say. His entire life stayed at his fingertips. He was one of those uncommon sorts for whom time is remarkably foreshortened, leaving what are sometimes called the "arches of the years" in each other's shadows. With each arch representing a decade behind him, it was only a short walk to the preceding decade, and traversing the lot of them was merely a stroll. He could wander almost anywhere in the few paragraphs of a single letter, from his mother dying when he was born to his father dying not long after and from there to his uncle's farm where he grew up. Times before he was born and before he could remember were filled in by his uncle and his grandfather. They soon became *his* stories, as if he had really been there.

He knew better than to share all of it with his young pen pal, but Felix could achieve something like escape velocity as he gathered momentum among those arching memories. Missteps were possible both in storytelling and in war with its land mines. He could only be so careful treading his way through. He never stepped on a landmine, but instead wound up behind barbed wire in a German prisoner-of-war stockade, where twice each week young women walked by carrying loaves of fresh-baked bread. The prisoners ignored the women and pined after the bread. He could still smell the bread. He could close his eyes and see expressions on the faces of his prison mates. He could also see his daughter's face in a time after that. He could stand at her bedside, where she lay dying. Though his hearing was so bad that others had to shout at him, he could even hear her voice as if whispered across a room only yesterday. All this he struggled to keep from his new Penelope.

If the morning or evening star happened to gleam through Felix' tunnel of arches, and if the moon or another planet happened to be quite close by, a casual observer might think these two companions close celestial neighbors, when they were simply in the same line of sight and in reality far apart. For Felix, viewing his own history, events were much like this, in his line of sight and yet sometimes far away from each other. Thus his memories were a mishmash of events, skewed out of their chronology and natural order, a clutter requiring historians to make sense of it, though it might have made more sense left the way Felix recounted in his letters to Penelope of Star Island.

"All he ever talks about are the weather, his school, and the farm he lives on with his aunt and uncle", she said to Marvin one Saturday

morning in the pole barn. Marvin thought that was quite a bit to
work into a letter.

"What's sarsaparilla?"

"It's sort of like root beer", said Marvin. "I don't think they make
it anymore."

Much of what Felix wrote to Penelope had been well rehearsed on
mail routes and wherever old-timers might gather in the village, foremost the barber shop, a bench in front of the fire hall, and Ed's Hotel,
whose residents all knew each other's tales by heart, having heard them
morning, noon, and evening in the downstairs tavern café, where they
gathered for meals, and repeated when a new face appeared on the
scene or the narrator forgot what he had recounted only last week.

Among other things Felix succeeded in *not* mentioning was Ed's
Hotel. Now and then he had been there as a boy of thirteen sipping
sarsaparilla while his uncle at the bar visited with its proprietor of that
era, a man who always wore a coat and tie while answering to the
disheveled-sounding sobriquet of Jigs. Penelope might hear about sarsaparilla, but Ed's was a land mine too close for comfort.

Like Jigs, the hotel itself was also a local anomaly: Nobody by the
name of Ed had ever owned it, and only sporadically had it been a
hotel. The ramshackle enterprise seemed never to have seen better
days, for it had been ramshackle from the day it opened, the year
President McKinley was inaugurated. It had stayed insistently ramshackle through the terms of fifteen subsequent presidents. The wonder was it had not burned down. Like many village buildings of the
pioneer era, the hotel had a clapboard false front, creating the illusion
it had a third floor above two real ones. Its false front was only the
most immediately noticeable of its several illusions.

It was more a rooming house than a hotel, and when, as occasionally happened, a traveling salesman in need of a bed for the night
would stop by and ask for Ed, he was often told that Ed had just
stepped out. This bit of simple fun at a stranger's expense wrapped
itself around the puzzle that Ed must have stepped in just long enough
to get his name on the place and then stepped out before anyone
could remember he had been there. The closest this history came to
Ed was its current owner, Fred. At least it rhymed.

Through a succession of owners whose first names sounded like
those of presidents—Grover, Woodrow, and Ike—followed by Jigs, who

dressed like a president, and finally Fred, the place had remained inexplicably Ed's. People referred to Ed as if his daily presence on the premises was a fact never to be questioned.

Ed served beer and hamburgers cooked in the old-fashioned way by flattening ground beef blobs on a greasy grill and then sliding them onto a split bun toasted in grease nearby. Ed had beef jerky and jars of pickled pig's feet; turkey gizzards; and, for the Christmas season, herring rollmops.

Over Ed's bar were tacked several faded placards whose corners curled around jokes so old that men grew senile in their presence. Both their fathers and their own sons had memorized them, not deliberately but as the result of long exposure, of multiple glances between sips of Ed's beer. Had you gone to church every Sunday throughout a long life, you would have seen more changes in the church than at Ed's, and you would have had faith of a sort in Ed, the man being as ubiquitous as God, more associated with practical necessity, and just as invisible a presence.

At the moment Ed's Hotel had no vacancies, a situation Fred found desirable, but for apprentice geezers a source of anxiety as they saw their lives drifting in that direction. Ed's eight upstairs rooms, four either side of a hallway, were all occupied as of a week ago, when the last of them became home for a retired railroad worker named Harry. On one side, rooms looked out upon the roof of an abandoned farm implement dealership; on Felix' side was the old train depot, which after years of neglect had been converted to a competing café. Each of Ed's rooms had a single bed, a small television, a dresser, a writing table, and but one chair. A sign over a stairway to the left of the bar said, "Residents Only".

Given the age of Ed's residents, this was less necessary for propriety's sake than good for business. Successive owners were sharp enough to see the advantage of having visiting friends and family gather downstairs in the tavern, which served as a public house, or pub in the old-fashioned sense of that word. Never in the history of Ed's had there been a female resident, and never would a woman have applied to live there.

This was but one of many unwritten understandings governing the life of rural villages like Clay Corners. A barber at the other end of Front Street had never cut a woman's hair or ever been asked to do so.

There had never been a male teacher in the village's school or a male librarian for its small community library in the same building.

Ed's might as well have been under the governance of an abbot, for it was de facto a secular monastery among whose monastic rituals were meals downstairs for residents at designated times and rules governing the use of its upstairs bathrooms at either end of the hallway, whose rank aromas were those old men bring with them and no amount of scrubbing or brushing can dispel, not even a regular Pine-Sol washdown whose medicinal odor would drift downstairs and linger well into the tavern's evening hours.

11

Grandpa Albert

Ralph's advice to Felix was of the sort encouraging people to head for a storm shelter while the sky is still clear. It wasn't going to make any sense before it made sense, which in this case was soon forthcoming. The unforeseen, as he put it, *did* have a way of happening.

In early June, Felix strolled into the post office and came out with his latest letter from Penelope, which had arrived sooner than he had expected. He went up to his room to read it under his magnifying glass. Halfway through its single page, he quit reading and made a beeline for Ralph's drugstore across the street.

Despite the CLOSED sign on its front door that Saturday afternoon, Felix rushed in. Ralph and his wife, Esther, were settling into an old wooden booth to have lunch in the manner of days gone by when the store had a soda fountain.

Neither of them could get a word in before Felix, as discombobulated as they had ever seen him, babbled on until he ended with "the two of them are going to be here next Saturday around this time", which in fact were the exact words he had blurted out at the beginning. Esther, a trained and experienced psychologist, continued eating and listened with an air of calm suggesting Felix was just now reporting the discovery of dust bunnies under his bed. Ralph, untrained in such arts, expressed something wordless with tapping fingers and facial expressions, including a bit of squinting, as he recalled saying something to Felix he was reluctant to quote verbatim. Even given the chance to get a word in edgewise, he wasn't the sort to say, "I told you so."

As the only person in Clay Corners with anything that might be taken for a medical background, Ralph was used to telling people things they didn't want to hear. He had become a sort of stand-in for

65

the doctor, dentist, chiropractor, and even the veterinarian the village had in its heyday. He was accustomed to being a Clay Corners version of socialized medicine, dispensing free advice and cautious diagnostic speculations in small, tentative doses, most of which suggested they consult with someone who knew more about it than he did, that *someone* being miles away and charging a fee they were trying to avoid by approaching Ralph instead.

He might also poke around in his cupboards for a bottle of horse liniment whose manufacturer went out of business a few years ago, bemoan the demise of Bromo-Seltzer, and speak with passion about the value of aspirin, whose dangers in his view had been grossly exaggerated by a medical establishment making a killing on more expensive and even more dangerous alternatives. Much of this he could manage to communicate by squinting, massaging the bridge of his nose, and tapping a countertop with his out-of-control fingers.

His customers—or patients, as they liked to think of themselves despite his protests to the contrary—were nostalgic about the days, before even aspirin was discovered, when people died of natural causes after living to a ripe old age. A world without Bromo-Seltzer and doctors making house calls was clearly a world gone off in the wrong direction. They all could remember grandparents of several generations ago who had lived longer than anyone since in their family, had never bothered with doctors, and had never been sick a day in their lives before the morning they died. Felix' Grandpa Albert was one such, and, in a vein far different, his memory was at this moment waiting a step or two offstage before entering the present conversation.

Jack rabbit Felix had lived these many years in his verdant meadow of easy familiarity with nary a gunshot or a hound at his heels. He had not thought of jumping up and bolting away from a scene since his German prisoner days. This solution was now the first thing entering his mind.

"The worst possible thing", said Ralph. "Set them loose in this town on their own with you missing, and they wouldn't have to ask more than one question of the first three people they met out there before they had your entire life story, beginning, by the way, with the seventy-two years you have so far not bothered to mention to that girl."

Finishing a last bite of his sandwich, Ralph gave the street outside a significant nod, as if he could already see Felix' biography running through a printing press out there.

"No, head in that direction, and the jig is up, I'd say."

The end of the jig was not the sort of thing anyone in Clay Corners wanted to hear from their stand-in physician, dentist, and all-around medical expert. He motioned for Felix, who had been standing up to this point, to join them in the booth, whose tall backs in years gone by had appealed to young couples concealing themselves while they shared a fountain soda.

"You've got to meet this head-on. Blazes, what are they coming here for?"

Felix pulled Penelope's last letter from his jacket pocket and slid it across to them as if the envelope by itself coming to a rest between their teacups explained it all. When silence all around followed this gesture, he finally choked out a few details.

"Penelope wants to meet young Felix, and her stepfather, Marvin, wants to see my Uncle Milton's Cord 810."

Penelope's name caught Ralph's ear, as her blue-and-red-striped envelope caught his eye.

"That's got to be the first airmail letter arriving here since I sold my last can of Dr. Lyon's Tooth Powder", Ralph said. "I imagine you delivered plenty of envelopes like that in your time. There were even a few left here in this store when we first moved in." He pointed across to what was once a stationery display and now was reduced to an odd assortment of out-of-style greeting cards. "Even have around here somewhere a few bottles of ink for fountain pens."

He would have continued this time travel but for Esther nudging him under the table. She had been studying the envelope as if it really did have much to say beyond any connection with dirigibles once traversing the Atlantic.

"No, you have to stand up to this and meet them as planned", said Ralph, returning to the problem at hand.

"I can't", said Felix.

"Of course you can, and you *must*, but you just cannot be Felix. It's as plain as the nose on your face—you have to be somebody else."

Felix' was in fact a sizable nose forming a necessary perch for his glasses with their thick lenses, but less plain to him was who that somebody else might be.

"You need to be Felix' grandpa!" Ralph said decidedly.

"I need to be Grandpa Albert?"

"The name hardly matters, but that's as good as any, I'd say."

Felix' grandfather had in fact been Albert, father of his Uncle Milton and his own dad, and one of those ancients who had survived by never seeing a doctor. Memories of him helped ease Felix into the spirit of Ralph's plan, and with that much in play, the rest fell in place in the time it took for Ralph and Esther to finish lunch and settle Felix' nerves with a cup of tea and their many reassurances.

In the words of a jolly old song they all remembered, Felix would be his own grandpa next Saturday, right in this very booth. Never before had this old building through its many permutations served as a theater, but it was about to hold its first-ever play, of the one-act sort.

Minutes later, across the street, Felix and Ralph sat at a corner table in Ed's tavern café while Fred studied them from a distance and pretended to be polishing his bar. They were answering Penelope's one-page letter with a single page of their own, mostly dictated by Ralph, since Felix continued to be at his unaccustomed loss for words.

"Why can't I just write and tell her that Uncle Milton and I are going somewhere next Saturday?"

"Because your Uncle Milton has been dead for forty years, and they will just postpone until some other Saturday", said Ralph, with his left-hand fingers for good measure tapping on Ed's tabletop.

He knew better than to leave the rest to Felix. Only with the letter safely slipped through the "Out-of-Town" mail slot at the village post office did he return to his pharmaceutical museum, while Felix headed upstairs for a nap.

Upstairs at Ralph's, Esther Corrigan had been engaged in research among her notebooks of sessions with counseling clients, securely locked in a cabinet of their apartment library. She had made a discovery that true to her professional calling she would not yet share with her husband, especially with him engaged in directing a play.

12

A Séance

Marvin had a plan of his own for Saturday. Standing in the doorway of June's home office, he shared with her the part she wouldn't question: Since the weather was good, he and Penelope were driving south to look at a car he had heard about. An instinctively honest sort, engaged in what felt like a deception, he said more than he needed to say and almost gave the game away when he mentioned "somewhere near St. Cloud". Fortunately, June's thoughts were elsewhere than on geography. She was happy to hear Penelope had been invited along. This would get her off the island for the day, and it seemed like something a real dad would do. Marvin, encouraged, flirted with the truth yet further.

"I think the owner has a boy about her age."

It seemed strange that he would know this from a car magazine ad, but this too failed to catch June's attention.

Having survived this far by telling the truth and seeing nothing but lies up ahead if he went further, he changed the subject to June's summer plans for Penelope. June was already at work on arrangements of the sort a school counselor had suggested. These would have her among girls her own age for two weeks at summer's beginning and then keep her occupied most weekdays after that, all the better if Marvin could invite her on a couple more of his car hunts. Having begun this exchange in something of a conspiracy with Penelope, he ended it drawn into a conspiracy with her mother.

A road trip from the North Shore of Lake Superior to farm country south of St. Cloud would normally be a journey veering ever more to the west as the miles went by. Marvin planned to approach Clay Corners by veering farther west than the shortest route, going past the village, and then approaching it from the south, as if road construction had forced a detour in fact forced by other circumstances.

Penelope paid little attention to directions, other than that they were going south—it had to be south because the farther they drove from the gigantic lake, with its own cool climate, the more they were leaving behind spring's last days and entering summer. Mile by mile more buds burst, until trees came fully into leaf. Behind them cows had been munching brown hay in gray mire behind barns, while up ahead they stood under shade trees in pastures of brilliant green. Dandelions of the north yielded to tulips and fields of young Alsace clover. These in turn yielded to lilacs blooming along yard borders and dogs lying in shade beside doorsteps. Fields not yet tilled for planting gave way to others where rows of corn and soybeans became more distinct by the hour, with some of them forming graceful curves on hillside contours and winding in spidery filaments around marshes where red-winged blackbirds perched on last year's cattails.

The White Whale's windows were eventually rolled down halfway. A warm breeze flooded over them, bringing with it now and then meadowlark song when they paused at country road intersections or crept along behind a farmer's tractor. Penelope could even wonder if the last of these might have been Uncle Milton's as they passed a sign announcing Clay Corners three miles ahead. She spotted an airplane overhead and thought surely the pilot was Uncle Milton.

In daydreams of his own, Marvin was already running his hands along the remarkable body lines of Uncle Milton's Cord. He loved the treasure-finding aspect of his hobby, against all odds the chance discovery of the genuine thing, but he was weak on the end where major restoration was required and amounted to rebuilding with new body parts manufactured for this purpose. He might replace a door handle or a glove box latch, but never an entire door. What he was best at was rebuilding engines and restoring working parts to a level last seen at the end of an assembly line. A Cord still being used for rides to school had to be in good mechanical shape, maybe as good as his 1960 Desoto, still reliable on two-hundred-mile road trips.

History, of course, tends to be least visible to those sitting in the middle of it, and while Marvin had the Cord in mind, those out and about when he and Penelope rolled into Clay Corners were gawking after them. Milton's Cord 810 would have been hardly more sensational than the finned Desoto White Whale pulling up and parking in front of Ralph's Corner Drug, where a CLOSED sign hung on its door. For the half hour Marvin was parked there, no one nearby could think of anything else. Fred peered from a tavern window, went back to fidget behind the bar, and then returned to peek out again.

Ten minutes or so after noon, the bell over Ralph's door tinkled. Marvin and Penelope stepped in and were greeted by a wiry little man with a full head of sandy brown hair and thick, wire-rimmed spectacles, Grandpa Albert by name. The drugstore interior was especially dark compared to the sunny street outside, deliberately so, Ralph having turned most of its lights off with the general notion that the less seen the better. At first, while their eyes adjusted, Marvin and Penelope could perceive little more than the gleaming orbs of Felix' glasses reflecting the sunlight at their backs.

For the second Saturday in a row Felix was speechless at first—considering the circumstances, one might have said stagestruck—meeting his pen pal for the first time. He had naturally imagined her in various ways resembling his own deceased daughter, none of them in the least resembling Penelope. Not yet knowing she was meeting Felix for the first time, Penelope at least didn't have this problem. At first all Felix could notice was her carrot-colored hair, not ever mentioned in her letters because up to this point the letters had been mostly about him. Ralph, out of sight around the corner in a storage room, longed for a script prompter, but thanks to Marvin's high spirits and Penelope's smile, the play moved forward, though far from the way the two of them imagined, as the word *measles* appeared among them in Felix' recollected script.

Young Felix, who planned to meet them here and guide them out to Uncle Milton's farm, had come down with the measles, diagnosed as such just this morning and too late to let them know. He was already covered with red spots and running a fever. He was quarantined; Uncle Milton was quarantined; the whole farm was quarantined. It was an especially virulent form of the disease. State health people were taking no chances. Grandpa Albert's informing them of this sounded so rehearsed that Ralph began to wonder if he would pull it off. Penelope was close to tears with the thought of her pen pal in such desperate straits. Marvin took her hand.

"The Cord 810?" he managed to ask, as heartless as that sounded at a time like this.

"Quarantined, too, I'm afraid", said Felix, now happy enough to declare everything in his corner of the world under quarantine. He had found his old tongue and was getting into the spirit of this play so far that he felt ready to improvise. In fact, he had stepped out of character and become his old self again. Ralph's script at this point called for him to lead them back as far as the screen door, expressing his regrets, and pleading a grandfather's needed assistance in such an emergency. He wasn't supposed to follow them out into the street because out there the whole town knew him, and anyone might greet him by name. The jig would be up for sure.

Felix could see the wisdom in that, but his old mail route sociability was taking charge. He was having too much fun to break this off quite so quickly in the safety of the shuttered drugstore, so he invited them to take a seat in Ralph's high-backed wooden booth for a few minutes while he sat across so they could catch their breaths before they headed home after such a long trip.

Set aside temporarily was Grandpa Albert's need to be elsewhere. He had just thought of a story he planned to tell Penelope in his next letter, one long enough to save him a good bit of writing under that magnifying glass. The play had evolved into the two-act variety, with an actor inclined toward the ham. Felix loved being his own grandpa. He loved speaking about himself in the third person. Ralph wanted to rush out with a bottled nostrum, one whiff of which would have sedated a charging rhino. The fingers of his left hand upon a pile of old calendars moved as quickly as any pianist's executing a rapidly ascending arpeggio.

"Felix was just saying to me only the other day—", said Felix when the bell over Ralph's door announced the entrance of Fred from Ed's.

The play having moved out of sight into the booth, Fred at first thought the store was empty. He squinted for signs of life. He had seen Felix cross the street and enter the closed drugstore, and he had seen the Desoto arrive. Thirty minutes later he decided to bring Felix something he had left on the hotel stairs landing. Maybe he needed it.

Fred, a Southerner, was by far the most gentlemanly of Ed's many owners, the most full of old-fashioned courtesy combined with good-natured curiosity nourishing flights of fancy and absurd speculations. Given a list of possible explanations for anything the least bit out of the ordinary, Fred could be trusted to embrace the most far-fetched.

He had long harbored the notion that Ed's had at least one ghost wandering around the premises on certain nights when wind or an insomniac tenant might have better explained the creaking he heard overhead in his downstairs bedroom. Like everyone else on Front Street that afternoon, he had been wondering about the white Desoto, but unlike everyone else, he saw a portent in its outlandish lines. Also unlike everyone else, he had an excuse for investigating.

"Felix?" he shouted from just inside the door. "Ralph?" he shouted, taking sufficient steps in to see Felix on his side of the booth facing the door.

"Hey, Felix," he said, "you must have dropped this coming down from your room on your way here. I thought you might need it."

He waved a familiar envelope in the air beneath an old ceiling fan. A further two steps had taken him within sight of Marvin and Penelope on the other side of the booth. His old-fashioned courtesy kicked in, buying a few seconds for his curiosity to penetrate this mystery of two strangers sitting with Felix, one of them a girl with orange hair. He glanced from one face to another and danced from one foot to another, waiting for somebody to say something. Since he held what amounted to a live grenade in hand, everyone else was dumbstruck.

Even as far outside Ralph's script as all this had wandered, Felix might have introduced Fred, except for finding himself stuck crosswise between his two identities: Felix as far as Fred was concerned and otherwise Grandpa Albert. Apart from a genial grin from Marvin, himself crosswise in an indescribable limbo between euphoria and amazement, nobody communicated anything. A ticking pendulum clock on a wall behind Ralph's cash register seemed suddenly louder. The nearby "Things Go Better with Coke" sign seemed suddenly sarcastic.

Out of lines for what had so far been a monologue, and with rescue nowhere near, Fred gave up and let go of his grenade, dropping onto the tabletop Penelope's most recent letter and the cause of all this in the first place. It lay there beneath all of their gazes in the glory of its unmistakable red-and-blue airmail piping.

"Felix, I'll see you later", he said. "We're having your favorite fried chicken tonight, Felix."

Fred's simple notions about old-fashioned Dixie courtesy required using first names as much as possible; it was not unusual for him to begin and end a sentence of direct address with the addressee's first

name. As far as he was concerned, first names worked a lot like liniment of the sort Ralph might sell: Massage with first names helped
soreness go away. He hesitated for a further moment. When even
tonight's fried chicken floating between two Felixes had no effect, he
stuck out a hand in the direction of Marvin.

"I'm Fred", he said and then by way of further courtesy explained
that Felix lived in his place across the street and kept everyone there
entertained with his stories.

With his eyes first on the letter and then on Felix, Marvin shook
Fred's hand, but without his usual firm grip.

"Name's Marvin", he said, still not looking Fred's way.

"Marvin, glad to meet you, Marvin", said Fred. "And the young
lady?"

"Penelope", said Marvin.

"Penelope, glad to meet you, too", said Fred. He cleared his throat,
looked at the hand that had just shaken Marvin's, and seemed about
to step back. "I've heard a lot about you, Penelope." With a feeling of
strangeness sinking in, Fred felt a damp chill sometimes associated with
meeting a ghost.

"And this here is Grandpa Albert", said Marvin in his wife's best
between-the-teeth manner.

Grandpa Albert attempted a smile and for some reason held out his
hand to shake Fred's.

"Of course ...", said Fred, who had also heard a lot about Grandpa
Albert. He didn't know what to make of it, but he had read enough
about ghosts to know touching them was risky. He stared at Felix'
hand. "Excuse the intrusion", he said and tiptoed away as people will
do when they have walked through the wrong door and stumbled
upon something not meant to be seen. Ralph's bell tinkled. Ralph
offstage cupped his ears with his hands, though little remained not to
hear. Silence took over.

Even at this point, a man less sincere than Felix might have saved
the day, even a man no better at acting. He could have remained
Grandpa Albert and said his middle name was Felix; all the people
around Ed's, where he lived these days, called him that. He could have
said young Felix gave him the letter to take so he would remember
their names. Ralph, in hiding, had all this flashing through his teem-
ing brain, along with a desire to strangle Fred the next time he saw

him. For Felix, though, he had to be himself again. Anything else would be too complicated.

"The jig's up, I guess", he said since he could not for the moment think of anything else.

"I'll say it is," said Marvin at his most indignant, "and you'll be lucky if this is the end of it." He was not sure what he meant by that, but it seemed to fit the occasion.

Both of them so taken by surprise had little else to say. Penelope was the least surprised, for ever since she had been sitting across from Grandpa Albert, she had been studying a ring he wore on his left index finger. It was a soldier's war souvenir fashioned from a shell casing with a cross deeply etched into it. Felix had mentioned how it had been passed down to him in his family, having once belonged to his father, and he always wore it for good luck. This time it brought the opposite, because of course he had forgotten his telling her about his lucky ring in the second letter he wrote. For Penelope, Grandpa Albert had begun to be Felix even before Fred appeared on the scene.

As she and Marvin were leaving, she turned to see the old man slumped over with his head in his hands. She called back to him.

"The spider? Was there ever the big spider?"

"A long time ago", he said. His glasses glistened with regret as he looked up at her.

"It's okay. Really, it's okay."

Marvin tugged her hand, the bell tinkled, the play ended, and a minute later the White Whale roared north out of the village on a highway toward St. Cloud.

Fred in his kitchen cutting up chicken missed this quick exit, but he already had more than enough to ponder. Separating drumsticks from thighs with a single clean cut was one thing, but separating the imagined from the real was something else entirely. Fred's brain wasn't sharp enough for that. Like everyone else, he had heard Felix talk about his deceased daughter, Penelope, a name not easy to forget. You didn't meet a girl by that name every time you turned around. Yet he had just met a Penelope, one with hair a color you would hardly ever see outside a dream. To Fred's way of thinking, it was like hair from another world. Then there was Marvin's clammy hand. Then there was Grandpa Albert, a legend who having lived so very long had left many memories around town. You need not rely on Felix for word of

Grandpa Albert. All of his current hotel occupants and almost everyone over the age of fifty remembered him and had a story or two to
share. He had just been introduced to someone named Grandpa Albert.
No matter that the man looked like Felix. Fred was quite sure ghosts
could take on appearances and disguise themselves any way they wanted,
and they could have hair any color they wanted. Their hands were
always clammy.

With Penelope and Grandpa Albert in the picture across the street,
what transpired at the drugstore seemed strange, as strange as a séance.
Combine this with a snow-white vehicle forty years old appearing
out of nowhere, and a man of Fred's superstitious bent could scare
himself thinking about it.

Less than an hour passed when the next strange thing occurred.
Felix came out of the drugstore with Ralph and Esther supporting
him either side. They helped him up to his room and left without
saying a word to Fred. Ralph ignored Fred's inquiry and appeared to
glare, casting a silent glance his way.

Twice more before night set in, Ralph returned to check on Felix,
who had not come downstairs for his favorite fried chicken. On his
second visit Ralph spoke with Fred.

"He's had a spell. I've given him something to settle his nerves. He
should sleep the rest of the night, but let me know if he wakes up and
seems agitated."

Ralph's calling it a "spell" confirmed Fred's suspicions: People coming out of séances often had such symptoms. For the moment, Ralph,
the druggist, had become both village physician and practitioner of
the black arts. His tone with Fred suggested he had also become its
debt collector. Ralph drew upon his arsenal of facial expressions to
discourage any questions. In the hotel tavern that evening, little beyond
the day's strange happenings was discussed, as Fred was regarded as for
once on the right track.

13

Taking the Road Not Taken

When Marvin quickly raced away from Clay Corners in his 1960 Desoto, he was so distracted that he took the highway he went out of his way to avoid on the way there. Rural scenes of late spring that earlier had seemed to float by like clouds on a windless day, now flashed by in a blur as if pushed by an approaching storm. Not a man to look back, Marvin was looking back, blaming himself, and of course missing what lay straight ahead. A man who usually looked before he leaped had already leaped without looking and was about to do it again. A dispassionate observer might have said it was inevitable: The surest way to run into something was to run away from it.

Penelope was the first to speak. A young lifetime of gazing out windows and watching the Great Lake from a boulder perch had been its own brand of athleticism. She had been thinking about those six letters from Felix, with their wavering lines now revealing how hard they must have been to write with glasses so thick and fingers so gnarled. She had been thinking about gum wrappers pressed into a foil ball long ago by the bent and grieving old man they had just left behind and most of all about the ring from his father, probably worn for fifty years longer than she thought it had been. Her thoughts formed a web of connections. Felix loved a father whom he said he barely remembered, or maybe he only loved his few memories. Either way, though, it was love.

It all connected to her own life, with its hints and suggestions from long ago and love reaching across a void to someone hardly known, trying to hold on to what little there had been. He had a brass ring. She had a welding mask stuck in a tree crotch and a picture with a hand in it. She sped through all this as the Desoto sped through the Clay County countryside.

"Marvin, I hope you won't do anything", she said. "He's not a bad man."

"I don't see how you can say that for sure."

"I'm sure of it", she said.

With both of them staring straight ahead through the White Whale's spaceship windows, this exchange halted abruptly on Marvin's side. They had come out of a wide curve between tree groves serving as farmyard windbreaks and onto a broad sweep of valley cropland broken by what seemed a gray fortress on the horizon. A road sign warned people about picking up hitchhikers. Marvin's unintended route from Clay Corners was taking them toward the one place he did not want to go near: Shade Creek Penitentiary.

His first impulse was to turn around and head back, but traffic coming toward them prevented it before another sign appeared, pointing the way to an inmate visitor's entrance. The prison itself rose up before them as if rushing out to meet them there. He vainly hoped Penelope was lost in thoughts too far away to notice. Instead she was lost in thoughts too close *not* to notice.

The Desoto sped on even more quickly than before, its eight pistons throbbing. Neither of them spoke as gray concrete walls and guard towers raced alongside with chained link fence, coiled barbed wire, and strobe lights flashing in bright sunlight at the edges of fields laid bare all around, not bare as farmers' fields awaiting the plow but bare as if seared and scorched in such a way that nothing again would ever grow there, a scene of devastation and despair. Marvin went temporarily blind. For a few seconds he could see nothing. By the time rows of spring corn and soybeans resumed their relentless Clay County presence, he had the Desoto up to eighty-five. He slowed to his usual fifty-five, quite amazed that its engine had not exploded.

He ought to have found Penelope's silence more deafening than his car going its fastest, but optimism was among the many wonderful ingredients in the recipe called "Marvin". He could never help seeing good things heading in the right direction, no matter the direction. When North Shore birds migrated south for the winter, he already anticipated their return for the summer. Watching the first snowfall, he thought of the apple blossoms that were sure to bloom in the spring. Miles passed in continued silence, and when Shade Creek Penitentiary was safely behind them, he exhaled his relief. Then Penelope spoke the saddest words he would ever in his happy, hopeful life hear.

"Is he?"

Marvin wouldn't give up without a struggle.

"Yeah, I'm afraid Felix is just that old guy we saw back there."

"Daddy, I mean . . ."

Marvin drove another mile, sped up to sixty, then slowed to fifty. He was close to becoming the second man to shed tears this past hour. The young spring corn just spreading its first leaves in tiny arches had become watery, blurred ribbons.

"Is he there . . . in that dreadful place?"

In all their years together, in all their chats about rabbits and dogs and cars, in all their talks about everything while washing dishes or strolling along the shoreline or lollygagging in the pole barn—never, ever had a word passed between them concerning her father. Her question penetrated to the deepest depths of his hopeful soul, and no matter how difficult it was to answer it, he knew he must.

"I'm sorry", he said, which was close as he could come to *yes, that's where your father is.*

She glanced at him, saw his torment, felt her own, and for his sake said nothing more for a while. They were on the southern outskirts of St. Cloud, more than forty miles from Clay Corners, when she next spoke.

"I wish Felix hadn't cried. I mean, it was a really good spider story, and those other things he wrote—I'm sure they were all true . . . a long time ago."

This was not exactly a change of subject. For both of them, thoughts of Felix and thoughts of Penelope's father in Shade Creek Penitentiary now formed a complex knot of threads intertwined and overlapping in ways defying attempts to unravel them into separate strands. They seemed to be thinking about both while thinking about neither, and they seemed to be grappling with deceptions and secrets surrounding both in which all of them were tangled in different ways. June had kept a secret, Aunt Charlotte had kept a secret, Bell Harbor had kept a secret, and so her father had stayed a secret Penelope pretended not to know. Felix had kept another secret. Penelope and Marvin had kept Felix a secret. Everyone was trying to conceal something, and now it all seemed to be unraveling without anyone tugging at its many loose ends.

"Don't be sad, Marvin. It wasn't ever a secret."

Marvin dodged one last time.

"You knew about Felix all along just from his letters?"

"I thought maybe Felix wasn't a boy, but no, Marvin, I mean Daddy. I knew about him. I just couldn't *say* I knew, not before today, and I didn't know for sure where he was."

The White Whale had a whale's appetite. Marvin stopped for gas in St. Cloud. While Penelope was returning from its convenience store with a bottle of Dr. Pepper, she heard a honk. From a car stopped at a red light, Sister Hilaria waved to her from an open backseat window. Penelope had but time enough to wave back before the light changed and Sister's car moved ahead out of view.

Marvin offered to pursue them, as pointless as that seemed given the traffic. He would have done anything to brighten their journey home. He would have stood on his head for the amusement of a single child and the lightening of the mood, right there between rows of gas pumps.

"No, Marvin," said Penelope, "it's okay just the way it happened. Really, it's okay."

She had no desire to change a thing, not any of it, from the moment the sun rose over the vast, shimmering lake to the moment she caught sight of Sister Hilaria. They pointed the Desoto northeast and, leaving summer behind them, soon returned to signs of emerging spring. With the sun near solstice making similarly long journeys, they arrived back on Star Island just as the lake waters brightened under a rising moon, whose shaft of light for a few moments held the profile of a ship toiling northeast from Duluth. The wooden bridge clattered beneath them, and they were home. Osgood barked. A light blazed in the window of June's home office. In the midst of great changes, the persistence of familiar things can seem remarkable.

14

The Last of It

Having lived so long in a local climate of perpetual summer, Felix had only once before been threatened with not hearing the last of something. He could not have known that Marvin had only once before made such threats. For this, both had to reach far back into an earlier time.

Felix, by far the better when it came to such reaching, was back in his prisoner days listening to something similar in German while staring at a Luger pointing his way. He had made the mistake of grinning when a guard sneezed. He hadn't grinned because the guard had a cold, but because the sneeze seemed to have a German accent.

Marvin had been in occasional disputes over playground equipment during recesses supervised by sisters in habits armed with rosaries. Otherwise he and Felix both could have been in line for the Sermon on the Mount's blessing of the peacemakers. Depending upon how experience is valued at extremes beyond the reassurance of Matthew 5:7, one or the other got the better preparation for their Saturday afternoon at Ralph's drugstore: Felix had been toughened waiting two years for his release, while Marvin had learned most storms blow over before next recess.

Their predicaments kept lights burning later than usual Saturday night, Marvin's in his pole barn and Felix' in the Corrigans' apartment above Ralph's Corner Drug. Marvin had Osgood sleeping underfoot while he cleaned the Desoto inside and out and changed its oil. Ralph and Esther had Felix resting across the street while his fate seemed to rest with them. Had the concerned parties been given the advantage of each other's company, Marvin's Desoto might have been driven a few more miles before its oil change, Ralph and Esther might have shaved a kilowatt or two off next month's light bill, and everyone would have gotten more sleep that night, thanks to knowing there was not as much to worry them as they might have feared.

Marvin couldn't turn to June without revealing a secret he had avoided explaining to Penelope before an explanation became unnecessary: Shade Creek Penitentiary had now spoken for him and said all that need be said about keeping Felix' letters hidden in the Frazer's glove box. He couldn't turn elsewhere—assuming he had known where to go—without bringing June into it. This stalemate left him stuck in a circle of his own, right back where he had begun this past March, except that Penelope now knew much more. At least he need not caution her about sharing her newest news with her mother.

Bedroom windows had long been darkened by the time Marvin flipped a switch in his pole barn, leaving Osgood to find his way by nose and a night light burning at his workbench. Penelope, lying in bed and staring at ceiling shadows, was awake well after both of them slept. Felix awoke in the middle of the night with everyone everywhere asleep and began writing under his magnifying glass.

Everyone slept later than usual Sunday morning, Felix thanks to having slipped a letter into the "Out-of-Town" mail slot and then gone back to bed some hours before Ralph awoke and slipped another letter into the same box. Penelope had also written and slipped a letter between pages of her journal. Marvin slept enjoying the peace to be found in realizing some things cannot be changed. Ralph, on his way back from the post office, woke Felix with a knock on his door. June, having enjoyed the blissful sleep only ignorance can afford, woke Marvin and Penelope with the fret that they might be late for Mass. So the day began all around.

With Marvin's 1955 Chevrolet Bel-Air back on the road, Marvin, June, and Penelope arrived at St. John Vianney just as those gathered were saying: "I confess to almighty God, and to you, my brothers and sisters, that I have greatly sinned in my thoughts and in my words, in what I have done, and in what I have failed to do." Having a horror of being late for anything, June considered among her failures being two minutes late for this Mass, and then dropped the matter as being more Marvin's fault. In view of yesterday's experiences, Marvin regretted ever reading his insurance policy magazine and resolved to burn its next issue. Later when the Mass came around to the Our Father, Penelope of course thought of having already forgiven Felix, who no longer seemed to have trespassed, and Marvin regarded the Cord 810 as one of those temptations not to be led into. Between Marvin's regrets and temptations, Father's homily this day centered on the many forms prayer could take, some of them surprising.

"You don't have to wear holes in your trousers from being on your knees or drive off the road because you're gazing toward heaven", he said. "St. John Bosco might have been praying while standing on his head."

Arriving late, the Listers had been unable to seat themselves in their accustomed location. Penelope found herself not only seated else-where but also seated on an aisle instead of between June and Marvin. The aisle angling to her right as it approached the front of the church provided a view of Sister Serena at the organ. Under Sister's bench was a cardboard box about twice the size of a shoebox. During a rather rambunctious *Gloria*, the box was shoved partway from under the bench. Penelope, approaching it at Communion, discovered her name written across its top. This determined the order of things after Mass, when Sister Serena, instead of looking for Penelope, found her already at her side as she lowered the organ lid.

Nothing could keep Penelope from telling Sister Serena about Felix' spider, even if the spider had been dead for seventy years or more, the barn had probably fallen down, and gum foil balls no longer made sense. She ignored those possibilities. Sister gave this monster a moment and then brightened with a guess having a long Latin name. Then she repeated almost word for word what Marvin had said in his perfect ignorance of spiders.

"They can get very large in places where flies and other insects are abundant. Sort of like living near an ice cream stand or having a mother who bakes cookies all the time", she said as June approached.

Sister Serena's knowledge of spiders being greater by far than her knowledge of Penelope's mother, she would not have known that June opened an oven door so seldom it would have been second only to the Frazer's glove box as a good hiding place. Sister could see, how-ever, that June was irritated. Was it because Penelope had approached Sister without her?

After an exchange of greetings, Sister Serena reached under the organ bench and handed the box to Penelope, who lifted one side of its lid and peered in cautiously as if a spider might have taken up residence there. Instead it contained tangled pieces of coppery metal hammered out as if on an anvil, a collection of large and small rings, something resembling a bracket with one side missing, and an arrow with its shaft broken.

Noting her puzzled expression, Sister Serena explained, "Sister Hilaria was doing some housecleaning as she was leaving and discovered this box with what we think might have been a weather vane, though where it came from no one can say. Father Ulrich has no memory of it. She thought maybe your dad could repair it and put it back together. Star Island would be a great place to mount a weather vane, if that's what it is. You will have to let us know."

Only June could have fathomed the many-layered irony in all this. Penelope set the box on the organ bench and opened it completely to have a better look. Meanwhile, Sister's gaze over her shoulder was following June on her way to the church foyer without having said goodbye.

"As for your spider," she said, "if you find out anything more, let me know about that, too. They are becoming quite rare, almost extinct, I suspect because of crop spraying."

At this point, Mr. Stiller approached, having finished gathering choir books into a cupboard.

"Hello, Penelope. I see you're registered for behind-the-wheel driver's training later on this summer?"

This wasn't bad news. In fact, it was good news, but *news* nonetheless, the first she had heard of it.

Outside across the street from the church, June settled into her seat and slammed the door with an impressive thud only an older car made mostly of steel can produce. She folded her arms in front of her, stared straight ahead, took deep breaths, and seemed to be saying, "Don't ask me." Marvin didn't ask. Penelope ran up a minute later with the box under her arm.

"Did Mom tell you what I have here?" she asked Marvin as she slid into the backseat with the box on her lap now.

"We don't have time for chitchat", said June before Marvin could answer.

Since this presumably included anything Marvin might say, he silently started the Bel-Air. A moment later he asked June the question he usually asks her on the way home after Sunday Mass: "Do you want to stop anywhere?" When this met with silence, he knew better than to repeat it.

Living on the North Shore all his life had taught him a lot about Lake Superior weather. More than a dozen years of marriage to June had taught him about another kind of weather, what he sometimes thought of as *June weather*, year around and as changeable as the month by that name. In both cases an old adage much repeated seemed to apply: He could not do anything about either weather and knew better than to try.

15

June in Two Junes

While Marvin's sawmill work world was almost entirely predictable, June's at Osgoode's Insurance Agency revolved around the unexpected. This allowed her to sell illusions of security to people convinced as Ralph had been that the unforeseen had a way of happening. Osgoode became wealthy because whatever his customers feared happening seldom actually happened. The insurance marketplace was like a gambling casino in which people were hoping to lose. When customers escaped a calamity, they breathed a sigh of relief and seldom looked back at the money they had spent needlessly.

June had lots of insurance advice and sold policies by the hundreds, but nothing she could come up with insured against the debris of her first marriage falling on her family years after. In the box on a seat beside Penelope were the fractured remains of a weather vane Penelope's father had made in his welding shop. It had been commissioned and paid for by parishioners as a going-away gift to Father James Spence, the parish priest who had baptized June and a week later married her and Warren.

A popular pastor, his reassignment the following year had met with general consternation. Parishioners had even discussed petitioning the bishop to keep him at Bell Harbor, but Father Spence, with his characteristic good humor, told them if he ever hoped to replace the bishop someday, they had better not proceed. There was no point in ruffling hierarchical feathers, even if he had no interest in becoming a bishop.

His departure proved to be a turning point in many ways, not all of them obvious. The old St. John Vianney Church burned mere months later, with Father Lyle on the scene returning to lead the parish for a second time. His first assignment there had been some twenty-five years earlier, in days when young Warren served as an altar boy.

June could not fathom why the weather vane had stayed behind with Father Lyle instead of going to the Iron Range with its intended owner. Equally inexplicable was how it came to be dismantled and stored in a box where Sister Hilaria would come upon it one day. The final mystery—or last straw, as June regarded it—was that Sister would think of giving it to Penelope. June was quite good at selling insurance using anecdotal evidence of life's unexpected twists and turns, but this turn of events seemed like a cruel, diabolical joke. When she couldn't view it any other way, she became more afraid than angry. She was too distant to hear it and much too upset, but somewhere a mouse was gnawing in a wall.

June had married Warren Hall in June. She was twenty-nine, and he had just turned thirty-four. Though they had both grown up in Bell Harbor, they only first met when they found themselves in the same apartment building in Duluth, where they had both moved in search of work. With Bell Harbor in common, they soon became acquainted. In the way that cities have of thrusting together people from the same small place, they began to identify people from back home they both knew and the various places where they might have been at the same time while managing somehow not to meet. Warren was certain that he could recall June's laughter from somewhere and had even overheard her Donald Duck imitation before coaxing it from her one afternoon on a Park Point beach.

Warren had been raised in the most Catholic of households, by parents who said family Rosaries at home, enrolled both their children in the parish school, involved themselves in parish life, and contributed to the support of missionaries. Anyone marrying their son inevitably would be Catholic. In fact, so insistent were Warren's parents likely to have been that Father Spence had questioned June with extra care about the freedom of her decision to convert.

Warren's friends called him War, a coincidence eventually reflecting what was going on inside him, where he seemed at war with himself. It was not, however, a declared war but rather one of the clandestine sort fought by obscure guerillas in out-of-the-way places. And so this only became evident a year after he and June married and moved to Star Island, into her old childhood home vacated by her parents, who had rented an apartment in a Bell Harbor complex for seniors. Warren set up his welding shop, and June prepared for the birth of their first child.

Warren was more than a welder of broken trailer hitches and the like brought his way from all around or left for repair at a Bell Harbor hardware store. He was an artisan fashioning objects from iron, copper, and brass; elaborate artistic creations, some as insanely complex as brightly painted mobiles and weather vanes with imaginative themes well beyond the inevitable crowing rooster. His largest mobile hung in the lobby of a bank, but not the one where June continued working. He could not keep up with orders for his decorative rural mailbox mounts, some of which had shown up as far away as Felix' mail route, brought back as souvenirs by tourists to the North Shore. He made most of the income he and June needed from the sale of these and some from routine welding jobs. The rest June provided from a job she continued until Penelope was born.

When their baby was two weeks old, Warren and June drove to the Iron Range so Father Spence could baptize her there. No one on hand for that happy occasion among friends could have predicted what soon followed. No insurance policy could have been written based on calculations of probability. No wariness of the sort Ralph advised could have encompassed such a possibility when Warren suddenly plunged from his Catholic ways. Not long afterward June was dressing for Sunday Mass and wondering if they should sit in an area set aside for parents with babies and small children.

"Forget about it", said Warren. "We aren't going anywhere this morning, or ever. Forget about all of it."

"Forget?" This time it was June being told to forget without knowing why or how. She had embraced her conversion with a convert's ardor. Was she now supposed to let go?

"Yes, all of it!"

He broke down in tears and slammed the door behind him on his way to the garage. Warren's war had finally been declared.

Many people in their twenties and thirties drift away from the religion into which they were born, some for a while and some forever. Warren's change of heart was not of this sort. It was a metaphorical version of a heart attack. It came out of nowhere without warning and changed his, June's, and Penelope's lives forever. Whatever St. Paul acquired in being knocked from his saddle, Warren seemed to have lost with equal suddenness. He had been hurled into an invisible abyss, and when he struggled up from deep within, he had lost not only his convictions but his personality along with them. The man June had married was no longer that man.

He became so wild and strange in the grip of ranting and rage that she began to fear for herself and their child. The orange light of his blazing forge cast shadows late into the night from the garage he had turned into his welding shop. Hammer rang on anvil until the baby awoke and cried. June retreated to the room farthest away. Haggard and worn, wild eyed and face stained with the marks of his welding mask, Warren would begin a new day just as the last had ended.

Nothing seemed to result from Warren's endless activity. Customers were turned away, and half-made mobiles lay scattered in tangles. Then word reached the island of a fire at old St. John Vianney. Its roof had collapsed, killing a church custodian as he was attempting to save some of its furnishings. Two days later, county sheriff's deputies appeared on Star Island to arrest Warren for arson and homicide in the death of the custodian.

June would struggle to put behind her the weeks and months following. She stood by Warren through much of it, weeping at hearings with his sister at her side. Warren, who had never denied guilt, drifted along the border of awareness. Some days he could seem detached and oblivious. Others he would concentrate as if the proceedings were as complex as a mobile he was attempting to assemble. Attorneys attempting to represent him found themselves in a whirlwind of client confusion and incoherence and community outrage. That the man was clearly out of his mind was irrelevant as the wheels of justice or something passing for justice ground forward.

The local political climate swung strongly in the direction of retribution. Late one evening, alone with her baby on Star Island, June heard gunshots. The next morning she discovered two bullet holes in the roadside mailbox beneath Warren's name. It was the sort of vicarious execution typical in remote rural settings, a kind of north woods voodoo whose intended victim was not June. Nonetheless, Charlotte joined her on the island and spent a fortnight.

Prosecution, reflecting public mood, had looked for blood revenge. The district attorney brought in an indictment for murder in conjunction with a felony crime. Warren's defense called in the Bell Harbor fire chief to testify that he had unequivocally warned the old custodian, Clarence, about the danger of entering the church even on the end where it seemed not to be burning. His testimony proved to be crucial in defense efforts to frame Clarence's death as a case of unintentional homicide. Eventually this view of the crime prevailed. About the crime of arson there had never been a question.

Despite his attorney's attempt to argue that Warren was schizophrenic at the time of his crimes and incapable of knowing what he was doing, all this supported by extensive expert psychiatric testimony, he was found guilty and sentenced for arson and negligent homicide, with his sentences *not* running concurrently. He might be eligible for parole in less than twenty years. In addition to his prison sentence, he was ordered to pay $500,000 in restitution to St. John Vianney Parish, an impossible sum. No provision was made for his treatment. The fire chief, citing hate mail and telephone threats, resigned his position and moved to another state.

During jury deliberations and the punishment phase of these proceedings, June, without warning, quit visiting Warren, broke off all contact with Charlotte, and was absent when sentencing was announced. A few days later, when sheriff's deputies left Bell Harbor with Warren on his way to prison, she was nowhere to be seen. As the months and first years of his incarceration went by, she neither wrote him nor visited. His letters to her went unopened and unanswered. A court order was put in place forbidding all contact with her daughter, not *his* any longer. His sister Charlotte was not only avoided but spurned. For June, Warren had ceased to exist.

The rebuilding of St. John Vianney Church and June's life occurred in tandem, while Father Lyle served as pastor a further three years. When he left, both projects were complete. Though he had replaced a popular priest, his presence was welcomed all around in the present circumstances. A strong and capable administrator of parish finances, he was well qualified to undertake the building of the new church, a project already in the planning stage as Warren Hall went off to serve his sentence.

With Father Lyle's assistance, June's marriage was annulled; a few months later she married Marvin Lister in a private ceremony one evening at the new St. John Vianney. Marvin adopted Penelope. With the name Lister obscuring her and her daughter's past and most of its associations, June found a secretarial position at the Osgoode Insurance Agency. Having buried the girl voted most fun to have around, she soon advanced using the principle that hard work has its rewards, one of them being forgetfulness. Within a year, Osgoode Agency seemed hardly capable of surviving a day without her.

The rebuilding process in the lives of Warren's family took longer, though few in the parish or Bell Harbor could be found directing any blame their way. Still, Warren was theirs, and that had to mean something. Within five years of the church burning, both his parents had died, disheartened and impoverished by the cost of their son's legal defense. Their daughter, Charlotte, moved into their home in a neighborhood near Lighthouse Consolidated School and, as much as her carrot red hair would permit, gradually blended back into the parish life of St. John Vianney.

The natural need of people to put a horror behind them eased this process. Nobody wanted to be reminded of the fire or think of the new church as their second on that site. Even Father Lyle, so much a part of the aftermath, seemed to fade away like a ship far out in the Great Lake, slipping into fog and mist. On the near eve of his retirement, well past the age of seventy and with infirmities easily detected, he was transferred outside the diocese to a parish in eastern Wisconsin "to be nearer to what remained of his own family", it was rumored. About the same time, Warren was transferred to Shade Creek, which offered familial distance, not closeness, and its own version of obscurity. Meantime, Sister Hilaria arrived at St. John Vianney School determined not to be in the least obscure.

With that in the past, so much of it hidden from view, June chaffed against the twist of fate by which that happy-go-lucky nun rummaging through classroom closets had discovered Warren's broken creation and somehow seen it as the sort of thing his daughter would like to have on Star Island. Marvin—Marvin of all people—was supposed to repair it. Here it was now heading home in the backseat of their car to the scene of its construction while people passing them honked and waved as if something very funny were happening.

Where some might have seen irony, she saw mockery and the cruelest cut of a fate blind to everything she had done to begin a new life and protect her daughter. It seemed to her that somewhere out in the darkest regions of space, Warren in orbit had begun his journey homeward, and she was helpless to prevent it.

16

Felix Is All Right!

Ralph's Corner Drug could have been a page in pharmacy history in a chapter titled "Midwestern, Pioneer Era, and Later". It had always been a drugstore of sorts in a weather-beaten building older by decades than even Felix. Like Ed's Hotel, it had passed through the hands of many owners, some of them patent medicine types, some described by locals as "horse doctors", and some bona fide chemists who during Prohibition peddled medicinal concoctions of mostly alcohol right under the sensitive noses of federal agents. A couple of them, such as one Mr. Knapp, had even been arrested, held briefly, and then released into a community where no man dispensing alcohol, legally or not, could be friendless for long.

Then came a string of new owners, along with a string of several wars, before Ralph and his wife remodeled its upstairs—formerly a shoe repair shop and before that a photography studio—into their living quarters, with even a den and home library no one would guess existed from the look of it on the outside, which had retained the tumbledown appearance of its earlier years.

Downstairs remained all pharmacy history, much of it in pill bottles and corked tubes unopened in memory, since most of Ralph's business had gone to strip malls and chains in the cities nearby, and most of his predecessors had never cleaned out the stock. These days Felix' friend might as well have been a curator in a museum of medicinal oddities and curiosities. On his shelves for sale yet were more than a few products no longer manufactured and only advertised in magazines that had long ago ceased publication.

Ralph liked having the place to himself much of the time, opening for business that hardly ever came through the door, and closing at the end of the day with only a few dollars more in his cash register than he began with. He had made his money years before and could well let someone else have it now. His wife, nearing retirement as a clinical psychologist and college teacher, brought in more than enough income to keep them going month by month. Thus Ralph was free to regard himself as the trained pharmacist with not much use for his training as he sold bottles of aspirin, cough medicine, and the like to local folk with colds and headaches and not needing enough else to drive very far for such relief. He still dispensed a few prescriptions to diehard customers, a few of whom were Felix' neighbors in Ed's Hotel, and many of these he would hand deliver around town with a manner suggesting he had much more to do, was on his way to doing it, and yet was not inconvenienced in the least. He wasn't the sort to hang around for a thank-you. With his deliveries out of the way, he might detour to have coffee with Felix. He could cut his hours back to what used to be called "banker's hours" and close down at noon Saturdays, hanging a sign to that effect on a front door where a bell overhead seldom tinkled anymore. His regular business hours notwithstanding, if anyone banged on his door to get a prescription filled in the middle of the night, he would be downstairs in his pajamas to let him in.

Esther Summersby Corrigan, or Bea, as she was known around the private college whose counseling department she headed, had a PhD in clinical psychology and a thirty-year career in mental health prac- tice and in teaching at the college and university level. In her present position she was a tenured professor, teaching both advanced courses and occasionally something for beginners, which, as she thought of it, got her back in touch with the sparkle, sizzle, and gunshots at starting lines. As if all this and looking after Ralph did not keep her busy enough, she sometimes appeared at Shade Creek Penitentiary to review test results, to render an expert opinion, and even to interview a pris- oner who was suspected of having a mental health problem in an envi- ronment where mental health issues were misunderstood, misinterpreted, and generally neglected.

For fourteen years she had been engaged in all this, ever since she and Ralph had decided to leave behind the stresses of urban life for the anticipated sleepiness of a rural village somewhere in Midwestern farming country. With her new college position, they had only needed to find exactly what they had found in the Clay Corners drugstore listed for sale at just the right moment. Ralph thought he had found the ideal place to plant himself and ease into his retirement. He could take naps between customers so few, while Esther kept going throughout the day and sometimes late into the night. Ralph might wake up before she came to bed and go downstairs, as if in drugstore cupboards and closets, on shelves, and in drawers he also found matters demanding his attention in the wee hours. It was never clear what these might have been.

The effort to save Felix from Marvin's threatened retribution had claimed their joint attention in a recent wee hour, Esther to write a letter and Ralph to look over her shoulder and fill in gaps. As it happened, there was only one gap, and he could not fill it. He was in the dark when it came to the names of Penelope's parents. Thanks to Fred, he had heard Marvin's name several times, but in a context so stressful had forgotten it at once. Felix asleep across the street was in the dark in another sense. Regardless, Esther thought it best not to tell him about the letter, finally addressed to the parents of Penelope Lister, Star Island, Bell Harbor.

"How did you get their address?" asked Ralph, who would have been equally unable to fill in that gap.

"I have my ways", said Esther, an answer doing nothing to dispel the mystery but seeming to satisfy Ralph, who wanted to call it a night.

Tuesday's mail brought two letters to the Listers' Star Island mailbox. Marvin picked them up and promptly took them into the pole barn.

Marvin could look at a pine saw log and as fast as a computer say how many board feet it contained and how to go about cutting it, depending what dimension lumber was wanted. He could listen to an automobile engine and explain what was going on inside it. When it came to the inner workings and dimensions of people, however, he was close to lost and wise enough to trust to instincts better than his, even the instincts of someone as young as Penelope, especially Penelope. She knew without him ever saying a word that he would rather have her call him Marvin than Dad, and she grasped when he needed to be alone tinkering with his cars.

She had suspected something about Felix well before they met him disguised as Grandpa Albert. Marvin had been fooled, but she had not. In retrospect, it was all plain enough to him—those old-fashioned *r*'s wearing little flags, his wavering handwritten lines, a ball made from chewing gum wrappers, and so on—but *only* in retrospect. Even bringing Charles Lindbergh into it failed to alert him. It was all true, but like the gigantic spider true a long time ago, as Felix himself had said at the end.

Perhaps Penelope was simply a good detective, or perhaps she could look at people and see their lines, dimensions, and possibilities the way Marvin could measure saw logs. Perhaps she could listen to their hearts and minds the way he could hear engines. Whatever explained it, Penelope's instinct concerning Felix was also becoming his conclusion, even before Tuesday's mail brought those two letters. Felix, as she put it, was not a bad man.

The pole barn's side door opened. Osgood barked as he always did, even though it was Penelope, this time bringing news of her mother's summer plans for her. The day's letters at this point, one opened and the other sealed, Marvin had hidden in the Frazer's glove box. Marvin had read the one addressed to parents with Osgood looking on waiting to be fed.

Penelope told Marvin that her mother had enrolled her in a two-week camp for Catholic girls at a place called Pine Shadows, some miles from Bell Harbor. She would be going there next Saturday morning. Following this adventure was a summer reading enrichment program at the Bell Harbor Public Library, and after that, behind-the-wheel driver's training with Mr. Stiller. What she did not know was how this frenzy of summer activity had resulted from a school counselor's suggestion that more be done to get her off Star Island and involved with other children. Marvin had heard it all from June. His thoughts being elsewhere and this surprise being no surprise, he struggled to appear as excited as Penelope.

"There's more news in the Frazer", he said, pointing over the top of his Studebaker pickup.

They wove their way through a maze of cars to the Frazer, parked beneath a skylight in a column of sunshine, a spot in the pole barn farthest from the house and June. Marvin rested his arms on the Frazer's open door while Penelope read Esther's letter. Half way through it, she dropped both pages in her lap and clapped her hands.

"Felix is all right!" she said. "I just knew he was!"

Yes, Esther, using words both professional and tender, had assured Marvin and June, who seemed unlikely ever to see these words, that

Felix was indeed the Felix everyone in Clay Corners and throughout the countryside all around knew, loved, and—as she put it—would have trusted with their life's most precious possessions, which she knew must be Penelope where her own parents were concerned. Then she added almost as an afterthought:

> As a mental health professional, I usually avoid popular presumptions in favor of clinical determinations, but Felix once had a daughter by the same name as yours—we've all heard his stories about her—who died when she was about the age of your Penelope. It's not good science to make the connection quite so quickly, but I think this was probably in the picture at the beginning.
> Yours sincerely,
> Dr. Esther Summersby Corrigan, PhD

Esther did not often use her prefix, but she made an exception in a case so vital to Felix' interest. She also left two phone numbers and an email address where she could be reached had they further questions or concerns.

Penelope's joy banished any remaining questions Marvin might have had. The way she looked at it became his way, too. What could be better than a pen pal who had lived so long that he knew about things as amazing and unheard of as a Cord 810 and a gigantic spider, now threatened with extinction, hanging in the doorway of Uncle Milton's barn?

Next from the Frazer glove box came the unopened letter Felix had mailed in the middle of the night. She did not have to read aloud from its single page of wavering lines. Simply by watching her read it, Marvin knew that the forgiveness requested had been granted.

17

Pine Shadows' Shadows

One of the many rivers draining into Lake Superior had made for itself a series of broad curves as it flowed from the depths of a national forest into a small woodland lake. Over the years its gentle current had caught unawares many a canoeist neglecting maps and trusting appearances at hand while paddling through Lake Surprise. The lake might have been so named for another reason, but what lay ahead would have been reason enough, for only two miles downstream the river began its turbulent descent, cascading among boulder-strewn rapids and tumbling over a series of falls into the Great Lake far below. Well before that happened, yellow signs were posted along its bank warning of dangers ahead and urging river travelers to disembark.

Nearby along the shore sprawled Pine Shadows, a summer camp for school children. Through the winter months Pine Shadows' shadows were usually cast upon layers of snow, whose crystal surface was broken only by trails of rabbits, deer, and an occasional fox or timber wolf. Its upended picnic tables leaned against tree trunks. Its cabins wore white bonnets. Its canoes were stored overhead upon crossbeams beneath a pavilion roof, with paddles bundled below. Its wooden boat docks were stacked in sections along a frozen shore. The metal fittings of its dangling flagpole halyard clanked against its pole, while each new winter storm rearranged the snowdrifts of ones that came before. Its equipment tucked away, the camp was left to the forces of nature.

In the summer Pine Shadows hummed with activity during two-week sessions. This year one of these would be the Residential Camp for Young Catholic Women, sponsored by a consortium of parishes within the diocese.

Fresh from her visit to Penelope's school, June had only to see it mentioned in a St. John Vianney church bulletin before enrolling

Penelope in a manner sometimes described as shooting first and asking questions later. Neither Marvin nor Penelope had been consulted. Uncharacteristically, June had not even consulted herself.

Three weeks later, just after noon on a Saturday, Penelope arrived on the scene about fifteen miles from Bell Harbor, toting a sleeping bag purchased for this occasion and a backpack containing all items on a checklist provided to parents, including completed medical information and registration forms. It was all there: June had approached this with her Osgoode Insurance efficiency. Pine Shadows staff observed that few parents showed up so well prepared.

Meanwhile, Marvin, standing some steps out of this picture and not knowing where to fit in, appeared to be staring at a tree trunk. He was absently browsing a bulletin tacked there, listing Pine Shadows staff for this two-week encampment. June called him out of what appeared to be a reverie. They were leaving to look at Penelope's quarters.

Penelope was the first of the campers to arrive at a cabin with the name Hikers painted on a varnished pine slab over its door. Along the way they had passed two other cabins with the names Paddlers and Explorers, respectively, over their doors. Hikers was nearest to the lake, a fact unnecessarily pointed out by June and lost upon Marvin, whose thoughts seemed elsewhere. It was one of those sleepy, sunny afternoons when a drying forest floor releases its spicy fragrances; distant woodpeckers drum, fall silent, and then drum again; buzzing insects flit between shadows in swatches of light; and young quaking aspen leaves rattle in breezes seeming to arise from nowhere and go nowhere. Nearby, waves could be heard licking the sandy shore. From June's point of view, none of this could be improved upon. Marvin seemed oblivious to it.

Hikers had been cleaned, organized, and prepared as if awaiting a military inspection. Penelope's assigned cot was by far the best located of the six in June's opinion, being nearest a window one could look out while lying in bed. She glanced around approvingly while reciting for Penelope's benefit the defensive statements of a parent marooning her child. Marvin stared at the ceiling between fretful glances toward the cabin door.

With the promise to return next weekend for an outdoor Sunday Mass with parents, Marvin and June left for Bell Harbor. Osgood had been allowed to ride along for an occasion so special. The congenial creature barked as they approached and pushed his nose through a window left open a few inches. June's car, a late model Toyota that she drove to work five times a week, was ironically the only one in which Osgood was permitted to ride, as long as he stayed on the floor. Of course had he been that obedient, his nose would not have protruded from the window opening. For once June didn't mind. During their journey home it was Marvin's turn to seem especially preoccupied.

Among the first campers to arrive at Pine Shadows, Penelope had Hikers to herself for a few minutes more. Moving around among its cots, bedside tables, chairs, lamps, wooden chests, and lockers was like traversing a compact maze. She peered into half-hidden corners, lifted lids, glanced out windows, and lingered in an open doorway, looking at a lake so compact and so much easier to comprehend than the one she was used to. She located a locker having a number matching her cot and began unpacking her gear. This solitary interlude abruptly ended when sunlight aslant the door cast the shadow of her cabin camp counselor approaching with sleeping bag and backpack of her own.

Since shadows display muted, unrepresentative hues and come in generic, often distorted shapes, it was a further second or two before this one revealed itself as belonging to Penelope's Aunt Charlotte. There was of course no rehearsing for the moment Penelope discovered herself looking at Charlotte and Charlotte at Penelope. This was not supposed to happen any more than Felix was supposed to be found out and Marvin was supposed to drive past Shade Creek.

The unforeseen seemed to be taking over all their lives.

Not making eye contact was as close as Penelope and Charlotte could come to not seeing each other. Penelope glanced at her shoes, and Charlotte for the first time at a list of girls assigned to her cabin, protruding from her backpack. Penelope's shoes were far from ready to run away, and Charlotte's list was unmistakably clear, her name at the top in bold letters and Penelope's below it, third in a group of five. When Charlotte looked up from that, their eyes met for the first time, the first time ever in fifteen years of living near each other, unless the day of the baby crib picture could be counted. Penelope offered her the tentative smile of someone embarrassed and thinking it best to smile.

Penelope stepped forward. Reaching across an immeasurable void, she held out her hand. When Charlotte took that trembling hand in hers, they both knew that there was no possibility of turning away, not now, not ever. Neither could say to the other, "I don't want to be with you." Something that had never been real had at last given way to something real all along. Once again, the jig was up. Charlotte, still standing in the doorway, took a step inside, and two heads of carrot-red hair found themselves together in a very small place.

They at that moment were no more at a loss for words than Marvin was with June as she drove the car back toward the wooden bridge. He had seen Charlotte's name under "Hikers" on the staff list. He had seen "Hikers" over the door of the cabin into which they stepped for a look at Penelope's home for the next two weeks. He could only roll this information into something like Felix' growing sphere of foil wrappers and tuck it away in the mental equivalent of the Frazer's glove box. He was attempting to do the impossible and by not thinking about it further. Not even a Cord 810 suddenly discovered in his pole barn would have achieved a goal so far beyond him.

Part Three

The Unforeseen

Still, thou art blest, compar'd wi' me!
The present only toucheth thee:
But Och! I backward cast my e'e,
On prospects drear!
An' forward, tho' I canna see,
I guess an' fear!

—Robert Burns, "To a Mouse"

18

Victims of Punishment

For the second time Tuesday evening Ralph said he wished Felix had not done it, and for the first time Esther said she knew of few instances where sincere apologies ever worsened something. "And Felix has sincerity written all over him. In any case I wish he hadn't bothered to tell you this afternoon. You've done nothing but fret ever since."

Ralph's runaway fingers tapped something unrhythmical on a table near his armrest where otherwise stood the evening glass of wine he usually finished before his wife finished hers. For all his wife's gentle counseling and consoling, he was only beginning to feel at ease, and his glass was half full. You would have thought Felix' problem with what he saw as its dire potential was his problem also. He entirely missed an implication imbedded in this perception: Felix had a way of attracting understanding, empathy, and friends who would stand by him. There was little cause for worry.

"The law these days is without mercy", said Ralph. "It's best not to take chances."

"Felix is eighty-five. Anyone that old is free to take a few chances. He's done nothing wrong. He won't be sent off to Shade Creek, and in that impossible event he would find himself among more friends than someone who had just won a lottery jackpot."

Esther wasn't suggesting that Felix had multiple friendships with convicted felons. In the fifteen years since its construction, Shade Creek Penitentiary had become Clay County's largest employer ten times over. Hardly a family on any of Felix' several rural mail routes had no one working there.

"Lot of good either friends or fortune would do him in such a place", said Ralph.

"Well, you will have no opportunity to test your theory at any rate", said Esther. "He's quite safe, and besides, Shade Creek is maximum security. No one his age would be sent there for the simple reason he wouldn't survive a week."

"Better to take him out and shoot him."

In his views of prisons and criminal justice, Ralph was echoing sentiments he had often heard his wife express. He was happy not to know about it firsthand, but he took to heart much she said and made it so much his own you might have thought it was his originally. She was even beginning to make him feel better about Felix' letter of apology to Penelope, viewed by him when he first heard of it as an instance of what *not* to do with sleeping dogs.

Even apart from Felix' imagined incarceration there, Shade Creek Penitentiary had spread enough gloom over Ralph's habitually buoyant outlook. Had he thought about the prison when they were moving into the area, he might have suggested that they settle elsewhere. Having a prison in the neighborhood, with so many local people working there, changed the tenor of everything.

Prison workers carried Shade Creek home with them like smells from a slaughter house or dust from a coal mine. Those at least might come out in the wash, but Shade Creek remained a permanent odor and stain. Around Clay Corners people were less likely to slow down for anyone crossing the street. They were quicker to take offense, drank more, gained weight, and laughed a lot less than they used to in days before the prison. Felix agreed that life was better in these parts when every village street ended in a farmer's field, old-timers dozed in sunshine on Front Street benches, and flies could be heard buzzing in screen doors.

"Give me that any day", said Ralph wistfully.

Ralph had embraced a new life in his very old drugstore as if it meant stepping into a Norman Rockwell painting. Had anyone questioned him closely, he might have admitted that Rockwell's world never really existed. He might have been insulted if anyone suggested he was fool enough to believe it ever had, but he would have argued that it represented a yearning many people shared, making the painter famous and attracting people like himself to what seemed its last outposts in places like Clay Corners. People wanted physicians like the one in Rockwell's painting listening to a doll's heartbeat while a little girl stood by as anxious as any mother. People wanted genial, overweight Irish cops like the one in *Runaway*, sitting next to a boy at a soda fountain resembling what had once been downstairs in Ralph's store. People wanted friends like Felix, which is why he had so many and why Ralph was happy to be among them. The problem was, there was always something like Shade Creek just outside the picture. This unfortunate fact helped Rockwell make his fame and fortune. Sometimes it kept Ralph awake at night.

Esther lived and worked outside the picture. Both by training and disposition she was slow to form conclusions, but once she reached them she took the determined direction of a swan in flight: She never hesitated to stick her neck out. She had reason to be familiar with crime and punishment. People often thought about the impact of crime, but seldom considered the impact of punishment. Politicians built their careers around being tough on crime. Careers could be ruined by being soft on punishment. Laws had been passed everywhere, extending prison sentences for nearly everything and everyone. Discussions about the innocent victims of crime never came around to considering the innocent victims of punishment. When a man went to prison, anyone who happened to love him went there with him and stayed there as long as they could, which often was far from as long as his sentence. Visits came fewer and farther between. Then guilt set in outside the walls and festered there.

Esther knew about this firsthand. Several times in her clinical career, she had provided counseling for someone with a loved one in prison struggling to cope with a life broken apart and changed forever. Prison visits could be like putting one's hand in a fire just at the moment it had begun to heal from its most recent burn.

The ravages of prison life in crowded, high-security facilities like Shade Creek could be read clearly on the faces of a son, a brother, a husband. The more innocent they seemed going in, the more unjust and needlessly severe the verdict, the less understandable it all was and the harder it was for those closest to them to persevere. No wonder victims of punishment were invisible anywhere outside a prison visiting room. No wonder they faded away, tried to forget, and would have been forgotten had they ever been remembered. Some things are too horrible to contemplate.

Wherever they had lived, Esther had occasionally provided jail and prison services, more out of compassion than for remuneration, which was slight given the meager amounts those institutions budgeted for mental health services. Shade Creek was typical. As many as 30 percent of its inmates were mentally ill, and many of these suffered from serious conditions going largely undiagnosed, untreated, and getting worse in the prison environment. Most of the severe cases had not received proper care before committing the crimes that sent them there, and once there, they received minimal treatment aimed more toward managing their behavior than improving their condition.

Prison life bordering on the inhumane made everything worse. In a world where inmates could no longer be shackled to walls, hurled into dark pits, tortured, or starved into submission, prison officials were looking for drugs that would accomplish the same while maintaining an appearance of an institutional location in a civilized society with regard for human dignity and well-being. Anyone spending a day in Shade Creek, or in any other prison, knew better.

Much of this had evolved in tandem with her education and career. When she and Ralph met in college, she had just changed her major from English to social psychology in an era when public attitudes toward long-term mental health care were also changing. Mental hospitals, once known as insane asylums, were attracting public concern, ostensibly for effectiveness and quality-of-life issues, but more so for how much it cost to provide such mediocre care around the clock. With new drugs appearing on the scene, promising to reduce costs while improving or at least managing many of the most serious conditions, "mainstreaming" became the rallying cry and goal. Patients were released to group homes, halfway houses, and sometimes their own families, assisted by case managers and social workers. It all looked so humane and wonderful to anyone who had seen Hollywood depictions of life in the crazy ward.

Like so many plans born of trendy idealism underpinned by taxpayer concerns and false readings, much of this foundered. Ralph had a favorite saying that applied here: "There is such a thing as reality." Esther had given lectures about the reality as opposed to the vision. The mentally ill had been scattered and gone underground. Their former homes, the large walled and gated edifices built on hillsides in the countryside in an earlier era, were harder to ignore than single-story houses with walkout basements inconspicuously located in residential areas. The public might gawk at a state mental fortress perched in its line of sight on the road ahead and wonder what was happening there. It might come up with derisive names like loony bin, funny farm, and nut house, but that at least was a sign of persistent awareness. People could drive by a group home or halfway house and never notice or give it a second thought. Such places never even rose to the level of joke and nickname, unless of course a campaign to prevent one from being located nearby became a news item. Most everyone embraced the notion that mentally ill or mentally impaired people should be encouraged to lead normal lives, as long as this was not attempted in *their* neighborhoods.

Esther had gone into clinical psychology, completed her dissertation, and found her first position at a veteran's hospital where the Vietnam War was still being fought engagement by engagement ten years after the fact by men who could not let go. Ralph was employed as an assistant pharmacist at a drugstore in the Chicago Loop. Hapless "loonies" and "funny farmers", having drifted away from domestic surroundings normal folk enjoyed, were already beginning to appear on street corners near the Palmer House Hotel. Esther meeting Ralph nearby some late afternoons often passed men in serious conversations with inner voices. From there it was but a short trip to the Cook County Jail.

Esther could see the woven circles of the mental health care establishment unwinding before her in many a man sitting in his own urine on a street corner. Years ago he must have started out in an understaffed state mental hospital, where at night sometimes the raving, ranting, and screaming of other patients awoke him, and sometimes his own awoke others. Then he had gone to an understaffed group home, where life seemed more like something thought up by children attempting to role-play being parents while their own were away. Thanks to medications he slept better. Then thanks to medications, he felt good enough to be out on his own. Feeling as good as all that, he quit taking his medications and skipped appointments with his case manager, who had too many cases anyway.

He began to feel insecure and thought he needed to protect himself. He heard voices warning him about zombies disguised as police officers. He waved a knife at one of these or shot at a police car he mistook for a hearse, using a gun he had found in a trash can, wrapped in a hooded sweatshirt and dumped there by a robber fleeing the scene of a convenience store holdup in which a clerk had been killed. Then he found himself in prison, where once again he was awakened by raving, ranting, and screaming and sometimes awoke others with his own.

It might have been much the same in the veteran's hospital where Esther worked but for the fact she and others like her were there, and none of their patients were serving a prison sentence, at least not yet.

Inmates who had committed crimes with 10 percent awareness were being punished with 110 percent sentences by a society that could be regarded as their partner in crime if anyone thought about it. Few people thought about it. Crime and compassion never mixed in the get-tough-on-crime world. Esther had lectured about that and sometimes been booed. The insanity defense, regarded as an evasion of responsibility, had vanished from a courtroom where sentences were longer than ever as the public pursued a policy of crime prevention based on false presumptions of rationality. No one seemed to see that the get-tough approach could not penetrate the scrambled thought processes of people who barely knew who they were or that serious treatment of mental illness was a civilized alternative approach to crime prevention.

Ralph had left his chair and was looking out a window at Ed's Hotel. After much thought, Esther decided to change the subject slightly, or at least to rotate it in another direction.

"I have met the young lady's father", she said.

"How on earth did you manage that? I was down in the store around a corner. Where were you when they came and went in that white-finned apparition?"

"Not the young lady's *stepfather*. Her *biological* father."

Neither Ralph nor Felix for that matter had been aware of the difference in Penelope's case. Ralph returned to his chair, sat down, and tugged at the bridge of his nose.

"At Shade Creek", said Esther. "He's incarcerated at Shade Creek, and his name is Warren Hall. I have notes from two interviews with him, both of them much too brief, but in each he mentioned a daughter Penelope living on the North Shore of Lake Superior. He is forbidden to contact her by court order. I am convinced his daughter was the young lady downstairs Saturday afternoon."

"Good Lord!" said Ralph, emptying what remained in his wine glass.

19

Of Course You Know

Some might call it by such aliases as blind fate, Providence, or serendipity, but whatever name it answers to, coincidence is often just around
the next corner. Often it stays there out of sight, an unacknowledged
partisan prompting events from offstage, both what happens and what
fails to happen, such as Charlotte and June not meeting during camper
registration at Pine Shadows.

If June had not had a two o'clock hair appointment in Bell Harbor,
if she and Marvin had not returned to their car by one path while
Charlotte approached Hikers by another, or if Charlotte's familiar lime
green Volkswagen with its St. Christopher statue on the dashboard
had been parked elsewhere than the other side of a campground twelve-
seater bus, Penelope's stay at Pine Shadows would have amounted to
less than two hours instead of the two weeks it was destined to be.
Since none of these things happened, June left the scene happy, while
Penelope and Charlotte became happier by the minute. Only Marvin
was miserable.

Neither Charlotte nor Penelope had a chance to say anything beyond
unintelligible gasps before another of the campers with her parents
joined them, giving both of them time to recover. The remaining
three campers, two with parents and one with her grandmother,
appeared at what might have been intervals in a well-organized parade.
Penelope found herself drawn into conversations with the other girls,
none of whom were from St. John Vianney, and Charlotte into conversations with the adults. All went smoothly in this state of preoccupied obliviousness until the lone grandmother, noting their shared hair
color, asked in a voice loud enough for everyone to hear whether
Charlotte was Penelope's mother. Silence ensued. A similarity so striking could not be called coincidence, so while both redheads blushed,

Charlotte acknowledged being her aunt in the tone of a burglar caught red-handed, or red-haired, depending on how one looked at it.

Even this turned out to be favorable in the way that a shared predicament can sometimes break down barriers. After the grandmother's departure and while the other girls were unpacking, aunt and niece stepped outside with minutes to spare before a general assembly of all campers and their squad counselors. This was their first chance to talk.

Introductions had never been necessary. They had seen each other from a distance around Bell Harbor dozens of times through the intervening years, with Penelope growing up and Charlotte aging in various ways, some having to do with a brother in prison. Each always knew who the other was and had pretended not to know. Each had kept track of the other through a long series of occasional sightings. This self-conscious history had left them both feeling like old friends. Penelope could have said, "I saw you last March carrying a guitar just as school let out." Charlotte could have said, "You and Marvin were waiting in one of his old cars in the drive-up line at a bank just after Easter." This could have gone on and on. They both had a list.

"I don't know whether to laugh or to cry", said Charlotte, resting her hand on Penelope's shoulder.

Truly she didn't know. There were reasons enough for both, looking back and looking ahead. Charlotte's thoughts kept circling toward her brother.

"But we can't talk about your dad no matter what. We can talk about anything else and anyone else, and if anyone ever asks about this, we must say we kept him out of it. The court order ... I'm sorry", said Charlotte.

She had never known how far it extended and to whom it applied.

"It's okay. It's really okay", said Penelope.

Charlotte wasn't so sure, but she would do nothing to jeopardize his parole chances. He could be eligible in less than three years.

"I can't be seen to be carrying messages back and forth."

Over the years of his imprisonment, she had been able honestly to deflect Warren's inevitable inquiries about his daughter.

"I can't tell you much because I don't know much."

"How is that possible?"

"I hardly ever see her, except from a distance."

"What does she look like?"

"She has hair the color of mine."

Now how would she handle his questions?

The two-week camp for young Catholic women was different from most encampments sponsored by various groups throughout the summer in that it was part traditional camp and part religious retreat. Days began and ended with group prayers. Religious education and Bible instruction could be found on a schedule otherwise including swimming, canoeing, tennis, camp crafts, and nature study. Recreational activities were directed by Pine Shadows staff, while religious activities and counseling duties were assigned to instructors from the participating parishes, which is how Aunt Charlotte and later on Sister Serena came on the scene. In addition to musician services, each provided religious education instruction: Charlotte for the younger children and Sister Serena on a different night for the older ones, including Penelope.

Planners of the camp's religious activities had attached no importance to placing counselors with girls from their respective parishes. In fact, this was discouraged in favor of breaking from established routines and adding to the novelty and excitement of the summer experience. Penelope and Charlotte winding up in the same group was not supposed to happen, but like so much else unforeseen, somehow it managed to happen.

They and the other Hikers trooped off on a scheduled tour of the campground, broke up for an open activity period, and returned to their cabin to wash up before an opening day cookout and campfire. They ate as a group at an assigned picnic table, but afterward, as the campfire was lit and songs began, the various camp squads dissolved when familiar faces were spotted in the crowd and parish friends beckoned.

Eventually Charlotte and Penelope were sitting alone on the same side of the picnic table while flame-driven shadows danced in trees all around them and firelight flickered over their faces and hands folded before them on the tabletop. The crackling campfire, though distant, invited intimacy, the surfacing of old memories, and a sharing of confidences long withheld. No better moment could have been designed.

The evening's entertainment included first a juggler using duck decoys and then a magician, who turned out to be the same performer in a different costume. Following the magician, as if a rabbit appearing from a hat, came Father James Spence representing one of the Iron Range schools.

Each night of the two-week encampment, a priest from one of the sponsoring parishes would give a Gospel reading and a homily. Father Spence led off the series with some thoughts on the value of distance, on how sometimes it was necessary to get farther away to see things better up close. Penelope thought of Shade Creek. Father Spence referred to Christ getting away from crowds at times. To finish on a personal note, he then reminded everyone of how vacation from school served just this purpose, and being at a summer camp took the benefits of distance even further.

At this point cheers erupted. After closing prayers, someone added birch wood to the campfire. Each log released a fountain of sparks and feathery embers spiraling into tree branches and drifting out over the lake. Shadows leaped as Hibbing students clustered around Father Spence.

"He's Marvin's cousin, and I suppose you know he baptized you", Charlotte whispered while gazing straight ahead.

Penelope had not known either. Marvin seldom talked about his extended family, and her baptism had always been part of the world to be forgotten.

"We drove to Eveleth for your baptism. He was assigned there at the time. Now he's in Hibbing. Before both he was at St. John Vianney."

Charlotte was about to say Father Lyle had recently been assigned there, as if this explained why Penelope's parents had gone elsewhere. She reconsidered and set off in what seemed a safer direction.

"Of course you know I'm your godmother."

Of course she had *not* known. Aunt Charlotte seemed to know more about her life than she herself did. Something like vertigo seemed to pass through her, starting at the top of her head and exiting from toes pointed straight at flames about the same color as the hair they shared. She took her aunt's hand as if to steady herself.

"A copy of your baptismal certificate was sent to St. John Vianney so that a record would be located in your home parish. I'm sure Father Ulrich could find it for you."

Father Spence, now serving as campfire emcee, began to introduce the campers representing parishes in the diocese. Given how parishes are named as a rule, this became a list of saints: St. Cecilia, St. Edward, St. Francis, and so on, with applause following each from its respective contingent scattered among the various camp cabin groups. Penelope and Charlotte both cheered for St. John Vianney, with others joining in from other sides of the campfire. Among them Penelope was happy not to discover Jackie Rae.

Meanwhile, Charlotte's thoughts lingered among memories of Penelope's baptism, the springtime trip to Eveleth on a road winding past vast Iron Range canyons carved into forested hillsides, her niece's tiny face sometimes turned her way, smiling from her mother's shoulder. This was a happier time, when without knowing it they all perched on the edge of catastrophe deeper than a mining pit.

"Philomena was quite a popular saint when I was your age."

"Philomena?"

"Yes, your patron saint, you know."

Charlotte had reminisced some distance from the possibility her niece might not know her baptismal name. As they were dressing the baby for her trip to Eveleth, June had confided to Charlotte that she thought the two names together too long.

"Penelope Philomena is too much of a mouthful," June had said with a shrug and then a look of resignation, "but you know your brother. When he gets something in his head, there's no stopping him. Otherwise we wouldn't be going anywhere today, and Father Lyle would do it. He doesn't like Father Lyle."

Charlotte was familiar with this. Warren had always been the sort to get things in his head, to latch onto things that didn't seem to have handles and then not be able to let go. She could remember him as a little boy retracing his steps to touch a sidewalk crack with his foot or a lamppost with his fingertips and then saying to her that he *must* do it or something bad would happen. They might have been on their way to church, or perhaps they were coming home.

"What will happen?" she would ask him.

He would bury his face in his hands and cry.

So they would go back together to touch the lamppost or to step on the crack.

"It's all right now. It will be all right", she would say to him, with her handkerchief wiping his tear-stained cheeks. "Nothing bad can happen now. We have fixed it."

Except it wasn't fixed.

She glanced at her niece, whose face was illuminated by a campfire, and wondered how much she knew of her father and the church fire. Asking her would lead to things best left undisclosed.

Penelope had always believed her middle name was Anne. All her school records identified her as Penelope Anne Lister. Sister Hilaria in the third grade had been the first to point out that her initials spelled the word PAL.

"So no matter what," Sister had said, "you will always be a pal!"

But when had she ever been Philomena?

"Get used to this name stuff", her mother had said. "It's what happens to women."

Having finished introductions of participating parish groups, Father Spence led the assembly in singing "When the Saints Go Marching In". This rousing anthem sputtered at first, spiraled off toward flat, almost died out, and then caught hold as more and more voices joined it, sending it in a crescendo up into the trees and across the lake, where it became an echo and then an echo of an echo and then the silence that follows loud sounds. As the song ended, scattered conversations resumed all around in the low, sonorous tones of talk around campfires in semidarkness when people speak while gazing at flames.

"The sound of your name ... is like a series of little hills", said Charlotte to the flames.

Penelope felt herself climbing some of those hills for the first time and peering at what might reveal itself on the other side. In an interval of no more than two hours on their first day together, Charlotte had become not just her godmother, but her fairy godmother, whose magic wand could change things from the ordinary to the extraordinary and back again in a twinkling.

She had taken her by the hand to a bridge named Messages Back and Forth and then told her she must not be seen to cross it. It stretched over an abyss called Things Never Known or Forgotten and from there into a land where many things were not as she thought or had imagined them to be. Her name was not what it had been ever since she learned to write it at the top of a school tablet. Her baptism was somewhere else. Her aunt was her godmother. Marvin's cousin was a priest. She needed time to let it all sink in. Before it could begin to do that, Father Spence approached.

"I would like to borrow your niece for a moment", he said, suddenly in front of them as if pulled once again from a magician's hat. He led Penelope away to a nearby picnic table, where they sat facing each other. He waved off two girls approaching. "I will join you in a second", he said.

He introduced himself as her stepdad's cousin.

"Of course you probably already knew that", he said.

And she did, though only from a few minutes ago.

"I suppose you know the story."

Of course she didn't know Marvin and her mother had met through him when he had returned to St. John Vianney to preside at a wedding of one of her mother's high school friends.

"I'm not sure how Marvin happened to be there", he said, and then he remembered. "It was one of his cars." The newlyweds had arranged to leave the church and drive around Bell Harbor in one of Marvin's antique cars. "So how is Marvin these days? Has he added to his collection?"

"Not since last year", said Penelope, before recalling that the Frazer had shown up more recently, but leaving it at that.

Father Spence smiled. "You couldn't have a better stepdad."

Penelope nodded without difficulty.

"Your dad was a fine man, too. I never expected I would meet his daughter when I came here this evening. I'm sure he would be very proud of you."

The past tense made it seem as if her father were dead, but he was not dead: It just had to sound that way whenever anyone talked about him. She still didn't know what, if anything, her father knew about her, except her hair was the same as Charlotte's. Would that make him proud?

The "No Trespassing" signs Charlotte had installed around her brother for the sake of his parole seemed not to apply to Father Spence, who strolled right past them.

"Your dad tied the most beautiful fishing flies I have ever seen. I still have a few of them. You don't want to use them for fishing. You just want to save them and look at them, and then he built me an amazing weather vane. Actually it was a combination weather vane and mobile, ingenious and artistic. I don't have it any longer, or I would send you a picture of it."

"A weather vane?"

"Yes, I'm afraid it might have been lost when I moved from St. John Vianney."

"In a box?" She swallowed hard.

"Well, there *were* lots of boxes. People think of us priests as leading pretty simple lives, but some of us are packrats."

Father Spence drifted in one direction and Penelope in another. She experienced a second episode of vertigo, finding herself in a first-ever conversation about her father, well inside a world she and Charlotte had agreed to avoid. She did her best to smile, but it seemed to her she was smiling through something like bars in a window with a bright light in her eyes. It wasn't that way when they had talked about Marvin.

With that and a few further questions of the sort adults usually ask at such times concerning school, summer plans, and so on, he got up, and they walked back to Charlotte.

Five evenings later, Charlotte and Penelope set out for a beach several cabins distant from Hikers and its inevitable interruptions. A full moon had slipped behind gauzy overcast, but provided light yet sufficient to illuminate their path and cast a metallic sheen upon the water. An east wind carried with it a chill from the distant Great Lake and the promise of rain overnight. Aunt and niece had both brought windbreakers and, within minutes of sitting down, put them on. These were nearly the same shade of green, a coincidence they found comforting.

Green was Charlotte's favorite color. She asked if it were also her niece's and learned that June had picked out her jacket. This Penelope added to her growing list of ironies the week had thrust before her, for example, that they both had toothbrushes with the same dentist's name inscribed on the handles. June had also chosen the dentist. For at least the past eight years Penelope, her aunt, and June had been sitting in the same waiting room, perhaps no more than days or mere hours apart. The dentist had never said to Penelope, not once, "Your aunt was just here for an appointment only last week." Such was life in Bell Harbor, where even an especially serious dentist seemed to be in on the game.

"Perhaps he was afraid he might lose a patient", Charlotte had theorized the morning of this discovery as they stood side by side brushing their teeth.

"If he had told you," Penelope asked, "what would you have done?"

"Nothing", said Charlotte between gargles of mouthwash. "I hate switching dentists."

"I think Mom would have taken me somewhere else."

In such ways the week had slipped by, with similar snippets during chance meetings scattered between morning assemblies and evening sing-alongs. From that first evening campfire until the moment they settled down on the sandy shore in their green jackets, aunt and niece had not found another interlude to be alone together. But wherever they were and whomever they were with, there always seemed to be nearby the invisible presence of the man they could not discuss. He lingered in the space between their glances, in their thoughts unrevealed, and in their silences between words to each other. Everyone else and everything else seemed a digression.

"There can never be too much green in this world", Charlotte said, settling on banter as the best approach to their impending goodbye. She mentioned she had an abundance of green possessions: Scarves, living room drapes, a handbag, and her lime colored car. "My mother used to say I liked green because it was the color of carrot tops. Maybe so; I don't know. But I never liked peas, and they're green enough, that's for sure."

She was postponing the inevitable. They both knew she could stay no longer, given the arrival of June and Marvin for the Sunday Mass. She would be leaving Pine Shadows next morning, to be replaced for the duration by Sister Serena. Charlotte picked up a pointed piece of driftwood and traced a treble clef in the sand.

Goodbyes can be easier when plans can be made to meet again. Charlotte and Penelope had no such plan, just jackets of the same color and the same dentist. Years might pass before they wound up in the same waiting room together, suggested Penelope. "It can't be. I won't let it happen that way", she added.

They had been talking in tones barely above a whisper, sitting side by side and looking out over the lake, the way people do when they come to a shore, but with each determined syllable Penelope's voice grew louder as she grew more agitated and determined. She pivoted to look at her aunt.

"It won't happen that way, will it, Aunt Charlotte?"

Charlotte had long ago learned that life hung by threads. What you thought would never happen could happen, and what you were certain would happen might never be so. Hope and fear alike had a flimsy connection with events. The years since her brother's imprisonment had been filled with things that could not possibly be, but nonetheless were. She had faced them alone. She was about to face one such tomorrow. Penelope's question invited harsh wisdom, but clamored for reassurance. She knew which to reach for at the moment.

"I don't know how or why or when, but I think we will meet again soon. So instead of us fretting, tell me more about this Felix." She drew another treble clef and added a music staff alongside it.

On their walk to the beach, Penelope had mentioned her pen pal. Except for the fact her mother knew nothing about Felix, Penelope omitted little as Charlotte encouraged her with well-placed questions, each one becoming a musical note in the sand. At last Clay Corners and Shade Creek came into the story, with Marvin's speeding past and then Sister Hilaria waving when they reached St. Cloud. The driftwood stick paused, and Penelope knew her aunt had made the connection.

Charlotte took a deep breath, exhaling it slowly and looking skyward as people do when a revelation gives them much to ponder. She might have been asking herself what Marvin had already asked himself that early spring evening while washing dishes with Penelope: *How could it be that of all places on earth, Felix came from the village nearest Shade Creek and Penelope's father?*

Up and down the shore either side of them, others had drifted to the lake at evening's end and were sitting in groups of two or three. Despite the absence of much in the way of mountains anywhere nearby, the camp song "I Love the Mountains" began to their left and was soon picked up by others on both sides till it rose in a chorus, echoing and reverberating across the lake so that it seemed also to be coming from the spruce forest on the other side.

> I love the mountains.
> I love the rolling hills.
> I love the flowers.
> I love the daffodils.

Down through the catalogue of many other loves ran the song with unabated joy as some of the girls knew additional lyrics. It went as far as oceans and came as near as daisies. It even included sugar peas because they rhymed with *breeze*. Then it started all over again, once more racing its way through many loves because nothing this merry could be sung only once. Voices tumbled like a cataract on its way to the Great Lake, then arose and fell like a breeze through treetops rushing from the lake to meet the cataract. By and by the many singers became three or four, then two and finally one, perched on the edge of silence and solitude only a lake at night can provide. Penelope, among the last to join in, was the last to notice it was over, and everyone else was clapping.

"You have a lovely voice", said Charlotte. "Mr. Stiller should put you in the choir."

When the conversation between aunt and niece journeyed from Mr. Stiller's choir back to Felix, Penelope told Charlotte about his father's ring and her desire to write him again. She paused at that point and, taking Charlotte's stick, drew a question mark in the sand.

Charlotte took the stick, or rather Penelope's hand still holding the stick, and wrote, "OK", beneath her question mark. Afterward she would wonder, until she had less reason for wondering, if she had been too quick to give reassurance. The Felix spell appeared to have long-distance, secondary effects.

They stood up, brushed the sand off their clothes, and returned to their cabin by a path less illuminated. A thickening cloud layer had slipped over the moon. A few fireflies blinked and drifted as points of light gliding through the leafy undergrowth. Charlotte took the lead. Distant lightning flared at their backs too far away for its thunder to be heard. A few yards from Hikers, at a point where their path intersected the one Marvin and June had taken, where they all might have met a Saturday ago and none of this would have happened, Charlotte stopped and turned to face her niece. They embraced.

"I am going to see your dad tomorrow", she whispered in her ear. That was all, except for a single tear hidden in shadow on her aunt's cheek. This was goodbye.

As Penelope fell asleep, a pair of loons called to each other from opposite ends of the lake with song at once ethereal and eerie, near at hand and farther away than distances alone could account for. Perhaps they too were seeking reassurance. Perhaps they too sang from their love of all things. They seemed to be asking, "Are you all right?" Rain pattered on the cabin roof. She slept.

Charlotte left before any of the Hikers awoke next morning to discover Sister Serena sitting among them prepared with the possibility of going on a spider hunt before the day was out. Meanwhile Charlotte was driving south to Shade Creek, word having reached her that her brother had been beaten by another inmate and was in the prison infirmary. She had two reasons for leaving Pine Shadows.

20

The Cat Gets Out

Marvin awoke Sunday morning like a man on his way to a root canal. All week he had been able to think of little else than Charlotte at camp with Penelope. The outdoor Mass was scheduled for ten o'clock, ahead of which parents would have a chance to visit with their daughters about the week just passed and the one ahead. The hoped-for rainstorm forcing cancellation of everything hadn't happened. June's Toyota hadn't broken down in the middle of nowhere. A tree hadn't fallen across the road. The world hadn't ended, or at least wouldn't end in time. Nothing getting in the way of the inevitable, Marvin began to rehearse speeches of reconciliation and appeasement long before they drove under a sign hung between lodge poles proclaiming their arrival at Pine Shadows.

Marvin wondered whether he was best located behind June or in front of her as they walked to the Hikers cabin, which came down to deciding whether he wanted to be run over by a truck or backed over by one. He settled for the latter. Other sets of parents were gathered in a circle in front of the cabin, with Penelope in the doorway waving as they approached and then beckoning to someone inside the circle, Aunt Charlotte for certain. Marvin winced and then looked longingly at the lake like a shipwrecked sailor scanning the horizon for signs of rescue. Penelope ran forward just as a gap appeared in the circle of parents, and from a universe other than the one Marvin contemplated, Sister Serena stepped out to greet them.

While she was visiting with June, he furtively peered into the cabin for signs of Charlotte. He half expected to see her under a cot or perhaps perched like a lynx on the open log rafters. When he failed to find a sign of her, his fear shifted elsewhere. He hadn't imagined it; he hadn't been fretting all week for nothing. She had to be at hand and about to pop into their midst. On their way to Mass, he looked for her among other groups converging in an open field, where camp chairs had been arranged in rows. His next target was a portable organ. Instead it was Sister Serena who had left their ranks and settled there within a group of girls holding guitars, flutes, and clarinets. At this point, with a minimum of lip movement, June suggested he quit fidgeting. Marvin began to believe the unbelievable.

As pastor of the nearest parish, Father Ulrich had volunteered to celebrate the Mass and to provide music. From a movable stairway normally serving as an entrance to campground offices in a trailer house, Father Ulrich read the Gospel for the Eleventh Sunday in Ordinary Time and followed with an amusing homily about canoeing with the Lord, whether things went better with the Lord in the stern seat paddling and steering or with you sitting there with the Lord in the front seat.

Sister Serena's ensemble led the congregation in spirited, upbeat hymns as befit such an occasion. A flock of geese flew over; the loons, apparently responding to organ piping, began a conversation about all this; and sunlight flowing through leafy branches covered parts of the congregation in damask shadows trembling as soft breezes came and went. Even Marvin began to relax in the midst of a scene that could hardly have been improved upon. Even Father Ulrich, a hard to impress old hand if ever there was one, seemed spellbound.

His acknowledgments at the end of Mass before the final blessing were especially effusive. He thanked the absent Benedictine monk who had filled in for him for ten o'clock Mass at St. John Vianney. He thanked the Pine Shadows staff and the parents of the campers; he thanked the young Catholic women for being at camp; he thanked the young musicians; and, last but not least, as it is almost always put, he thanked Sister Serena for replacing Charlotte Hall at the organ on such short notice.

Marvin awoke from a pleasant Sunday doze as one who had discovered a hornet buzzing under his collar. June sat up straight; Penelope skipped four or five breaths and as many heartbeats. Even at that, though, all was not lost: The cat had not yet escaped its bag or at least had only its head sticking out. Father Ulrich had only mentioned Sister Serena at the organ instead of Charlotte. It might have ended right there with sufficient ambiguity in place all around to forestall disaster had not the inquisitive grandmother among the Hikers group turned around and asked Penelope, "Where's that red-haired aunt who was here with you last week?"

"May almighty God bless you, the Father, and the Son, and the Holy Spirit", said Father Ulrich, making the Sign of the Cross in the air above them. "Go in peace, glorifying the Lord by your life."

"Thanks be to God", responded the congregation, all but Marvin, Penelope, and June.

The former two were too stunned to speak, while June was too enflamed and very far from going in peace. Marvin took Penelope's hand. June took a deep breath and pursued Father Ulrich. Fortunately for all concerned, she had to wait several minutes and a hundred or so breaths while the rest of the congregation filed past and greeted him. The minutes passed slowly, and subsequent breaths were not especially deep, but in the time this consumed, she had assumed the brittle efficiency of her Osgoode Insurance side.

"Father, my daughter appears to have been here with Charlotte Hall all last week. How did that happen?"

June might have been asking an insurance claimant who had fallen asleep at the wheel, "How did you happen to run off the road?" Equally caught by surprise, Father Ulrich had been bathing in a flood of euphoria and glad tidings. At first his defenses were in disarray. He had a habit of raising both his bushy eyebrows when confronting a mystery. This would elevate them a full inch above the dark rims of his glasses, where they stood at the moment perched in a sort of apogee of bewilderment.

The mysteries capable of bewildering him were rarely of the theological kind. Only recently, on Trinity Sunday, Father had handled the three Persons in one God as deftly as an experienced juggler with only three objects in play. Many a less experienced priest might have stayed up late the night before, searching for a metaphor to elucidate the dogma, but not Father Ulrich. Give him problems like the Trinity any day over the sort human relationships managed to create. Those were the ones that elevated his eyebrows. Those were the inexplicable ones, for which homely metaphors would never suffice.

"I really don't know how it happened. Are you sure it happened?"

The most desirable solution to a problem like this is a discovery at the level of false or mistaken report. Father recalled the recent case of a parishioner reporting her purse having been stolen only to discover her husband had carried it to their car in his folded overcoat.

"I heard it myself from a lady at the end of Mass", said June.

In a strange way, from that point forward, this exchange took the form of something of daily occurrence under the Osgoode Insurance Agency roof, except Father Ulrich seemed to be occupying June's chair behind a desk answering questions and occasionally referring to policy provisions with June, a customer in search of answers, discovering that a particular misfortune wasn't covered and blame couldn't be assigned.

"I'm sure it wasn't intentional", said Father Ulrich. "With so many parishes in the picture—"

"Someone has to be responsible for this", said June through her teeth.

Insurance policies, as she well knew, sometimes sought refuge in acts of God, chance occurrences for which no one can be held directly responsible.

"Perhaps the Lord wanted it to happen this way."

"I will be the judge of that!" snapped June.

"No, I think the Lord will", said Father Ulrich, himself on the verge of not so priestly impatience because he was due back at St. John Vianney for the noon Mass, and it was now half past eleven.

Perhaps this circumstance was also part of a greater design at work, for he found himself saying something to June he had wanted occasion to say to her for a long time.

"We build walls, sometimes too tall and too thick. The Lord tears them down. The Lord unites what we would keep apart."

At this point June's anger turned to tears, though whether of indignation or frustration only she could have said. Her ventriloquism failed. Her Osgoode persona crumbled. Father's impatience had released an avalanche.

"No harm ever came of tearing down walls", he declared as if descending from a mountain. "Only good can come of it, for your daughter and for you."

His words seemed to echo though he spoke just above a whisper. He glanced at his watch.

Except for a squadron of large dragonflies and campground workers collecting chairs, Father and June were now alone in the playing field, with Penelope and Sister Serena approaching from a few steps away and Marvin maneuvering the church's portable organ in its case on a handcart toward Father Ulrich's car, stopping every few yards to rest and glance over his shoulder.

Sister Serena, a tiny woman in her early forties, was afraid of nothing. She had the keen eyes and steady hands of a watchmaker. When she lit church candles, her match never missed the wick. Had she taken instead the name Joan of Arc, it could only have been seen as a redundancy given the level of determination, courage, and force of concentration her face displayed whether examining the intricacies of a spiderweb, holding a bat by its wings to release it from its wanderings in St. John Vianney, stepping into the middle of a schoolyard brawl, or joining Father Ulrich and June at a moment when simply on account of her intervening the old priest would have recommended her for canonization.

"I'm sure it's all right, Mrs. Lister. I've been with Penelope since yesterday, and I have never seen her happier."

This of course was the last thing June wanted to hear: Penelope was supposed to be miserable. Helpless and outnumbered, she glanced from face to face looking for signs of agreement or at least understanding. When this wasn't forthcoming, she stifled a sob.

"Mom, it's all right", said Penelope. "It's okay. It really is. Don't worry."

She took her mother's hand, lowered it to her side, and hugged her. Since affection was not all that common between mother and daughter coming from either side, this had an effect beyond words. She led her mother away, speaking with her further as they went.

"Thank you, Sister", said Father Ulrich.

"Sometimes," said Sister Serena paraphrasing a poem she liked, "*would* is not heartwood."

Father Ulrich found himself pondering the mystery of that as he drove a bit over the speed limit in the direction of Bell Harbor. One of these days he would have to ask Sister Serena to explain. Penelope and the other Hikers went off on a spider hunt. Marvin and June drove home in silence, with her sometimes in tears again, clutching a rolled Mass program. Out on Star Island, he put his arm around her on their way into the house.

"We're very lucky", he said when he couldn't think of anything else to say, and at the same time wondering why he said it since it didn't make much sense at the moment. At least June didn't challenge him on that point. Later that afternoon, out in the pole barn, he had a long talk with Osgood and found himself wishing Penelope were home.

Lake Surprise had lived up to its name. Sister Serena had lived up to hers.

21

The Felix Spell

Anyone wanting to rile Felix need only remind him that Shade Creek Penitentiary had been built on the site of his Uncle Milton's farm. No one wanted to rile him, but he did not need reminders: He thought of it often enough without assistance, the more so since he had been writing Penelope and reminiscing a lot.

He had inherited from his childless uncle the farm, its two airplanes, and even the Cord 810, and he had fought the state's plans to purchase the land, which for some reason involved the proximity of a railroad forming its southern and western property lines. Why that should matter was beyond understanding as far as Felix was concerned, and even the state's construction planners were ambiguous in their explanations. One would have thought it somehow vital to the course of punishment that prisoners should hear trains passing in the middle of the night and be reminded of their lost freedom.

At last and inevitably the state got its way. Felix, facing formal condemnation proceedings, sold 638 of its 640 acres, Uncle Milton's house, his farm buildings, and his airplane landing strip, down to a wind sock that once spun from a pole in the middle of his cow pasture: Lock, stock, and barrel, as they say. He succeeded in keeping two acres of woodlot and a watery hollow formed by the other Shade Creek as it flowed under a railroad bridge out of sight of the prison complex, yet close enough that some days shouts of guards and prisoners could be heard.

Uncle Milton had constructed there a large farm storage building of corrugated sheet metal and semicircular trusses near what was now a disused railroad siding with brush and small trees growing between its creosoted timber ties. A stranger in the area standing on the creek bank, gazing uphill from there through the woodlot, might never have guessed that a prison boundary with chain-link fence and coiled barbed wire lay just beyond its crest. If he happened to hear men shouting, he would not have known what to make of it. These two isolated acres were what remained of Uncle Milton's farm, and Felix in later years had spent many an interlude there immersed in thoughts of bygone days and treasuring remnants of his boyhood still housed in the storage building. Otherwise everything else seemed to be imprisoned at Shade Creek along with its inmates—Warren Hall among them—as if somehow Felix' own past were as guilty as theirs.

Esther had advised her husband not to tell him about Penelope's father imprisoned nearby. She was sure it would complicate matters in ways unforeseen.

Ralph took her advice to heart and kept this to himself whenever he ran into Felix. One can imagine his amazement when he hung the CLOSED sign on his store door a few days later, walked over to the Depot Café, and heard from Felix that Penelope's real father was not the man who drove that white Desoto, but another.

"In the pen up the road", said Felix with a nod in that general direction. He did not mince words, and Ralph did not have to pretend surprise.

Felix' information had not come from reading Ralph's mind or eavesdropping on his conversations with Esther. Nor had it come by chance or by way of gossip, though these were possibilities since Felix knew practically the entire Shade Creek labor force. Its source was none other than Penelope herself, whose letter from summer camp had arrived in yesterday's mail.

Recent events having lowered Felix' expectations where his post office box was concerned, he hadn't bothered before late afternoon to pick up what he thought would be the usual junk mail. The presence of another of Marvin's striking airmail envelopes propelled him back to the hotel at a pace twice his in leaving there. Nine times out of ten, or maybe ninety-nine times out of a hundred, there wouldn't have been another letter, but Penelope and Felix were equal to such odds. She had found a grandfather, and Felix a Penelope. Neither was about to let go.

The correspondence of Penelope and Felix had entered a further stage, and as so often happens in relationships forming by chance and enduring through turmoil, a newfound intimacy emerges among survivors. Penelope and Felix had washed up upon a common shore after what seemed a shipwreck.

Felix was familiar with this. Decades after his prison camp experience, he continued to hear from those captured with him: Christmas cards, a phone call once in a while from one who had been drinking, an annual visit from an Iowa buddy who made a point of stopping at Clay Corners on his way to a family cabin in northern Minnesota. More than a decade had passed since he had last heard from any of them. In what had become an informal Last Man's Club, Felix might have become its last man. Perhaps this could have been predicted. Felix, enlisting when he was but seventeen, had been the youngest recruit, and prison life ages men more quickly than life on the outside. Esther Corrigan had an armload of statistics to prove this. Those two years sleeping on concrete floors behind German barbed wire had put ten on most of them.

Even before Shade Creek blighted the scene, thoughts of prison and prisoners had special resonance with Felix. And Penelope had both disclosed her father's presence in the middle of Uncle Milton's farm and mentioned that he was forbidden by court order to have any contact with her. This touched a further chord with Felix, needing no explanation beyond the old ring on his finger and an inscription on a gravestone in the nearby cemetery, where orders of an even higher court ruled.

"Are you going to write back?" asked Ralph.

"Already have", said Felix, pointing in the direction of the post office.

With this news in hand, Ralph hurried back to his drugstore to deliver what he expected would be the day's broadside. Instead he found Esther home from the college, fuming with a lead story of her own, coincidentally also involving letters.

"Do you know what State Departments of Corrections have up their sleeves now?" she asked.

Ralph of course had no idea, but glanced at his own sleeves as if the answer might be found there.

"If this becomes policy, a further step in the dehumanization of the prison experience: Loved ones will no longer be able to send hand-written letters", said Esther in the middle of what had been a soliloquy during her drive home.

"Whose loved ones?" asked a bewildered Ralph.

"Anybody's and also anybody's anybody. As I understand it, even a small child won't be able to send a birthday card. Except for attorneys' communications, nothing personal will any longer reach prisoners by regular mail."

Esther had long been a critic of the unnecessarily brutal conditions of prison life, affecting the mental health of inmates and their long-range chances of assuming anything like a normal life if and when they were released. Departments of Corrections didn't correct much of anything in that sense of the word and usually made things worse. An example was this news, drawn to her attention by a colleague in the sociology department, namely, that prison systems all over the country might be prohibiting handwritten letters from family and friends and allowing only Internet messages.

As Esther saw it, in the outside world, with so many people these days communicating this way regardless, the proposed change might seem trivial, but prison policy makers ought to have known that an inmate's world was a surreal alternative world, not the real one. Time and again, the entire criminal justice system failed to take this into account when considering matters great and small, from the length of prison sentences to the significance of a handwritten personal letter in the hands of a relationship-starved convict.

"That someone so much as bothered . . . to stick a stamp on an envelope", said Esther.

Ralph poured them each a cup of tea. "Would you like to have a little brandy in that?" Ralph poured some into his cup.

Esther declined. "So Grandma can't write. She can't look for that special stamp that might brighten the day for her grandson. Instead she must find someone in the family with a computer—she herself doesn't know how to use one—who can convert her message to a digital, heartwarming form. And as is so often the case, the Departments of Corrections pass this off as of great benefit all around when in fact it saves them the trouble of dealing with regular mail. Piffle, I say!" She paused to sip her tea. "Grandma becomes another victim of punishment. As if for the inmate whose bipolarity might have gotten him there in the first place, incarceration, regimentation, social deprivation, and overcrowding weren't enough reason to feel depressed."

Ralph had long ago learned there was little use in suggesting Esther calm down in the course of what he regarded as one of her teakettle moments. She had to be allowed to blow off steam and gradually settle down. Any intervention on his part would have the effect of turning up the flame again.

Given his contradictory combination of pragmatism and nostalgism, Ralph could see both sides of it: The practicality of prison email and the tenderness of Grandma with her commemorative stamps, especially old ones in an antique desk drawer saved for special occasions and now requiring a strip of five where one would have been sufficient postage back in the days of Smith Brothers cough drops in their original white box. Of course he didn't need an advanced degree in psychology to follow his wife's reasoning, though in this instance, with its dependence on symbolism, nuance, and aesthetics, she seemed more beholden to her days as an English major. She herself would have said it had mostly to do with Jung, not poetry per se.

Esther seemed to sense his ambivalence. "Would you rather get a real birthday card in the mail from your sister or one of those e-cards? What means more, an emailed letter from a friend or an old-fashioned letter?"

"I see where you're headed with this."

"And you're on the outside."

At last Esther fell silent, examining the bottom of her cup in the manner of a reader of tea leaves. Ralph changing the subject seemed not to be changing the subject at all. They both had letters in mind.

"Penelope has answered Felix' letter", he said.

"I'm not at all surprised", said Esther, still peering into her cup. "There was something about this that seemed not ready to end."

"She told him about her father at Shade Creek."

This did surprise Esther, or perhaps more accurately, it set her to speculating about Penelope. "She's made of some pretty exceptional stuff, I'd say. Still, she seems to have fallen under the Felix spell."

"Who hasn't?" said Ralph. "If the man had sold lightning rods door to door around here, they'd still be buying them even if every house in Clay County had burned to the ground by this time. She also told him her father was under a court order forbidding contact with her."

"It's in my notes. It's about all he wanted to talk about", said Esther. "Will Felix write her back?"

"In the mail, fresh from under his magnifying glass."

"Well, as I was saying, there's nothing quite the same as a personal letter. Would you mind warming the kettle?"

For Esther there was also something that might have been called the Ralph spell. She set down her teacup and gazed at him with eyes that might have been those of forty years ago, looking at the young pharmacy student sitting across from her in a student union. She didn't need brandy; she only needed Ralph.

Next morning, while rummaging through a crate of old nostrums pulled from under a shelf, Ralph lost track of the CLOSED sign on his drugstore door, where it remained till well past ten, when a customer looking for Alka-Seltzer and mouthwash tapped on its glass and peered in under his hand.

"I wish they still made Bromo-Seltzer", said Ralph. "That always did the trick."

The hangover victim, younger by far and with his ears ringing, had no idea what Ralph was talking about. Guiding him out, Ralph noticed a lime green Volkswagen Beetle parked in front of Ed's with what appeared to be a statue on its dash.

22

Climate Change

In fairness to Fred, proprietor of Ed's, life around Clay Corners did not come up with much to feed his natural curiosity. When it did come up with something, he had stockpiled so much curiosity he could hardly contain himself. Felix sitting over in his tavern café having coffee with a woman of striking red hair had taken over both his thought processes and motor skills. He forgot about the rubbish he should have put out in the alley for this week's pickup, and he had broken a beer glass while rinsing it.

Hair of Charlotte Hall's color was unforgettable, as was Penelope's. So Fred couldn't put down to coincidence that he had seen that same red hair over at Ralph's recently. He even looked out to see if by chance that 1960 white Desoto had rolled back into town. Adding to the mystery in some ways was its replacement in the form of a lime green VW. He decided that the woman must be the girl's mother. This much was easy, but what did Felix have in common with them both? Who had been the driver of the Desoto racing out of town at the end of a meeting at Ralph's, where normally no one ever met? Then there had been the CLOSED sign on the front door, which somehow had not been meant for them. The mystery of it all compounded itself as he glanced Felix' way, where the red-haired woman appeared to be crying and was daubing her eyes with a tissue.

Fred saw only one available conclusion: Felix, ever amazing and unpredictable Felix, younger than his many years, had a secret life. The red-haired woman was his lover. The red-haired girl was his daughter, named for an earlier daughter of the same name. The man driving the Desoto was a jealous husband who had discovered the truth at last. What any of this had to do with the ghost of Grandpa Albert brought Fred to the limits of his analytical powers.

This had been Charlotte's second journey to Shade Creek in three weeks. The first had come routinely at the end of the school year and before her assignment as a camp counselor. Then came the report of her brother's beating by another inmate. This news hadn't been a complete surprise. It had happened once before, during his first year as a prisoner. Many a night ever since Charlotte had lain awake worrying about it happening again.

When a message arrived in a sealed envelope handed her by Pine Shadows staff, she almost knew what it would say before reading it. During previous visits Warren had intimated fear for his personal safety, for he found himself caught up in prison gang rivalries on the one hand and difficulties with guards during episodes of mental illness overwhelming his medications. Sometimes his medications themselves seemed to trigger confrontations. (Esther could have told her how typical this was for the most seriously mentally ill inmates, whose erratic behavior was likely to be misunderstood and misinterpreted by other inmates and prison guards alike.)

A year ago, he had been placed in solitary confinement with visiting privileges suspended for behavior he couldn't remember. He ran afoul of the gangs for much the same behavior. The lives of prison guards weren't easy, and little about the situation encouraged them to distinguish between the involuntary and the belligerent, the catatonic and the defiant. Prison gangs didn't recruit psychologists to help them interpret violations of a pecking order. It was easy enough for outwardly normal people to run afoul and amuck in a prison world accurately described as another planet.

Prisons had their own weather and a magnetic polarity rendering useless the ordinary compass and weather vanes of the sort Warren once built. Nothing there made any sense. Life had to be learned all over again, actually two lives. Prison authorities had one set of rules, with its rewards and penalties, prison inmates another. The former had been developed by bureaucrats and pragmatists, the latter by sociopaths, psychopaths, and petty megalomaniacs. Throw into this mix chronic rage and resentment, cynicism and despair, and isolation from loved ones in a loveless world devoid of healing properties. Someone with Warren's problems and artistic sensitivities was almost certain to find himself crosswise, so much so that Shade Creek was his third state prison assignment. If he could survive four more years, with parole it might be his last.

Charlotte found her brother bruised and battered but resting and seemingly out of danger in the prison infirmary. X-rays and scans were being sent somewhere for further analysis. While navigating Shade Creek visitor's security procedures on her way, she had overheard a screener mention the name Felix to another standing by: *He had run into Felix yesterday.* The world no longer contained many Felixes. The much smaller world of nearby Clay Corners could have had few if any.

Charlotte had been plodding her usual way along a dreary, familiar path with its waymarks of inspection and regulation posted on walls and in handouts: LEAVE JACKETS, SWEATERS, HANDBAGS, AND CELL PHONES IN LOCKERS PROVIDED; FORM-FITTING, REVEALING CLOTHING NOT PERMITTED; NO FOOD AND DRINK ALLOWED; ALL PACKETS AND PACKAGES SUBJECT TO FURTHER INSPECTION; CONTRABAND WILL BE CON-FISCATED AND MAY RESULT IN DENIAL OF VISITATION PRIVILEGES; GREETINGS LIMITED TO A BRIEF KISS ON CHEEK OR A HUG; VIOLATORS SUBJECT TO PROSECU-TION; and so on.

Necessary as all this might have been from the penitentiary's point of view, nothing could have been devised to make a visitor feel more unwelcome and more like running away and forgetting the whole thing. After eleven years Charlotte had every warning memorized. She seemed to be passing by Stations of the Cross on the way to the Good Thief's crucifixion.

It had all become a blur because it could only be traversed as a blur. If you thought about it, you would never get through it, and the person you came to see would never see you, so it was all the more surprising—or perhaps unsurprising for anyone believing in miracles—to hear by chance the name Felix, which was like a match struck in darkness. Charlotte lit up. Had she seen this coming and rehearsed for it, nothing would have happened. In a world where silence and com-plicity got you through to the other side, she would never have dared speak up. Prison staff were as serious as mortuary technicians. Since they worked in a world where friendly sorts were the most likely to be up to something, you only answered their questions and skipped the usual pleasantries.

Therefore no one was more amazed than Charlotte when she blurted, "Not Felix from Clay Corners?"

Equally unlooked for was the result, for never in her many Shade Creek experiences had she been met with a smile from anyone, let alone a snippet of conversation passing for normal. The Felix spell had struck.

"You know Felix?"

"He's a friend of the family", said Charlotte, not quite lying, with her feet remaining firmly planted in a world of the unrehearsed, otherwise impossible to say, and miraculous.

"And a friend of just about everyone working here", said the screener, smiling again.

She glanced at Charlotte's ID.

"Bell Harbor? I didn't know he delivered mail way up there. The guy sure gets around."

A screener listening from the other side of a metal detector smiled. As if smiles and good thoughts added extra carbon dioxide to the world, a slight warming had taken place in the Shade Creek climate. Charlotte passed through security with less fuss than she had ever experienced.

Reflecting on all this after the two-hour visit with her brother, she decided to stay overnight in the area. Penelope's pen pal appeared to have been enshrined like a smiling Buddha in the heart of the dark mystery called Shade Creek.

In Clay Corners the next morning, she hadn't needed to make more than one inquiry about the whereabouts of Felix before being directed to Ed's. Felix turned out to be such a willing listener that he was well on his way to nodding through her whole story by the time Fred broke the beer glass. Each succeeding chapter made him more determined to help any way he could.

Suddenly godlike, Felix nevertheless was not immune to the absence of purpose and the growing sense of helplessness old age imparts. A man who had always wanted to do, he chafed even more than most under the burden of unable to do. Add to that a bred-in habit of gallantry—courtesy of his Uncle Milton—in a life affording few opportunities beyond an occasional chance to hold a door for a woman perhaps half his age, and Felix at times could feel sidelined and useless.

Penelope's aunt had brought him a chance to get back in the game. Here was a woman in tears needing help, and helping her was something he could do, not only for her but also for Penelope. In fact, while Charlotte struggled to ask of him something relatively easy to accomplish, he was already mulling a project much more ambitious. "Warren is really a good man", Felix had heard her say three times, two more than needed for him to believe it. "Penelope is an amazing young lady", he had no need to hear even once. "Perhaps if people working at the prison knew you were somehow concerned about Warren . . ."

"He's *family*. He is for a fact", said Felix, picking up on that part of Charlotte's story and warming to the idea. "Tell your brother he will be hearing from me."

Charlotte drove out of Clay Corners on the highway passing Shade Creek without a clear sense of what Felix had in mind. She did not have to wait very long to find out. By the time she arrived at the city limits of Bell Harbor, he had already asked a prison custodian, once a dairy farmer on his mail route, to get him a Shade Creek visitor's application form. He had run into the man at the post office while mailing a further letter to Penelope.

"You know somebody out there?"

"Name of Warren Hall", said Felix. "I'm a family friend. Just learned he was there."

It all made some sense, not a lot of sense, but enough sense, especially coming from a man known to be as good as his word.

Anybody who has ever worked for an institution learns—sometimes the hard way—that custodians will spread the word more quickly than anyone. Never tell a custodian something you do not want to go around from door to door pushed at the end of floor polisher or broom. If you want word to get out, a custodian will beat newsletters, bulletin boards, and the Internet any day. Felix hadn't the benefit of that experience, but he had instinct and good luck in abundance to make up for it.

23

Slender Threads

The trip home from Pine Shadows summer camp and eight o'clock Sunday Mass the next morning resembled a two-act play of the sort where the actors are also its audience. Everyone seemed to be acting and simultaneously observing performances of the other actors. There were no ovations at the end, no curtain calls, and no encores.

Except for its first moment, when Marvin struggled to say, "Gentlemen, start your engines!", the Pine Shadows trip was silent pantomime with background music. Delivered as a half-hearted aside, his was perhaps the worst performance of the next thirty-six hours. Bravado so feigned in a man craving sincerity and most of the time achieving it could only sound pathetic. When he realized how pathetic, he turned on the radio of his 1955 Chevy Bel Air. Nothing else was heard before they arrived in the pole barn turnaround, where June opened her door on the right, Penelope in the backseat opened hers on the left, and Osgood barked. Osgood's was by far the best performance.

Sunday Mass followed intermission and featured actors as yet unseen. Whether by chance or after reflection upon circumstance, Father Ulrich's homily explored the mysterious workings of grace in people's lives that lead to Divine Providence being interpreted as accident or coincidence. Removing his glasses and gazing out over the assembly as he concluded, he said in a voice assuming Shakespearean proportions, "Sooner or later, we all have to recognize that God is smarter than we are."

Meanwhile he pretended June, Marvin, and Penelope were not sitting directly in front of him a few feet away. Both June and Marvin shifted in their seats as if on cue, leaving Penelope between them with more room than she usually had. This being a choir Sunday, Mr. Stiller did not so much dust the choir as wax and polish it. Having never been within twenty miles of Pine Shadows the past two weeks, he seemed to have picked up tuning fork vibrations from Sister Serena sitting nearby. The latter, at the end of Mass, turned Penelope's way and smiled before hurrying through the church side entrance as if Felix' spider had just been spotted in a web over the convent door. In the vestibule Father Ulrich found himself engaged in deep and animated conversation with a group of Bell Harbor summer tourists, beginning as the Listers approached and ending soon after.

The play continued through a further pantomime on the way home, where Osgood barked as usual when they arrived in the turnaround. All this concluded with key members of the cast falling asleep: Father Ulrich on a sofa in the rectory, happy for once *not* to have a Sunday dinner invitation; Penelope while lying across her bed writing in her journal; Marvin after reading the funny papers; and Osgood on his accustomed carpet remnant under a pole barn workbench.

Later, Marvin joined Penelope in the pole barn, where she found two letters from Felix waiting in the Frazer's glove box. Only Sister Serena and June had stayed awake the whole time. June immersed herself among Osgoode insurance affairs, in whose fine print distraction was to be found. Sister Serena, with the other St. John Vianney Sisters, walked downhill to an outcropping offering a view of the lake far below and a procession of migrating birds high above following its curving shoreline.

"One came on the heels of the other", said Marvin, an observation applying equally to Felix' letters and to migrating shorebirds at that very moment in the gun-sight gaze of Sister Serena. Marvin's nap with a newspaper over his face had left him still bouncing between relief that he had been home before June in time to retrieve Felix' letters and worry about the outcome had he not been. His thoughts might have been taken as a theater critic's review of the performance just concluded, with some ruminations on psychodrama. Everything seemed to be hanging by ever more slender threads.

"I guess Felix doesn't know about our little secret", he said sheepishly, there being more than one secret—a multitude, in fact—with none of them seeming *little*, and Felix not knowing the half of them. "Otherwise he would have waited to write till camp was over."

In light of his Pine Shadows experience a Sunday ago, Marvin had been especially troubled by the tangle of secrecy he had succeeded in weaving around himself, or someone had succeeded in weaving around him. Either way he was left feeling helpless. No matter how he looked at it, his circumstances were becoming too complicated for a man who appreciated simplicity as much as he did and liked a life with the smooth, unbroken lines of his favorite cars. If Aunt Charlotte could pop up out of nowhere, any one of Marvin's detested secrets might do the same like prairie dogs in a desert colony. In any instant up ahead June might learn about Felix' many letters, or the trip to Clay Corners, or his mistaken drive past Shade Creek.

He would rather have driven the Frazer over a North Shore cliff than have her find the letters inside the glove box, not because he didn't value the Frazer, or because he was afraid of exposure, or even because he hadn't much time for secrecy—all in fact the case—but for the sake of their happy home life and June, who had said hardly a word to Penelope on the drive home from camp or in the day and a half since. Aunt Charlotte had been one surprise too many and seemed to have induced a catatonic state.

June was one of those people who did not get over things with time but seemed to have them weigh ever more heavily, the way a loaded backpack might after being carried a long distance. The circles in which she became trapped became downward spirals to a point becoming pointless. As it had been with Warren when at first she could stand by him, and then later when she attempted to put behind her forever the part of her life he had occupied, so with every passing day she said less about Charlotte at Pine Shadows, and the less she said, the more it weighed upon her.

Penelope glanced up from the second of Felix' letters and wondered if she should share its news with Marvin. She was sitting in the Frazer's front passenger seat. He was three cars away at his workbench reading a car magazine.

With the Frazer's glove box open, just beyond her knees lay the stack of Felix' other letters, the card from Sister Hilaria, and the little biography of St. John Vianney, left behind when she meant to take it to camp with her. She now understood why Felix needed to be a secret from the start, but there was no reason for Sister Hilaria to be a secret. Once a whirlpool started in that direction, things of all sorts were sucked in. Clay Corners was too close to Shade Creek for her mother to know about Felix. This was Marvin's bad luck when he was trying to be helpful, but in ways it was also *good luck*: Her father somehow seemed more real, and now Aunt Charlotte had met Felix.

If the outdoor Mass had come and gone without Marvin and her mother finding out about Aunt Charlotte, she would never have told them. There wouldn't have been any point in it. Keeping it to herself didn't exactly make it a secret when it was just something she didn't bring up. Maybe Charlotte's going to Clay Corners was another such thing. There was no reason to add to the bundle of things poor Marvin had to conceal from her mother. She shut the glove box and threaded her way through the rows of cars back to the workbench.

Looking up from his magazine, as if reading her mind and shaming her without intending to, he told her he had known about Charlotte all along.

"I'm sure you would have told me first chance," he said, "but it was right there tacked to a tree, not ten feet from your mom, under my nose and plain as day. I hardly slept a wink all week."

This struck her as a further instance of mind reading. For the sake of Marvin's sleep, Charlotte and Felix' meeting this past weekend would remain unrevealed.

There wasn't much to say about it anyway, because Felix had been vague, mentioning it but offering few details beyond that Charlotte seemed surprised he already knew about her brother in Shade Creek. He didn't say if he told her how he knew it. He didn't say what brought Charlotte to the vicinity or why she had stopped in Clay Corners to meet him. His letter had a sort of breathlessness about it, and strangest of all, as if this explained everything he hadn't bothered to explain, he made an odd request: He wanted Penelope to write a letter in which she provided a lot of details about herself.

One would think he was doing research for a book called *The Life and Times of Penelope Lister.* Up to this point he had seemed uninterested in that, the game of correspondence tennis still being of the sort with Felix serving and mostly about *his* life and times. He had made his childhood so interesting that hers seemed too dull to bring up. She couldn't match riding copilot alongside Uncle Milton or the spider or putting a copper coin on the railroad track to see what happened to it when a train came by. When it came to herself, what was there to write him about?

"What did Felix have to say?" Just as Marvin asked, June called to him from the pole barn turnaround.

His question would go unanswered the rest of the day and into the next week. Penelope was happy to leave it so. June's voice awakened Osgood from a Sunday afternoon nap with his front paws over his head as if he had tired of the complexity besetting Marvin and Penelope. He looked up at her, cocked his head, and then bounded after Marvin just as the latter started a lawnmower.

Alone in the pole barn, Penelope began an inspection of its many shelves, running the length of its sides and filled with car parts; cans; bottles; tubes of every description; and taciturn, nondescript cardboard boxes revealing nothing about their contents beyond an unreadable Marvin scribble. She concentrated on these, searching for Sister Hilaria's box, with "Penelope" written on one side and "geography" on the other, last seen on one end of the workbench when she left for summer camp. Marvin had mowed half of their very large lawn before she had looked over, under, behind, and even inside boxes with nothing written on them. What might have been her father's weather vane was nowhere to be found.

Prolonged futile searching for something—as Esther Corrigan might point out in one of those basic classes she loved to teach now and then—can lead to actual chemical changes in the brain. These in turn can trigger episodes of anxiety, uncertainty, ennui, and loss of confidence. Penelope felt herself in the grip of all four. All of a sudden she was tired of everything, even writing Felix, who now seemed to have given her a homework assignment. What was she supposed to do: Find an even bigger spider or make Osgood into something rivaling Uncle Milton's Russian wolfhound? Could flying a kite with Sister Hilaria ever beat flying upside down in a biplane? Her collection of Lake Superior agates might be worth mentioning.

She left the pole barn by a seldom-used backdoor leading to a path in the woods behind their house. At the end of the path, where it bent to the left, she hesitated before plunging ahead to where her father's welding mask suddenly met her gaze from its tree-crotch perch beyond the rusty bed springs. She had to be in a mood to do this, to stand there with what could almost pass for her father himself looking at her. The tree trunk supporting his mask might have been his body, with his feet hidden in the flotsam and jetsam of a sunken Great Lakes freighter. The V-shaped tree branches could be his arms stretched high to greet her. The sun's reflection on the mask's dark lens could seem to be his eyes casting fiery glances. Only now and then could she bear it. Only now and then could she be brave enough or uncertain enough to be in need of the strange reassurance this concocted image could give her. She stepped forward, climbing a mound of discarded car parts, old batteries, and tires to the lower edge of the bed springs leaning against the tree. In brute defiance of what proximity usually achieves, the closer she got, the more intense the image of her father became, the more it seemed that he was actually standing there in his own discarded past at Star Island, with his eyes flaming through the welding mask.

Then came an event unforeseen and coincidental, of the sort Father Ulrich might have had in mind in this morning's homily. She stumbled and fell to her knees with one arm up to her elbow in a matted pile of last year's pine needles and leaves. While brushing herself off, she caught a glint of bright metal from deep within the hole her arm had made. After some digging around there, she pulled up a corroded aluminum box about six inches by twelve, opening on one side by a hinged lid. Within was something like a candy box with tiny compartments in two layers, each one filled not with a chocolate but with a bright, feathered object wound around with colored thread attached to a fishhook. A few were stained from rain and melting snow seeping in over the many years, but others were as perfect as the day her father added them to this collection of his fishing flies.

Having given up in frustration her search for one thing, she found by accident another. "God", as Father had said, "is smarter than we are."

24

Time Travel

The tendency of plans to stray off in a direction other than the one envisioned was far from limited to Pine Shadows summer camp. June should have known. She had also seen this aplenty while processing insurance claims: The cautious driver rear-ended while driving ten miles an hour below the speed limit; the owner of a new four-wheel-drive vehicle spinning into a ditch; and just over a year ago, the hand-gun purchased for family protection killing the child who mistook it for a toy. She had filing cabinets and a computer hard drive filled with such stories, most of them less tragic than the last of these, but still examples worthy of a Father Ulrich homily. Church doors are not the only ones behind which lessons are routinely left.

Those trained as Esther Corrigan would explain much of the world's apparent disregard for anticipated outcomes to absent realism at the planning stage. Human nature and chaos theory had been left out of the equation. Ralph as usual arrived at the heart of the matter without the aid of psychology texts. "First, find out where people walk, then put the sidewalks in", he would sometimes observe, looking up from his newspaper or at the end of a story Esther brought home from the college. Many a street in an older city follows the path a cow first took one morning centuries ago to avoid a barking dog.

A cow had no role in the location of the road between Star Island and Bell Harbor, but a portion had once been an old game trail used by animals descending from the forest heights to drink from the lake. Later it had been used by Indians hunting these animals and still later by Voyageurs trading with the Indians. Still later came loggers and prospectors. In the present day, absent these previous travelers with their various aims and ambitions, the twists and turns of the road as it approached Bell Harbor from the north made little apparent sense beyond the obvious placement of a pine-covered outcropping more easily gone around than climbed over.

Pursuing her own aims and ambitions, June, with Penelope alongside, drove the winding road to Bell Harbor on Monday morning. Few unrehearsed words passed between them along the way. Most of these concerned June's needlessly repeated instructions about how the day was supposed to go: In summary, the library reading program until twelve thirty; then simply the library, where surely Penelope could find plenty to interest her; and then the summer school activity bus stopping in front of the library at two thirty for her trip home. Her micromanaging did not seem excessive in light of Penelope's recent tendency to run off without explanation.

This much having been gone through within a mile beyond the wooden bridge, silence had taken over. Both sides sensed, however, something building slowly between them, like the fine on an overdue library book one had checked out and not found the time to read. The critical moment was reached coincidentally in front of the library's drive-by book return when Penelope opened the door to get out without her habitual goodbye kiss on Mom's expectant cheek.

"I just want you to know I don't believe a word of it!" said June through her teeth, looking straight ahead with both hands on the wheel as if she were still in heavy traffic.

Penelope did not have to ask what this referred to. Of course it was Aunt Charlotte and her dad: *Not Marvin*, but the one she was supposed to forget. Of course it was Pine Shadows despite what she, Sister Serena, Father Ulrich, and probably Marvin had said about it over and over to reassure her. Wheeling away, she ran to the library steps, with the car door slammed behind her saying all that she could think of to say.

Inside at this early hour was welcoming silence. Something like the safety and security of a church drew her in and wrapped itself around her. Penelope did not look back to see her mother, still at the book return, slumped over her steering wheel until a car behind her honked, and she drove away to the insurance agency.

The Bell Harbor Public Library was one of hundreds across the world built with funds provided by philanthropist Andrew Carnegie. Like many of its Midwestern counterparts, it could be counted among Bell Harbor's most architecturally interesting buildings. It was in fact the city's only building with a dome, albeit an unobtrusive one most

likely to be noticed from inside. Four wings composed its reference
and periodicals areas, its children's library, a reading room reduced in
size to make way for computers and microfiche readers, and the library's
main book collection. To approach all this from a broad granite stairway leading up from its main entrance could be as transcendent as
entering a small cathedral or county courthouse designed to symbol-
ize and to proclaim its importance and special purpose. Church buildings were designed to proclaim faith and worship, and courthouses
justice and the rule of law. Libraries such as Bell Harbor's proclaimed
civilized learning. Its was a gentle, undemanding creed.

The summer school reading program had been funded by a grant
from an iron ore mining foundation aiming to encourage children in
reading the classics, while acquainting them with the library's many
resources. Participants were to be involved in discussion groups, dra-
matizations, and various contests focusing on selected scenes from some
of the world's notable works of fiction, biography, and history. Like so
many projects of idealistic intent, this proved to be more ambitious
than could be accomplished in ten mornings in two weeks. Even par-
tially carried out, though, its value was indisputable.

Given the misfortunes of June so far in executing her summer plans
for Penelope, one would have expected to find on the program's summer reading list selections from *Great Expectations* and *The Count of
Monte Cristo*, along with other novels and histories featuring the lives
of prisoners and their ultimate redemption. This turned out not to be
the case. The nearest thing to a prisoner appeared in a biography of
Harry Houdini, who imprisoned himself for the sheer challenge of
escaping. June could have reviewed the program's entire reading list
without the fear or regret Pine Shadows had brought her way. Like
Houdini, after mischances and unintended blunders, she appeared to
have at last escaped.

June had even engaged in reconnaissance, phoning the library to
ask for Charlotte Hall just in case among her many part-time jobs she
might be working there. Small town connections and interconnec-
tions tied Bell Harbor in knots everywhere. Everyone seemed to know
everyone. Half the town was cousins with the other half. Inbreeding
was a local joke, with no one quite sure how funny it was. It was
impossible to step on only one set of toes. Pine Shadows and Warren's
resurrected weather vane had made the case for caution.

"No one on our staff by that name", she was told after a nerve-racking pause. "Have you tried the church?"

The receptionist on the other end turned out to be Mr. Stiller's wife. Of course June wondered if Emily Stiller had recognized her voice. June's through her teeth was as distinctive as Emily's through her nose.

June would have felt equally at ease with the reading program's aim to highlight library services. Like everything else, these sessions involved activities designed to establish lifelong connections with the everyday lives of participants. On Thursday, participants were asked to search Bell Harbor *Daily Sentinel* microfiche to find out what else happened the day they were born. Since there were but three microfiche readers and twelve participants, Penelope and two others had to wait until Friday for their turn. Penelope used the rest of Thursday afternoon to write to Felix. Meanwhile at Clay Corners, Felix had begun making two daily trips to the post office, where he would peer through a tiny window in his box at the end of the day when normally nothing would be there regardless. On one such afternoon the village post-master, noting Felix' impatience, confronted him.

"It's always all out by ten o'clock, Felix", he said. "*You of all people* ought to know that."

"But sometimes things get into the wrong box and show up later."

"Not very often since you retired", said the postmaster. The letter Felix was looking for was on its way, sent from a mailbox near the library on Thursday as Penelope waited for the summer activity bus.

The next afternoon, the fated day, the very last of the public library reading program, she settled finally into her seat in front of a micro-fiche reader. Its large gray-green screen and controls for shrinking, enlarging, focusing, and moving forward and back through days, weeks, and years imparted the imagined sense of being in a spaceship engaged in interstellar time travel. She began to wish she had delayed writing to Felix until she could include this adventure. While not on a par with many of his, it at least had in its favor an invention that did not exist in his boyhood years, possibly involving a device he had never used.

She had installed in her reader a spool containing *Daily Sentinel* issues spanning three years, the first of these being the year of her birth. The forward and reverse control, a tiny lever permitting time travel, had slow and high speed settings at its extreme left and right ends. Penelope chose the high speed setting at first and flew into a world where she had her first teeth, made her first steps, and was photographed in her baby crib with her father's hand resting on its railing. She moved the lever the other way, held it for a few seconds, and found herself in a world before she existed among newspaper ads with models whose hairstyles and clothing seemed interplanetary if not intergalactic. Racing in the other direction, she once again over-shot the mark and landed her time machine on a *Sentinel* front page devoted entirely to the St. John Vianney Church fire, with a banner headline proclaiming its destruction. Below to the right was a picture of its roof with flames shooting through into a dark sky; to the left a secondary headline: "Church Custodian Dies in Roof Collapse"; below that: "Arson Suspected, Investigation Underway"; to the lower left of that another picture showing the old church by sunrise as a smolder-ing, burned-out shell.

She switched to the slow speed setting. Her time machine inched forward to another front page bearing the headline "Star Island Res-ident Arrested", its lead story with her father's picture wrapped within a paragraph beginning: "A local welder and artisan has been arrested on suspicion of setting fire to St. John Vianney Church." She closed her eyes, opened them, closed them again, and then opened them. Between times nothing had changed. Nothing now would ever change. Only in a world of time travel could innocence be lost so quickly, framed within blinks of an eye.

What she had never known she now knew, and there was no going back to when she had not known it, even though this was only seconds behind her. It was all like what Felix had once said about the giant spider hanging in the barn doorway: So frightening you froze right in your tracks looking at it, and when it finally let go of you, you could not keep from coming back to it. Day by day she moved forward and sometimes back for a second look, caught between belief and disbelief, transfixed to the very end, and unable to pull away till well after the activity bus had departed from its library stop.

Daily Sentinel accounts of the fire and the processes it set in motion, while not exactly biased, had taken advantage of an occasion to sell more than its usual number of newspapers. Stories reflected the mood of an outraged Catholic community and dwelled so heavily on the history and beauty of the old church that Bell Harbor seemed to have lost both its cathedral and its "little chapel in the moonlight". Not only had a cherished building gone up in flames, but also generations of memories—its baptisms, weddings, and eulogies of loved ones—as if memories themselves had suddenly become flammable. Local Catholics stepped forward to share their heartfelt sentiments with a reporter. No tangible value could be attached to such a loss. Even Bell Harbor Protestants were reported to be dismayed.

The old custodian might have been St. John Vianney himself, so great were his songs of praise in the aftermath. He had rushed inside to rescue a few of the church's many treasures and never come out. He had worked at the church long past his retirement age, not because he needed the money, but for reasons of dedication and attachment, so said the newspaper, and who could doubt it? A martyr for sure, the custodian was at the same time not just any martyr, but one who left behind hordes of friends and now could not be buried from the church he had so long served. Thus had the newspaper pandered to its readers' thirst for sentiment and sensation and fanned the flames of another sort of fire, while—as they say in the journalistic trade—"getting the story out". Retribution was in the air.

Bell Harbor was a dull place most of the time in an era when ore boats seldom sank during ferocious storms, and when they did sink were usually out of sight somewhere. The week's most noteworthy local items might be speculation about the impact of gasoline prices on the local tourist trade and meeting minutes of a school board deliberating over the purchase of a snow blower and an elementary school teacher's request for maternity leave.

The allure of a really good local crime story well beyond the occasional burglary or abandoned car on Front Street was irresistible. Local police, having grown fat while standing around "keeping an eye on things", had something to investigate for a change. The police chief, the county sheriff—involved since Star Island was county real estate—and the *Sentinel's* editor-in chief all left their desks to take turns in the public eye. The ubiquitous source wishing to remain anonymous suggested the FBI had taken an interest in the case. Insurance investigators were on the scene and had asked for cooperation from the public. Everyone was cooperating with everyone. It became a feast of community cooperation, there being nothing quite like violence to bring out the best in local citizenry.

Twenty parish stalwarts stepped forward to offer their service as the old custodian's pallbearers. His funeral Mass took place before an overflow crowd in the community auditorium. Father Lyle officiated, assisted by Father Spence. Bell Harbor's mayor, not himself a Catholic, spoke of a community pulling together in the face of tragedy, as he put it, "irrespective of creed and race". No matter that those in attendance who weren't Catholic were at least Protestant, with nary a Jew or a heathen in the picture and the only nonwhite a Fond-du-Lac Indian member of the mayor's human relations committee, in a *Sentinel* photograph looking as if he yearned for days prior to the white man's arrival.

News reports of local tragedies on this scale inevitably leave room for the human interest perspective. Not having exhausted that side of it in its thoughts about the custodian and lost memories, a subsequent issue of the newspaper turned to Father Lyle, with a picture of him surveying the ruins and an account of his long association with the parish.

"There was always something special about St. John Vianney", he was quoted as saying, his words containing the unintended suggestion that the parish had been simultaneously destroyed along with its church building. "It's a great privilege to be leading this parish for a second time", said Father Lyle. "I look forward to helping it rebuild."

Among his St. John Vianney congregation, Father Lyle had preached moderation, understanding, and forgiveness to people now attending Mass while seated on folding chairs in the school gymnasium. The destruction of the church and even the death of its genial custodian were somehow part of God's plan. In the course of time, he said, even things so senseless would make sense. Hardly any of his listeners seemed prepared to agree. None of them could have sensed the irony in Father Lyle's sentiment. Had it been otherwise, he might never have said it. A grim detail had been all but buried in the smoldering debris of the parish church, bulldozed over and smoothed out, with the new church built on top of it.

Then appeared the final newsworthy twist, not mentioned by this notably discreet priest but included in an article published the day of Warren Hall's first court appearance: The alleged arsonist's parents were highly respected St. John Vianney parishioners. This seemed to add to the horror.

All this had been duly reported by the vigilant *Sentinel* and was now read by Penelope before she could tear herself away. When she finally looked up, it was as if raising her head from a battlefield after the battle, eerily empty with a fog settling in, veiling its shattered landscape. The other reading program participants had left for the day. The program's director had resumed her regular duties at her work-station beneath the dome as if nothing had happened and all of it had been a dream. Penelope herself, returning to earth in her time machine, hardly knew where she was. She never had gotten back to the day she was born, and only at the end was she aware she had been crying. Her fingers in knots were wet with tears.

25

The Ones That Matter

Charlotte Hall lived the life of many musicians cobbling together a modest income. Her handful of part-time jobs included working as St. John Vianney Church organist and religious education teacher; as an occasional organist for funerals and weddings, both there and at other Bell Harbor churches; and as a teacher of studio lessons in piano and organ from her home.

The last of the week's students had just been picked up by a parent when her doorbell rang. She glanced around to see what her student might have left behind. With nothing in sight, she went to the door and discovered Penelope waiting on the other side, left behind at Pine Shadows three weeks ago. She had last seen her niece sleeping peacefully as she tiptoed out to greet Sister Serena, who had arrived at sunrise with a backpack and a butterfly net. The agitated, bedraggled creature in front of her might have just awakened from a nightmare.

Glancing both ways up and down the street as if admitting an escaped convict or a member of a banned organization, she let her niece in and quickly shut the door.

"Aunt Charlotte," Penelope said, "I will *not* not talk about my father!"

Penelope's anguished cry was somewhere between a demand and a plea, as well as between protest and capitulation. Within her a tide had been rising and moving against a river current as she had half run and half walked the three blocks from the library to Charlotte's house. The current was detached, dreamy, and inclined to meander while traversing a landscape of her lifetime, an innocent longing no more connected to anything than a cloud is attached to the earth over which its shadow passes or a river is attached to its riverbed. The tide now pushing against the current had gravity and hard fact on its side. What had happened really had happened: *Her father had burned down the old church.*

This fact thrust itself against everything she had ever imagined about him with the force of real events never revealed to her. The secrecy enveloping her father had left her free to think whatever she wanted about him. He seemed to be in prison not for committing a crime but so he would continue being a secret. She could daydream till he became a fairytale with a happy ending she had only to await. The tale now seemed to be over, but its ending was not happy. It seemed all the worse because she had been allowed to think whatever she wanted while going to school next door those six years and while on her knees in the new church Sunday after Sunday with everyone around her knowing the truth. They all knew and hadn't told her, even Sister Hilaria, even Marvin. The lifelong void had been filled and would never again be empty.

"Why didn't someone tell me?" She looked at Charlotte and stifled a sob.

"Perhaps because they love you, my dear, at least the ones who matter."

Charlotte need not be told what this was about. Her week with Penelope avoiding all talk about her father had yet managed to reveal how little her niece had been told. Before it was over she had even admitted not knowing her real middle name. Charlotte led her to the nearest chair in her living room, the one parents usually sat in if they wanted to wait through a lesson. Penelope fell into it with her arms extended upon its arms, her hands clenched into fists, her face red, and her eyes enflamed.

"I *will* talk about him!" she exclaimed.

"Of course you will", said Charlotte, without knowing why she said it, except she would have said anything to calm her. "What has happened?"

"I know what he did, and it's so terrible!"

June might have said *terrible* was the collapse of her efforts to protect her daughter for the past fourteen years. This was the moment she had wanted to avoid. The distraught girl in Charlotte's house proved how right she had been all along. Had she loved her daughter less, she might have felt vindicated, but she would have taken no pleasure in the scene unfolding before Charlotte.

With the full weight of her father's guilt upon Penelope, there was no going back to retrieve something like lost innocence. Having imagined so many things while free to imagine, she had now begun to discern the face of evil and a vicious smirk lurking behind her father's welding mask. Prior to this day, she had always felt the more she knew about him, the more she would understand. Somewhere in her incomplete picture of him could be found the possibility of redemption. This could no longer be found.

The more signs of disillusion Charlotte detected in her niece's rambling narrative of library time travel, the more compelled she felt to talk about her brother. Her view would not have sold so many newspapers and was one most Bell Harbor townspeople, in no mood for compassion, hadn't wanted to hear, but Warren's daughter needed to hear it. The time had come.

"Yes, we *will* talk about him", she said.

She slid a piano bench near Penelope's chair, held her hand, at times let go, and then held it again as she struggled with point of view and perspective in a wavering narrative she knew by heart but had seldom recited to anyone. From one sentence to another, the subject was Warren, my brother, his parents, your grandparents, or your dad. In isolation, with sometimes pauses between, this created the impression they were actually all different people. In a sense this was true, since one was the Star Island resident, subject of newspaper accounts; another a sibling Charlotte had known, loved all her life, and visited in prison the past fourteen years; others were parents whose lives had been destroyed defending him; still others were grandparents and a father Penelope could not remember.

Charlotte's story was infused with fond memories and affection; from Penelope's viewpoint all three versions were describing a stranger. The overall effect was that of a portrait painted by a modern artist with multiple perspectives creating a series of flickering gestalts. Penelope could hold onto one for barely a second before another snapped into view.

"*His* parents . . . *our* whole family had always been exceptionally close to St. John Vianney parish life. *My father* had served for many years as a church trustee. Your *grandma* was a fixture in the choir and at church social functions."

While days passed and Warren Hall sat in a jail cell awaiting arraignment, his parents were generally housebound, with an unusual number of cars filled with gawking passengers creeping by on their hitherto quiet residential street.

Though the police investigation reportedly focused on Warren's possible motive, why he had picked the church remained from beginning to end a mystery, helping to make the case he had simply been out of his mind. This both explained everything and explained nothing.

Perhaps it might have been instead the courthouse, the library where Penelope had just been, the school, any building he thought empty at that hour, and yet it didn't seem to be the random act the *Daily Sentinel* described. Coming from Star Island, he would have had to drive past all three on his way to the church.

Charlotte knew—though it had never come up anywhere—that Warren had had a tremendous confrontation with Father Lyle a few days after a copy of Penelope's baptismal certificate arrived in the parish office. Something had been ignited within him whose flames would spread to the church itself. Warren himself had only revealed this much later in one of their first prison visits. Apparently Father Lyle had been silent about it when police questioned him, looking for a motive that hardly seemed necessary given the confused, incoherent responses of the confessed arsonist. Charlotte paused at Penelope's side and looked up at her living room ceiling as if pleading for guidance from some higher power residing there.

"Had I known about it at the time of the investigation, and had anyone asked me, I'm not sure I would have told them", she said. "It might have helped people understand why my brother did it, but he would have been guilty regardless, and it even might have hurt his court case because a motive, any motive, would have made him appear more rational than he could possibly have been."

Warren's parents had spent their life savings defending him in court with a team of psychiatrists and a Duluth attorney brought in when the Bell Harbor one seemed unable or unwilling to proceed with an insanity defense. "It doesn't work these days", he told us. "The Duluth attorney agreed, but was willing to give it a try since there seemed to be no alternative."

"It went on and on, through changes of plea, a denied request for a change of venue, psychiatric testimony from both sides, and plea bargaining. It seemed as if it would never end, and when it finally

ended, your grandparents were broke, we were all brokenhearted, and
your dad went to prison maybe for a few years less than he might
have. What saved him from a longer sentence or maybe even a life
term was not his mental condition, which seemed to count for nothing, but the testimony of the Fire Department chief, who told of
warning the custodian not to go back into the church, it being too
dangerous even though most of the fire seemed to be on the other
end. This made Warren less to blame for his death."

She got up from the piano bench and crossed her living room to
a small corner table. She returned from there with a picture of her
father with his parents, the first she had ever seen of her grandparents and only the second of him, both within the past two hours.
Though he was still in high school at the time, as Charlotte explained,
he didn't look that much younger than the alleged arsonist on the
front page of the *Daily Sentinel*, yet old enough to be her father at
that point.

"He's not a bad man, Penelope. I visit him almost every month,
and despite what he's been through and is still going through every
day in that dreadful place, he stays the same gentle, loving man I knew
as a brother. I can't tell you what to think or to believe or who to
love, but there was more to this than what you read in the newspaper
today, much, much more."

She glanced at her watch. "We had best be on our way."

A half hour later the lime green Volkswagen pulled into the pole
barn turnaround. With no one else home yet, Osgood was its only
witness. Penelope leaned across to hug her aunt.

"I believe you, Aunt Charlotte", she said. "Thank you for everything you've said today. I'm okay. I'm *really* okay."

Charlotte was not so confident that she could drive straight home
without stopping at St. John Vianney. Father Ulrich was not in his
office, but she and Sister Serena sat for a time on a parish bench with
a view of the Great Lake.

In the meantime Marvin arrived home earlier than usual, having
driven past Charlotte heading the other way on the outskirts of Bell
Harbor. He made a phone call and then hurried into the pole barn.
An hour after that June arrived. Outside, behind the house feeding
her lopsided lop, Penelope heard her car door slam. A few seconds
later June came out the back door.

"How *did* you get home?" she demanded. "The bus driver called me when you didn't show up at the library. I drove over there, called your dad at the sawmill, and even called the police."

Penelope slowly raised the two rabbit ears, the one still an inch longer than the other. Still without answering she closed the lid of the rabbit cage, setting its latch ever so carefully, before looking straight at her mother.

"Aunt Charlotte gave me a ride home", she said.

"How dare she!"

"No, Mom, *I* will dare, and I will never, ever let you tell me I can't have her in my life!" She broke away, ran into the house, went to her room, and shut the door, leaving her mother standing outside staring at *the rabbit*.

Marvin in the kitchen, as Penelope flew past him, had made a point of being close enough to hear this. He seemed to have three options: Follow Penelope to try calming her, join June outside to try calming her, or ignore the whole thing. June, speaking to him through a screen door, decided this for him.

"After this behavior I am not going to take her to driver's training", said June. "I won't have it. She can wait till this fall sometime."

Marvin looked up from his chair at the kitchen table, attempted a smile, and then said something slightly un-Marvin-like. "Then I guess I will have to", he said.

"She's not going. I won't have it." June stepped into the kitchen.

"*I* will take her then."

"You can't. I won't have it. I'm her mother."

At this point, without attempting his usual smile, Marvin stood up and said something distinctly un-Marvin-like. "And if I'm not her father, why do you insist that she calls me Dad?"

Part Four

The Black Bus and the Roman Collar

I will lead the blind by ways they have not known,
along unfamiliar paths I will guide them;
I will turn the darkness into light before them
and make the rough places smooth.
These are the things I will do; I will not forsake them.

—Isaiah 42:16

26

Dead Ends and Cul-de-sacs

Twelve times a day, seven days a week, a black bus with yellow lettering on its sides drove through Clay Corners and stopped in the parking lot of the Depot Café to drop off and pick up prison workers. Its yellow letters identified the bus as belonging to Shade Creek Penitentiary. Its passengers were Clay County residents living nearby, going on and coming off full- and part-time work shifts. Prison management preferred this as a way to reduce the number of cars in its employee parking lot, making security on that end easier.

Security was a god at Shade Creek, feared, worshipped all around, and enshrined in repetitive rituals more symbolic than necessary. No one had ever escaped Shade Creek. No one would ever escape: Prisoners were transferred to other facilities euphemistically described as correctional, were paroled after serving long terms, or died there. There was no other way out short of alien abduction or feats of bilocation. Nothing could be brought in, and nothing came out. Even the air in the prison workers' lungs seemed to linger behind as they boarded the black bus for Clay Corners.

A powerful, redundant symbol, the black prison bus nevertheless had its loyal following. Employees saved money on gas and saved time getting through the prison's security perimeter. While waiting for the bus or upon arriving home, some of them patronized the Depot Café, and a few even showed up at Ed's just across the road. The proprietors of both were therefore happy with the extra business this arrangement brought in and did not mind having so many cars parked nearby for hours at a time.

The prison bus, as it came to be called in the more than five years since it began its Clay Corners comings and goings, had changed the atmosphere of the village, especially along its Front Street. An orange school bus might have been uplifting, as it brought with it the promise of youth at school and a semblance of hope, even if the more barbaric among them shouted from its windows and threw pop cans in the same way as those riding in the back of Larry's Lighthouse Consolidated bus. At least it was a school bus.

The prison bus seemed to bring despair with it. Nobody shouted from its windows. It might have been loaded with mannequins on their way to a department store. It did not help that the law required it to be painted some color other than school bus orange and that instead of being blue or green or even peppermint striped, it wound up being black. And it did not help that when it backed up to get out of the Depot's parking lot, it emitted a series of beeps expressing what Esther Corrigan might have seen as a hypocritical regard for safety. It also didn't help that it shifted gears two or three times on its way out of town, leaving a blue gray trail of diesel exhaust.

Ralph had a theory about vehicles beeping when they backed up: For every life saved by that infernal sound, five people died of annoyance. The ones who were not run over were drunks or morons yakking on their cell phones. Those who died of annoyance were poets and thinkers. Even though Shade Creek brought income into Clay Corners, most of it strayed away to cash registers in the larger cities nearby, leaving the black bus as its most tangible reminder. Hardly a merchant on Front Street other than the tavern keeper could have told you when prison payday arrived. Old-timers thought the village worse off for having Shade Creek nearby. Nobody needed to be reminded how much better life used to be, but about the time they managed to forget, the black bus returned again to remind them.

No one disliked the prison bus more than Ralph Corrigan, who would swear at it under his breath and complain he could hardly look out his drugstore window without catching a mood-altering glimpse. A man of habitually buoyant personality, albeit on the curmudgeonly side, he always sank a bit beneath the waves at those moments. He would sooner have lived near an international airport and heard the sounds of wide-body jets taking off. At least the jets were going somewhere. The prison bus was all about dead ends and impossible cul-de-sacs. The village dogs, as much as they seemed to share his aversion, only made things worse. They had taken to barking at it, with one or another sometimes chasing after it as it rolled out of town. When they barked and howled at noon and 6 P.M. as a village siren wailed from its mount high up on the water tower, this was understandable since it probably hurt their ears. Their hatred of the prison bus expressed something primordial and instinctive.

Then there were the prison employees themselves filing on and off, stoop shouldered, overweight, and silent. Anyone witnessing this would never know Minnesota was not a state with capital punishment among its crime deterrence tools. They seemed to be heading for an execution or returning from one that had not gone well. Looking at them, Felix was sometimes reminded of his German prisoner-of-war camp experiences. As unpleasant as that memory was, it failed to compete with the loss of his Uncle Milton's farm, the other thing he thought of whenever he saw the prison bus. At least he had a present use for it, since with eyesight as bad as his, he could not drive any longer.

His Shade Creek visitor's application had been approved, signed by the granddaughter of an old friend who had died some years ago. She had written a greeting across one corner of the form letter he received. Did he remember she named her pet goat after him? Of course he remembered, it not being every day a man is so honored. Penelope's letter had also arrived, five pages of it with more information about herself than could be found in his other six letters combined. Enclosed was something he had not requested, making it all the more valuable: A recent school portrait of the sort classmates exchange. It was all settled, everything in place for his visit with Warren Hall. He would ride the noon prison bus to Shade Creek and, depending on how things went, ride the two or four o'clock bus back to Clay Corners. The prison bus was intended for prison employees only, but only the warden could open more Shade Creek doors than Felix, even a bus door. Besides, he knew the warden's secretary.

After a bright sunrise gave way to clouds followed by a featureless gray overcast, Clay Corners lay sodden beneath an all-day rain. Weather of this sort stirred restlessness in Ralph, who had shuffled away much of the morning in his drugstore store, working his way from back to front to back again, pausing at intervals to straighten shelves in no need of straightening and filled with things he would never sell. With equally nothing in mind, he peered out windows in the front and into cabinets in the rear, all the while barely listening to an antique radio he kept on a shelf high up over the wooden booth. The weather being such as to discourage all but the most desperate in search of remedies, he hadn't had a customer all morning and was on his way to a nap upstairs when the hated black hulk lumbered by without its usual village dog fanfare. Those ardent despisers had all taken shelter.

Being of the opinion that a CLOSED sign hanging askew in his door created a bad impression, Ralph had returned to the front door to straighten it in time to see Felix sitting by a window just behind the bus driver and already engaging him in conversation. This ought to have surprised him more than it did, but several times in the past two weeks he had spotted Felix in the Depot Café in the company of prison workers, most of them friends from his mail route days. He seemed to be making a special point of being with them instead of his usual village cronies. He also seemed to be avoiding Ralph, his almost daily trips into the drugstore having been dropped from his routine. The man was up to something, and whatever it was, he did not want Ralph asking about it.

He said as much to Esther when she arrived home.

"He visited Warren Hall today", she said, while hanging up her raincoat.

"How did you hear about that?"

"He's not the only one with connections out there."

Esther had a counseling intern working at Shade Creek of whom she had inquired about Warren Hall. Arriving back on campus today as Esther was leaving, the intern had brought several reports.

"Our Felix has made quite an impression by posing as a family friend of Warren's and now even visiting him. Warren could use a friend; he's not doing very well. Of course we're the only ones who know Felix is posing—at least I think he is—unless being his daughter's eighty-five-year-old pen pal makes his case."

Neither of the Corrigans knew about Charlotte's visit with Felix, so this left them with a few dots they could not yet connect. Fred of Ed's, who had seen Felix return from Shade Creek on the four o'clock bus, knew about Charlotte but had connected the wrong dots. Meanwhile Felix was sowing confusion without intending to and also reaping it.

"Anyway, my intern saw him today after Felix' visit. She was brought in to help get Warren back on the right side of prison life after a beating he took two or three weeks ago, something I am not sure I would even know how to do. He shouldn't be there."

"For God's sake, a beating?"

"Inmates as ill as he is at times get crosswise with everything and everybody. That's the long and short of it. It's a wonder he hasn't been killed by this time. They just keep moving him from one pen to another or one building to another. Shade Creek is his third prison at least. My intern was supposed to be helping him deal with the effects of his beating, but instead it was all about Felix' visit. Warren did not handle it very well. Not surprising. There's more."

At that moment more had to wait as a buzzer at the drugstore entrance intended for urgent business called Ralph downstairs. Under the CLOSED sign peering in stood Felix, with his hat dripping rainwater and his thick glasses fogged over.

"I've got to talk to you and Esther", he said.

Ralph took Felix' hat and a soaked rain poncho from his rural mail delivery days, hung them over a back of the wooden booth, turned off the radio he had left on, and led Felix upstairs.

"It might work better if you came looking for advice *before* you did something", said Ralph, not for the first time.

Like many a person on what could be seen as an errand of mercy, Felix had fantasized about its happy outcome: Gratitude would spill over; he would have to shrug off a slew of thank-yous; Warren would be his friend; Warren's sister, who had not been informed of his plan to hand over Penelope's letters, would be overwhelmed with appreciation; Penelope, equally uninformed, would be crying grateful tears; prison workers would pat him on the back as he climbed back onto the bus.

Pipedreams of this sort left him unprepared for a visit that took a bad turn at the outset and never recovered, ending in an argument of sorts, sufficient to unravel him and send him home to Ed's wishing he had never left in the first place. Up in his room he wrote a short letter under his magnifying glass. The letter went on its way to Charlotte Hall, and Felix from the post office crossed the street to Ralph's just as the prison bus rolled through Front Street on its next run, trailing rainwater and mist, but still no dogs.

"I should have left well enough alone", said Felix, without quite knowing what *well enough* might have been.

Esther had put the kettle on, but, after seeing Felix, poured him a glass of wine.

Felix' plan had relied heavily on the usual Felix magic, which for him was not magic at all but simply his genuine warmth and interest in other people. This worked as expected with everyone who knew him at Shade Creek and spilled over among those who did not know him. Old acquaintances viewed him as something like a rainbow on a day of rain as this had been. For many he brought to mind a time before Shade Creek when they made less money but were happier even if they were not prepared to admit it. Warren, who had heard about Felix from his sister and for her sake agreed to a visit she had not foreseen, was not among these. He was unconvinced Felix intended to do him a good turn and had not instead shown up to taunt him with knowing much more about his daughter than her own father did.

Prison visiting facilities were deliberately designed not to be casual or comfortable. They sat facing each other in a sparsely furnished room under constant surveillance. The packet of letters Felix gave to Warren at the outset had been inspected with dramatic flair. The man inspecting them, once a farmer living near the southern extremity of Felix' mail route, had rolled his eyes as if they were filled with contraband. Warren flipped through the seven of them as if they were next month's bills. He pulled out the school picture, managed a smile, and then glared at Felix.

As glares go, it was not a very good one. His facial bruises were still evident. Felix, knowing of the beating was prepared for this, but unprepared for how the man looked otherwise, ashen and frail, older than a sister who was several years older than he. Everything about him was gray: His hair; his eyes; and his complexion, with its bruises simply a deeper shade of gray. His hands trembled and danced as if playing an invisible musical instrument sitting across his lap. The agitation flickering over him from his fingers to the lines of his mouth and into his eyes could have been taken as anger or fear: If anger, on the point of explosion; if fear, on the point of panic attack. He spoke slowly and with evident difficulty. The movement of his lips and the words coming from them seemed to be from separate languages.

"Is this supposed to make me happy?"

"There's a lot in there about your daughter," said Felix in the way of an answer, "especially in the last one."

"Look, I don't know how she met you or how my sister met you, but if you think I'm happy that Penelope can write you and not me, and that I cannot write her, and she cannot visit—"

"That doesn't make me happy. I know how it is, and that's why I'm here."

They sat facing each other ten feet apart beneath the glare of fluorescent lights running in three strips the width of the room. The distance between them from Felix' perspective seemed to be lengthening by the second. None of this was the way he thought it would be.

"You can't possibly know!"

He flung the packet of letters at Felix. For a second or two Marvin's airmail letters became truly airborne, skittering in several directions around the room. Penelope's school picture lay as a rectangular blur at Felix' feet.

A prison guard came in. "I'm going to have to end this, Felix. Settle down, Mister", he said to Warren.

Felix was on all fours attempting to gather the letters. With the guard's help, he soon had them in hand and was back in his chair.

"Give me another minute, Matt", he said.

Matt had been a filling station garage mechanic in Clay Corners before the station became a convenience store and he quit the car-repair business. He had worked on the last of Felix' mail delivery cars. He had been on the same bus taking Felix to Shade Creek and getting off had asked him if he still drove with his foot on the brake pedal, a joke now ten years old. He too seemed older than he should have been, standing in an open doorway of the visiting room with his arms crossed while giving Felix the minute he requested. Everyone at Shade Creek seemed older and grayer.

With the packet of Penelope's letters in hand, with her picture now in an envelope other than the one it came in, and with Warren farther away than ever, as if sitting at the other end of a long, narrow hallway, Felix, himself feeling bereft and afraid, had this to say, his own voice trembling and echoing: "I came out here to bring you word from your daughter. I came here to share that. I had a daughter named Penelope a long time ago. She died about the age of your Penelope."

Actually she had died when several years younger, but for Felix age difference didn't matter, not with eternity in the picture.

"Nobody will *ever* come to me with word from her. I will *never* see her again, in this life at any rate. You're lucky as far as that goes."

He had left the packet on his chair seat and, without looking back, left Penelope's father sitting there. By his calculation, they had been visiting somewhere in the vicinity of his Uncle Milton's granary.

"Perhaps it's far from as bad as you think", said Esther. "It must have come as a shock to him."

"Yes," said Ralph, "give it a few days." This was standard advice from someone dispensing medicine.

"I still wish I hadn't done it", said Felix, with his eyes looking from the one to the other through his thick lenses. "I am too much of a meddler. That's my problem."

"You're a tender-hearted man," said Esther, "and that is never a problem. I would not be a bit surprised to hear he is reading those letters right now and quite happy to have them."

This in fact had turned out to be the case, encouraged by the insistence of Matt, the former garage mechanic.

"You're forgetting something, Mister", he had said to Warren, who was leaving without Penelope's letters. "An old man goes to all the trouble to get them to you, you could at least take them with."

As a leftover from his mechanic days, Matt had brought to Shade Creek the hectoring mode he had sometimes used with irresponsible teenage drivers neglecting or otherwise abusing cars their parents bought for them.

An hour or so later, the rain having stopped, Ralph escorted Felix back to Ed's. The sun breaking through the low cloudbank at day's end shot an orange shaft down the center of Front Street, casting their shadows as they crossed it.

"Let's have coffee tomorrow", said Ralph with his hand on Felix' shoulder.

Back upstairs in the drugstore, Esther was in the kitchen preparing a dinner they had planned to eat two hours ago.

"You said there's more."

"Yes", said Esther, with her back to him and a bowl in her hands. "Warren Hall is dying, terminally ill."

"Terminal?"

"Terminal."

"Good Lord!"

27

Walking the Tracks

Two days later the lime green Volkswagen was once again parked in front of Ed's. It was Saturday afternoon, and the woman with the orange-red hair was once again sitting with Felix at a table in the tavern. Charlotte had been summoned to Shade Creek for an update on her brother's medical problems. In view of the most recent test results, these were much more serious than previously thought. Before she got around to that part of it, she told Felix that his packet of letters had been read over and over and that Warren seemed to have forgotten the argument Felix mentioned in the fretful note he had written her afterward.

"So you can quit worrying about it", she said. "I'm sure he's very grateful, as am I. He just has a hard time some days, but I really think people out there connecting him with you has made a change for the better."

Felix beamed and gestured Fred's way for a refill of coffee cups. Fred, normally on the lookout for any signs of insolence among his boarders, was happy to oblige with the chance this afforded to move closer for a few seconds, in the course of which nothing further was said, giving him all the more reason to suspect secrecy in the picture. When people quit talking while you were pouring coffee, they had to be hiding something.

"In her last letter," said Felix as soon as Fred was out of the way again, "Penelope even mentioned finding a collection of his old fishing flies and tucking them away in her room. Reminded me of my Uncle Milton and how he used to travel up your way and fish in those trout streams. Maybe they even fished the same stream some weekend. Who knows?" Felix' wistful speculations along these lines overlooked the fact that his uncle's trout fishing days were in an era before Warren could toddle, let alone stand in a trout stream wearing waders.

Charlotte caught this discrepancy, but rather than blunt his enthusiasm, she let it go. As for Penelope's letters, had Felix advised her of that part of his plan, she would have discouraged it as a possible breach of the court order affecting Warren's parole prospects. By the time she left Shade Creek, this was the least of her worries: Warren would never make it to his parole eligibility. It had even crossed her mind to bring Penelope to Shade Creek if she could arrange it. News of the sort she had just been given at least brought some freedom with it. Under the general heading of the silver linings sometimes said to be discovered in clouds, perhaps Penelope and her father could be reunited. She had long looked in vain for any sign of precious metal where her brother's circumstances were concerned. There she had only seen iron bars, steel-clad doors, and the cold stares of prison staff.

Watching all this from the sidelines of his tavern bar, Fred was once again speculating. His speculation reached the breaking point when they left and crossed the street to Ralph's Corner Drug, where the CLOSED sign had been hanging in its door since noon. As was their habit on Saturdays, Ralph and Esther were sitting in the old wooden booth having lunch when they saw Felix at the door with a red-headed woman.

"This is Charlotte Hall," said Felix, "Warren's sister. We need some advice."

He looked at Ralph as if to say, this time I'm asking *before* I do something. The fact was he did not know what to do. Ralph climbed out of the booth and shook Charlotte's hand.

"I'm sorry to interrupt", said Charlotte.

"We were just finishing up", said Esther, about to admit she had previously met Charlotte's brother and then deciding against it for the time being.

She led Felix and Charlotte upstairs. Ralph followed, pondering the tendency of small, simple things to develop over time the complexity of a coral reef. Three months had passed since he first heard about Felix writing a young girl living two hundred miles away. Now they were all connected to his pen pal's family in increasingly intricate ways. Every move someone made only multiplied the connections. Soon they would all be sending Christmas cards to each other, showing up at family reunions, and having group pictures taken. A branch stuck crosswise in a mountain stream thousands of years later could create a waterfall.

Upstairs something like a dot-to-dot picture was forming as Charlotte told the story of her brother from Cub Scout to prison inmate, tying one event to another and completing the picture with these apparent extremes at the beginning and end. Word that Warren had been an altar boy during Father Lyle's first St. John Vianney assignment raised an eyebrow Esther quickly lowered. No one seemed to notice. Esther already knew bits of this from her two intake interviews with Warren, but avoided mentioning it. Interesting her especially were Charlotte's recollections of her brother's early signs of obsessive-compulsive disorder, not specifically described as such by her but clearly present from an early age.

"Did anyone ever look into that?" she asked.

"We thought he would grow out of it, and as the years went by he seemed to."

Esther knew this was hardly ever the case. It simply went underground, disguising itself in different behaviors over time, some of which became more private and therefore less outwardly noticeable.

Felix had heard an abbreviated version of Warren's life from Charlotte on her first visit to Clay Corners, but seemed to be hearing it for the first time. Prior to this Ralph had heard next to nothing. Felix and Ralph listened and said nothing. Esther asked a few further questions, but otherwise seemed to be keeping thoughts to herself. Charlotte discovered the heart-lifting freedom of sharing burdens long kept to herself in Bell Harbor, where—except for Sister Serena and now and then Father Ulrich—she had been living bound and gagged as far as her brother's affairs were concerned. She could even pour out the anguish she felt arriving at her conclusion.

"Now he's going to die in there. He will never be free!"

This thought passed like a tremor through the four of them, followed by a few seconds of silence. Ralph's left-hand fingers began to dance on his chair arm. Felix pondered his shoes. Esther was the first to speak.

"At times like this, my dear, it's best to focus on the short range: *What* needs to be done now."

Not being the sort to dangle false hopes, Esther feared Warren's dying there might prove to be the case.

"There's no looking back either, but your brother's case is a travesty of justice as far as I'm concerned, not that it helps to say so at this point. It's obvious something happened to him when he was so very young." Esther teetered on the edge of a teakettle moment. Ralph, seeing the signs, cleared his throat.

She left it at that, but glancing at Charlotte began to wonder if she had told the whole story as far as she knew it. Did Warren's sister know or suspect what she herself had begun to suspect? The puzzle pieces fell neatly in place, though perhaps too neatly. Esther, a reader of detective novels, knew how easily everything could add up but amount to no more than arithmetic. If life were that simple, there would be little need for detectives, or for clinical psychologists, for that matter. Things could make too much sense: A little boy afraid "something bad" might happen and going through rituals to fend it off; a parish priest from his days as an altar boy returning after an interval of many years; then a conflagration soon after.

Charlotte's remaining with her church despite knowing, or guessing, that a priest had violated her brother could seem like a battered wife scenario, but Esther was wary of diagnostic clichés and shallow judgments diminishing such virtues as loyalty and dedication. Not a particularly religious person herself, she nevertheless respected the consolations of that durable mystery called faith. It was too easy to call martyrs plain fools.

"There is such a thing as compassionate leave or medical parole, as it's called in some states", said Esther, moving into safer territory by far than the punishment of mentally ill, possible abuse victims by a society unwilling or unable to treat them by civilized standards.

"The problem with compassionate leave is the endless red tape. It would challenge a team of lawyers, let alone a family member with no experience in such matters. Then there are the politics involved, both local and otherwise, and the taboo of appearing soft on crime. The one point in our favor is that it saves the state money. This always helps, you can be sure, even if nothing else will."

Once more the kettle began to heat. Once more Ralph cleared his throat.

"You, my dear," said Esther, "are a victim of punishment, as is Penelope, and even that poor girl's mother. I'm afraid the state won't give that a second thought. Mention it to anyone from arresting officer, through prosecuting attorney and judge, all the way to a prison guard on the other end with the rest of the world in between, and no one will know what's troubling you."

"Could Crossman help?" Felix asked, unaccountably brightening at the prospect of getting lawyers involved.

Lawyer Crossman lived out in the country on something of an estate with its own nine-hole golf course on one of his old mail routes.

"Completely out of his league", said Esther.

"At this point nearly everything is", observed Ralph.

Wayne Crossman Sr., attorney-at-law, was an anachronism and throwback to an earlier era at Clay Corners. A village once having a doctor, a dentist, a locally owned bank, a Ford dealership, two hardware stores, and two grocery stores, and now having none of these, still had an attorney, albeit one not to be depended upon when it came to much beyond writing up a will or a quit claim deed.

His Clay Corners law office had begun as a branch of the larger firm in a nearby city where Crossman had once been a partner. Much of the time it had been manned by a secretary-receptionist who made appointments for the two afternoons a week Crossman would be there on his way home. She served as a notary and processed documents for clients to come in and sign in the meantime. When Crossman retired from the law firm, he kept his Clay Corners office—grown as fusty and aimless as he had become over the years—sitting there still those two afternoons a week beneath the gray, bushy eyebrows old attorneys seem to acquire, unable apparently to let completely go of lawyering long after it had let go of him.

Nevertheless, Felix knew things about Crossman the others did not know, for example, that he had a son in a Minneapolis law firm of whom the old man himself once bragged to Felix while leaning on a golf putter by his mailbox, "He's a powerhouse. If you are ever in a pickle or about to be sent up the river, he's your man."

This of course was Crossman's idea of a joke. Still Crossman junior had taken on the defense of Uncle Milton's farm when Shade Creek was to be built there, and even though the farm was lost, he had gotten Felix compensation beyond all expectations.

"Let me do some research and check with some of my contacts", said Esther.

She wrote Charlotte's address and phone number on a small card and slid it into a handbag hanging from a coat rack behind her.

"Meantime, I think the two of you should stay for dinner."

"I should be leaving. I have to be back to play the organ tomorrow at St. John Vianney."

"And no one else can get some worshipful noise out of that contraption?"

A call to Sister Serena soon settled that part of it, leaving Charlotte free to have dinner and spend the night in the Corrigans' guest room at Esther's further insistence. With Sister Serena now in the conversation, as well as Father Ulrich, of whom Charlotte spoke with utmost respect and regard, the picture Esther had been forming became yet clearer.

As the evening wore along after Felix' departure for Ed's, Ralph noted sleepily over a second glass of wine that what had begun as Charlotte and Esther had now become Charlotte and Bea. The coral reef continued to grow.

Later that night, long after the other boarders at Ed's had fallen asleep, Felix sat by his bedroom window, looking out over the vacant lot toward the Depot Café, where the old railroad tracks used to be. In his mind he walked those tracks back to his Uncle Milton's farm, tore down Shade Creek, freed Warren Hall, and put the farm back in its place. He had a plan to accomplish at least part of this.

28

Walkers in the Night

About the same time Felix was staring out the window of his room, Marvin woke up and stared at the ceiling of his. In both visions there was much to keep a man awake while others slept.

Out on Star Island something like the calm after a storm had settled in. In fact, a summer thunderstorm had just passed over, thundering and gasping its last as its squall line slammed up against cool air piled like a snow-capped mountain over the Great Lake's still frigid surface. The other storm, the one on Marvin's mind, had met a similar fate over the suddenly frigid surface of Lister family affairs.

June and Penelope had quit talking, in favor of the safer approach of thinking things that were not being said. Marvin, doing his best to stay out of it, spent more time among his cars in the pole barn. Cleaned inside and out and gleaming from bumper to bumper and hubcap to hubcap—at least those able to gleam and those having hubcaps—they had never looked so good. One would have thought he was taking the whole fleet to a car show in St. Cloud this coming Saturday. Since Penelope would be riding along to visit Sister Hilaria, he had chosen the 1955 Chevy Bel Air, the easiest for her to drive in most respects except for its standard transmission, which would give her experience using a clutch and shifting.

Behind-the-wheel driver's training never taught the subtleties of gear shifting. Mr. Stiller would have found alternative summer income had anyone suggested it. His life already appeared sufficiently at risk riding around Bell Harbor with four students, three of whom would be texting on their cell phones out of sight in the backseat while he was trying to keep Penelope on the right side of the road. Marvin, in contrast, regarded learning to use a clutch as a skill no less basic than tying one's shoes.

"You don't know how to drive until you can make a left turn with a stick shift", he said to Penelope with conviction. June, having relented, without talking about it, would take Penelope to her driver's training in Bell Harbor tomorrow morning, just as she had done this morning. After that, Penelope was supposed to wait for the summer school activity bus, this time at the school, since that's where its route began. The school was six blocks from the public library. Halfway between was her Aunt Charlotte's house. Six blocks in the other direction was St. John Vianney Church. Penelope had lots of options for spending the three hours between the end of driver's training and her bus ride home. She was not talking about it. June was not asking about it either.

Marvin's ceiling normally had little to say when he awoke in the middle of the night. He could glance up without fear or regret, but tonight his ceiling admonished him for how complex, compressed, and compartmentalized life on Star Island had become. He should have stuck to tinkering with cars. Tinkering with people's lives, his good intentions notwithstanding, lay well beyond his skills. He had wanted to make Star Island life less isolating for Penelope, and look at the mess he made of everything instead. He failed to consider that it might yet prove to be a fruitful mess, at least viewed from a distance greater than his ceiling.

The next issue of his life insurance magazine, arriving in the day's mail, had reminded him of the innocent suggestion behind all this. Here was the tumbling pebble leading to the avalanche. Instead of putting it in its usual place at the bottom of his magazine pile, he tossed it into a barrel stove, where at least it would help kindle a fire the next time he needed one. To affect Star Island life as much as the previous issue, the fire would have to burn down his pole barn. At least a lot of secrets would burn with it. If secrets kept accumulating at the present rate, he would soon need an additional car to contain them all. Had he known of Ralph Corrigan's musings along similar lines, they would have found much about which to philosophize on his next visit to Clay Corners. The way things were going, there was bound to be a next visit.

He glanced at June asleep beside him and did a further calculation of how much she did not know and then added it to the consequence of her ever finding out. It had grown from the last time he added it up, but it did not stop with her. Penelope (he thought) did not know the broken weather vane from Sister Hilaria had been constructed by her father. She did not know it was hidden in the Frazer's trunk, the best he could manage when June told him to get rid of it. This, of course, went further since Marvin knew nothing of what Penelope had heard from Father Spence at Pine Shadows, not even that his priest cousin had spoken to her there. What Penelope knew about her father was anybody's guess at this point. If Marvin worked up the courage to ask her sometime, she would be reluctant to say. She knew he was already too much in the middle of it, between her and her mother. Everywhere he looked there seemed to be something someone did not know or did know and had to keep quiet, and he could only look as far as Star Island.

No one on that outpost as yet knew Warren Hall was dying. No one knew he had in hand from Felix the packet of Penelope's letters. Only Felix knew what his next move would be.

As was the case some nights when Marvin tossed and turned, he decided to get up and go for a walk. With Osgood from the pole barn trotting alongside, he took a familiar path to the lakeshore, finding his way with a hanging lantern of the sort campers use. His feet knew the way, as did Osgood's nose. Had Marvin left the lantern behind, he would hardly have missed a step of a journey made so often. He could have put Osgood on a lead and simply followed behind. At first he walked among birch and aspen, with the lantern swinging from his belt, casting shadows either side ahead of him and setting lower branches aglow. Nearer the lake he passed through a black spruce grove and from there onward toward the looming hulks of dark boulders nearest the shore, several hundred feet from the pole barn.

The peculiar feature of a walk at night, especially on a night as dark as this, is the way the other senses fill in where vision cannot go. There was the flutter of unseen birds disturbed by his passing by, Osgood's methodical panting and the clicking of his nails as they passed over rocks, and finally the various hoots and toots of shorebirds and ships signaling to each other. The lake, whether turbulent or sullen and quiet, was always as inescapably present as the heavens whose moods it reflected.

Living near a body of water as large as Lake Superior was like living with a second sky, this one at one's feet sprawling forward to meet the other with all the resonances and imaginings that brought to mind.

Slapping against its shoreline and licking at its rocks, the lake could almost always be heard before it was seen. Some days it would roar; others it would whisper as if having secrets to share. When it was invisible under darkness or hidden in a mist, you could hear it; when you had no other reason to know it was there, you could smell its wet breath among lichens and mosses and glistening chunks of driftwood. Marvin knew all this like a poem he had memorized in his youth. You could not live as close as he had always been without knowing every line of it by heart.

Having done this so often, he had a favorite place to sit. The passing storm leaving it too wet this time, he stood a few minutes with Osgood at his side. There were in fact two ships far out on the lake, the one—from the length and low silhouette of it—an ore boat heading out from port, the other a freighter, chunkier and riding higher in the water heading in. Lights flashed between, horns sounded, in a ritual of coming and going, before the ore boat slipped behind a low cloud bank forming from warm rain upon the cold lake. The freighter he could follow far longer as it moved southwest of Star Island toward a disused lighthouse built on a stony pinnacle. Finding in all this a simplicity and a predictability, Marvin savored the sense of things going on as they always had. He turned back toward home.

As he and Osgood came out of the birch and aspen grove, he could see the pole barn lights. He recalled having turned them off. Inside he found June waiting for him, sitting in the Desoto where Penelope often sat and read. At least the Frazer was three cars away on the other side. The pole barn being Marvin's world and occasionally Penelope's world, June, who lived in a world of undeclared boundaries and borders, seldom showed up there. Yet here she was at three in the morning. At least Osgood had been kind enough not to bark at her.

"How was the walk?" she asked as nonchalantly as if this was something they always did in the middle of the night.

"Couldn't sleep", said Marvin as he extinguished the lantern and hung it from a hook above his workbench.

"Me neither", said June, getting out of the Desoto and losing whatever nonchalance she possessed while sitting in it. "Everything's falling apart, Marvin, and I don't know what to do to get my daughter back."

Marvin did not come equipped with ready responses to statements like this. The Esther Corrigans and Fathers Ulrich and Spence of this world have them at hand in their tool boxes. One among them might have said, "I'm sure it's not as bad as all that." Another might have suggested, "Separation is the natural course between parents and their teenage children. It's just what happens, so don't blame yourself. She will be back, and besides, you're not *really* losing her." Then of course something aphoristic might have come from the likes of Ralph, along the lines of Little Bo Peep and her lost sheep. Life had a way of going in circles. You had to let go of something before it could come back.

Marvin had none of these thoughts within reach. He did have June within reach, so instead he took her in his arms and hugged her, brushing her hair from her forehead and planting a kiss there.

"Penelope's a good kid," he said, "and no matter what, I am sure she loves her mother. She needs to do what she needs to do, and maybe we need to let her go do it. It will be all right in the end." He was not all that sure, but for June's sake he had to say it.

"I had to start over from somewhere", June said. "I could not start from where I was, so I had to start from nowhere. Oh, Marvin, I am so afraid. I don't want to lose her. She is all I have other than you."

He held her close and kissed her again. "It will be all right", he said again. "You will always have us both." Not even Esther Corrigan and Father Ulrich could have topped that.

Knowing Penelope as he did and June might have—and knowing himself—he knew this would always be true. The daughter who would not give up on a father she could not remember would never let go of anyone who cared about her as they did. They all were living beyond the end of something begun long ago. There might have been other ways to begin with, but there was no going back to undo it and to try alternatives. Marvin, who sawed logs into lumber for a living, did not need a Sunday homily to tell him that. Once he made his cut, there was no going back to start another way. A pile of boards could never be turned back into a tree trunk.

Set into motion by the tiniest inadvertent nudge, a change was rippling through all their lives as if the three of them were dangling figures in a weather vane mobile of Warren's creation. June was turning her face from it, looking outward and away. Marvin was looking through

it toward her. Penelope was spinning between them. When the weather
vane stopped rotating and revolving, they would all be in different
places. He glanced over her shoulder across the roof of the White
Whale and the Studebaker truck box, then over the roof of the Henry J.
to that of the Frazer.

In that moment he might have let go of all its secrets. It crossed his
mind to be done with it. Osgood had fallen asleep beneath the workbench. A new squall line was rushing east to meet the lake. He could
see lightning flickering in windows on that side of the pole barn.

"We should get into the house before it starts raining again."

The girl once voted most fun to be with, now the efficient mainstay of Osgoode Insurance, wandering around in the middle of the
night lost somewhere between these two images of herself, was led
back to the house. Marvin would sometimes think back to this moment
and wonder if he had done the right thing by not leading her instead
to the Frazer and its secrets. He was not a man to look for comfort in
metaphors. The lake was a lake; the sky was the sky; the lighthouse
was simply a lighthouse. There was poetry enough in all of it as it
was.

29

An Unseen Hand

The not discussed, unmentioned, and unknown were accumulating elsewhere than in the Frazer's glove box and trunk and were not so easily swept from view as those had been.

Father Ulrich had never met Warren, but his fate and inevitably Charlotte's and that of St. John Vianney remained intertwined in a way he found all the more troubling for knowing more about it than most. Some of his parishioners still grumbled about the man's twenty-year sentence being much less than he deserved. They were quite happy to think of him locked up whenever they thought of him at all. They were equally happy to suggest throwing the key away. Father Ulrich did his best to nudge them beyond such thoughts. He might imply that churches in general needed a good fire now and then. "The dove and the flame", he would say, as if those two symbols for the Holy Spirit explained what he meant and made Warren Hall something of a reformer.

He had replaced framed photographs of the old St. John Vianney hung in a hallway of the parish center with pictures of the new under construction. A watercolor of the old church by a local artist was moved to the rectory dining room, where few would ever see it. He pressured parish trustees to remove from its accounts receivable list the half-million-dollar restitution Warren had been ordered to repay as part of his sentence. When Charlotte had attempted to apply a tax refund toward that spell-binding debt, he returned her check and gave her a raise.

"Not on my watch", he said, drawing upon an old expression of his navy chaplain uncle.

A tall man of gaunt features some might describe as owly, Father Ulrich peered like a conscience over the shoulders of his parishioners, determined to urge them toward their better instincts. His chaplain uncle, equally tall though long deceased, peered like a conscience over his. Whenever he thought he was not doing his best, he would imagine what his uncle would have expected of him. St. John Vianney—neither battleship nor penitentiary—was by comparison a safe harbor. "Pull your socks up", his uncle could say with a stern look. The chaplain had no time for self-pity.

"I was once a lad in school like ours over there", said Father Ulrich, pointing from a window of the parish hall with his back to the assembled trustees. "The dictator Joseph Stalin died, and our teacher Sister Almeda led us into the church that very afternoon to pray for his soul. Now there was a monster by all accounts, and there we were on our knees asking God to be merciful, and there was the good Sister teaching a lesson we all need to learn, one that I myself would have been too cowardly to attempt. We will strike from the parish accounts Warren Hall's restitution."

A motion was made and seconded, and the proposal was approved by a single vote.

Father Ulrich's view of prison life had not been burnished by personal experience as Charlotte's and Esther Corrigan's had been. It arose from his innate sense of fairness and justice and had a purely theological formation: "Your brother serves to remind us all of the need for mercy, compassion, and forgiveness. Among the corporal works, to visit the imprisoned is about the least practiced, least understood, and most overlooked."

He kept from Charlotte the story that his uncle went from war in the Pacific to prison chaplain and, after serving as such, expressed a preference for war: The latter made no sense, while prison made too much sense: "The foul rationality of retribution in misguided pursuit of righteousness", as his uncle described it. "Some at least who went to war came back the better for it, while prison never redeemed anyone. They were always the worse for having been there."

Father Ulrich reserved that thought for others in his congregation when Warren's name or that of Clarence, the custodian, popped up and the old thirst for vengeance reappeared. He would remember both of them in a Mass said every year on the anniversary of Clarence's death. He made no secret of his intentions.

"After a year or two in one of those pens, my uncle was never the same", he said.

The old chaplain might joke that after he said Mass for them, at least his congregation went back to their cells, and he heard no more from them that day; but it seemed even at the time a sad thing to say, and as the months went by his uncle talked about prison life less and less. Five years passed.

Penelope had not been told about her father's beating. Charlotte could not do that without exposing her niece to the brutal reality of his prison life, with its horrors best left unimagined. Where could one so young and innocent go with a vision so terrible? What solace could be found there? She herself had taken years learning to live with it and even now still had nightmares in which her brother reached out to her with cries of help made all the more horrifying by the helplessness she felt. Here was not merely the paralytic sense one sometimes experiences in dreams, needing to run from the approaching train but unable to move. Much worse was to waken, to know it had not been a dream, to see it coming again and again, and to be able to move and yet unable to act. She once said to Father Ulrich, who from time to time inquired about her brother, "People can't possibly know what it's like to have a loved one in prison. Your heart goes there with them."

"With your heart for his companion, Charlotte, he will survive."

When Charlotte returned from her most recent trip to Shade Creek, she brought yet more news she was unsure about sharing with her niece, who might be showing up any minute now, that minute being about the time she appeared after yesterday's driver's training.

Whatever obstacles that had once existed discouraging contact between aunt and niece had dissolved and been replaced by the kind of intense intimacy that can only form between people who are not supposed to be together. June's strategy had achieved ironically an effect opposite her intent. This presented Charlotte with problems she had not previously had. She was the only person in Penelope's life having day-to-day knowledge of her father. If the girl wanted to know something, what was she supposed to tell her? Revealing nothing when they never saw each other had been by far the easier course. How could she tell her he was dying of a disease directly related to a prison life too dreadful to describe?

No closer to knowing whether to say and what to say than she had been yesterday, she sidestepped mention of Warren with an offer to

teach Penelope a first lesson on her antique reed organ, whose decorative scroll work and inlaid ivory stops had caught Penelope's eye.
Within a half hour, Penelope was playing the right hand part of
Beethoven's *Ode to Joy*. When Charlotte suggested it, Penelope thought
this was much more advanced than it was and far from a good way to
get started. Anyone seeing her sitting there, with her feet firmly planted
on its two pedals and her hands poised above the keys, would never
have guessed this was her first lesson. She seemed to belong there just
as she seemed to belong to life with all its complexity.

After *Ode to Joy* they worked on several versions of *Amen*, at the
conclusion of which she raced back to school to catch the summer
activity bus. Charlotte, watching from her living room window as she
crossed a street and headed uphill, could not but feel grateful. At last
they were together, facing what must be faced, even with the extra
burdens that brought.

Fortunately her niece did not know of her most recent trip to Shade
Creek, so saying nothing when she showed up again today was still an
option, but it did not seem like a very good one, and the longer she
went without saying something, the less satisfactory it seemed. The
easiest part to reveal was that Felix had given her letters to her father.
She might even like to hear it. Her father's medical condition was
another matter entirely. How could Charlotte tell her, and where would
she go for comfort once she knew? Certainly not home, where the
man's name could not even be mentioned.

This seemed to call for more advice from Father Ulrich. She made
an appointment to meet with him Friday morning and had just gotten
off the phone with the parish secretary when her own rang. A secretary
calling from a Minneapolis law firm wanted to schedule an appointment with her for this coming Thursday afternoon in Bell Harbor.

"An interested third party who wishes to remain anonymous has
asked us to assist you and your brother with his application for compassionate leave."

"We have not applied yet. I can't possibly afford a lawyer", said
Charlotte.

"Our legal fees are being paid by the interested third party", said
the secretary. "You will not be charged for our services, but in order
to get started, our attorneys need some background you can provide."

"Who is this interested third party?"

"Wishes to remain anonymous."

"Can I call you back in a few minutes?"

Charlotte searched around in her purse for Esther Corrigan's office number and left a message on her voice mail: "Bea, this is Charlotte Hall. Can you call when you have a moment? Urgent."

At that point Charlotte's doorbell rang. Penelope stood on her front step with a student driving report from Mr. Stiller in hand.

"I parallel parked today without knocking down any flags", she said with a voice like a bird singing.

Another lesson on the reed organ followed, in the course of which they were both laughing as Charlotte demonstrated some keyboard flourishes and Penelope picked them up at her first attempt. From there they moved on to more serious work.

June's three-part plan for her daughter's summer activities had unbeknown to her and unplanned by any of them developed a fourth unofficial part. Penelope pumped the organ's foot pedals. Soon Charlotte's house resonated with the *Ode to Joy*. The *Amens* followed, just as yesterday, and from there a doxology, something a bit more complicated. Then the phone rang. Charlotte let it go unanswered.

"I never let the phone interrupt my lessons", she said. "If it is important, they will call back. Let's try a doxology you have probably heard Sister Serena play. You will really like this one, a bit like parallel parking."

Minutes after Penelope left to catch her bus, the phone rang. "Charlotte, this is Bea. I am sorry I could not call any sooner. I was in class. What's up?"

"I'm not sure", said Charlotte. "That's why I called. Is there any chance the Department of Corrections itself would initiate the compassionate leave process for Warren?"

"Highly unlikely. His family would have to be involved from the outset."

"Well, *somebody* has started something", said Charlotte, who described the call from the Twin Cities law office.

An hour or so later, Esther called Charlotte again. "I have been checking out this law firm online and with an attorney we have on staff here. They are legitimate in every way, about $500 an hour legitimate, said to be one of the best in the Twin Cities. I cannot imagine where this is coming from." Actually, she had only just begun to imagine.

"What should I do?"

"My advice is to meet with whoever is heading your way on Thursday, be clear about your money circumstances, and proceed with caution. Call me afterward. Do not sign anything."

"Who could possibly be paying for this?"

Esther did not yet have an answer, unless Ralph had been playing the lottery, won a jackpot, and kept it secret from her. She left campus early, arriving home just as he returned from a prescription delivery at Ed's.

"Does Felix have any money socked away somewhere that you know of?" she asked.

"If he did, do you think he would be living over there?"

"Probably. It would be just like him. Somebody seems to have just decided to throw a bundle at our Warren Hall problem, and since we did not do it, and his sister does not have it, and hardly anybody else knows what is going on, I am thinking it must be Felix."

"Felix? If Felix has money, why am I always paying for coffee?"

"That might be why he has money. Everybody has been doing that all his life."

"He has holes in his trousers."

"Another reason."

"He has probably never had anything to do with lawyers."

"Now *there* is a very good reason."

30

Of Course of Course

Wayne Crossman's son, legal bulldog that he was, on his way to becoming a legal titan, nevertheless had not yet risen to the level of having his name listed among the full partners of his Twin Cities law firm, a generations-old firm bearing names distinctly Irish. Its offices had once occupied an entire floor of the Foshay Tower, and its attorneys filled several tables after hours at the nearby Court Bar, a lawyers' watering hole. Thus its listed names, five of them in fact, provided by Charlotte did not form an immediate connection with Clay Corners. This might have helped them bring the matter to earth somewhere nearer to Felix than they could arrive by the process of elimination Esther was attempting to employ.

Fred of Ed's might have added to speculation with news that two men in suits and ties, one of them wearing argyle socks, had met with Felix yesterday in his tavern. They stayed so long that one of them took off his coat and hung it from the back of his chair. He wore suspenders, and the other one, with the voice of an admiral or a disk jockey, asked him to leave a coffee pot at their table. Actually it had sounded more like a command. The guy in the suspenders had been taking notes on a legal pad. They were all business, with not a laugh among them during the two hours that went by. Fred's opinion was that Felix was up to his ears in a paternity case involving the two redheads.

He was almost prepared to jump into the middle of it for the sake of his next rent payment when he saw the old man signing papers, one after another, as if he was admitting guilt and giving the farm away. It was the closest Fred came to the truth of the drama playing out before him. Felix was in fact putting a substantial portion of the money from his uncle's farm at the disposal of the law firm where

Crossman junior was building his bulldog reputation and by stages his father's bushy eyebrows. The man taking notes was Crossman junior.

Thursday afternoon, two days later, both men were in Bell Harbor, one of them poring over documents at the courthouse, while the other interviewed Charlotte Hall. Penelope had been gone no more than an hour when he arrived at her door, a time so arranged that her niece would be out of the way. As it happened, Penelope came into the conversation regardless.

"Your brother's daughter?" Young Crossman examined his notes. "There is a court order in place preventing him from having contact with her."

Charlotte nodded with a perceptible shudder as if there was something yet to fear in that fact.

"It might not be a problem as is, but we would like to ask the court to quash that order. Your niece is how old?"

"She just turned fifteen this past spring."

"Fifteen years and four months approximately", Crossman wrote on his legal pad. "A responsible child?" he asked.

"Very much so. She was just here for an organ lesson." Charlotte pointed to the reed organ in her dining room. "I hope that is okay."

"Okay?"

"In view of the court order, I mean."

"Strengthens our request to have it quashed. The child already has ongoing contact with her father's family."

He took more notes. Some young attorneys no longer used legal pads, preferring to enter notes on a laptop. Young as he was, Crossman could be regarded as old school, around his long-established law firm the *only* school. He even wore suspenders, clearly visible under his unbuttoned suit coat.

"At her age, a judge would probably honor her wishes in this matter. Had she had any contact with her father?"

"None." Charlotte thought about mentioning the packet of letters and decided against it.

"Well, no matter. Do you think she has any interest where her father is concerned?"

"Definitely, but her mother would object, I'm sure."

Crossman frowned and took more notes. "We will be getting back to that one. Then there is the matter of court-ordered restitution. Let's see ... a half million dollars I think was stipulated." He flipped back a few pages in his legal pad. "I don't suppose any of that has been paid."

"My parents bankrupted themselves just trying to keep him from a longer prison sentence."

"Of course, of course", said Crossman. "We will be looking into it as part of the larger picture. The more obstacles we can clear out of your brother's path, the better our chances."

"Are they very good?"

"Touch and go," said Crossman, "but I think we have a shot at it. Last year in the entire country there were no more than a hundred medical paroles granted. There are no guarantees, but you have a lot of firepower in the picture on your brother's side—utterly fascinating instrument", said Crossman, nodding in the direction of the reed organ as if it represented firepower of another sort. "By coincidence my dad plays one of those, as a hobby, you might say. I grew up with it in our house. I can still see Dad in his slippers playing it. Even learned to bang out a few things myself. Mostly old horror movie sounds: Great when you're a kid and you want to scare your friends. Dad, though, is serious about it and quite good. Plays Bach and such. Your occupation?"

"Church organist and music teacher."

"Of course, of course", said Crossman, taking more notes.

Charlotte had not been asked to sign anything. When she asked about attorneys' fees, Crossman smiled like Santa Claus minus his white beard.

"All paid. Pro bono as far as you and your brother are concerned. You will never see a bill, even if we succeed in bringing your brother home. No promises, of course, but there is plenty of firepower in the picture."

He did not explain what he meant by firepower, but she took him to mean the interested third party's money and the legal services that would purchase. He glanced at his watch.

"Would you mind if I tried the organ for old time's sake?"

"Be my guest", said Charlotte, expecting to hear horror movie sounds.

He sat down, removed his shoes, and with his feet in argyle socks on the foot pedals played instead a Bach prelude as beautifully as she had ever heard. He seemed to lose himself in the sounds filling up her house. All the while he gazed at the picture of Warren with his parents as if Bach's notes were written there.

"Your brother?"

"Yes."

"I have an appointment with him first thing next week. I suppose he has put on a few years since that was taken."

"A few ... especially recently."

"Of course, of course."

"You're pretty good", she said of his musicianship, attempting to change the subject.

"I only know the first part," he said, lowering the roll-top lid, "but coming from a music teacher that is a high compliment. I will have to mention it to Dad next time I see him, which should be next week after I see your brother. Lives nearby, near Clay Corners. Ever been there?"

"I pass through all the time."

"Of course, of course", said Crossman discreetly fishing while tying his shoes.

How Felix, the old retired mail delivery guy, had gotten involved with all this and was willing to spend a fortune if necessary had been the number one question around tables after hours at the Court Bar. Unlike Fred of Ed's, Crossman was not the sort to speculate. Nevertheless, he found it a fascinating aberration in the usually mundane and predictable world where he worked, where even a few years of lawyering exhausted most possibilities, leaving only the inevitable.

Without extracting more in the way of motive than he had already in hand from Felix, and offering assurances she would be hearing further from him, personally or from someone on the legal team, he shook her hand and left.

"Legal team? He said legal team?" Esther asked. "A Bach prelude?"

"Played it perfectly. I think he could give *me* lessons. Who could possibly be paying for this?"

"Have you ever read *Great Expectations* by Charles Dickens?"

Charlotte had seen the old black-and-white film.

"Good enough", said Esther. "For now, let us just say you have a mysterious benefactor, like the young lad in the movie, and I do not see any harm coming your way."

Esther put down the phone and turned to Ralph sitting by. "I think I just compared Felix to an escaped convict. Did you know Wayne Crossman had a son in the law trade?"

Ralph shook his head. "Never heard of him."

"That brings it as close to home as the other end of Front Street. If not Felix, who else?"

3 1

Victims of Crime

Father Ulrich had always been a certain way, "old school" in the opinion of the current parish priest crop, some of whom were his senior. He had become the outsider on the inside or perhaps simply beside the point. He knew it was true, and he did not in the least mind hearing it now and then when his fellow creatures gathered and teasing came his way. In fact, he was proud to be conspicuously old school and happy to have it acknowledged.

He wore his Roman collar in an era when many priests had shed theirs, favoring the anonymous garb of mostly older men with arms protruding from blousy shirtsleeves. His uncle, who probably slept in his Roman collar, would have sneeringly called it mufti and thrown in sheer cowardice for good measure. While many would deny the trend toward less clerical garb had spread in tandem with the priest sexual abuse scandal, Father Ulrich suspected as much. The behavior of errant priests was a curse under which they all lived and worked, the guilty and innocent alike. The innocent were fated to be living examples of guilt by association, except no baptism would wash this guilt away.

At least Adam, whatever explained his fig leaf, had not been called a pedophile. Father Ulrich had never been called that to his face, but he knew some people suspected it of every priest they met. He understood the attraction of being mistaken for a vacuum cleaner salesman in the present environment and did not think it cowardice. The problem was his mufti-clad colleagues never quite pulled it off. Their casual clothes were too self-consciously casual: They looked like priests in disguise, as if the indelible mark said to have been conferred by Holy Orders showed through seersucker and twill. Regardless, it was never intended to be a scarlet letter, and he would not attempt to conceal it.

He sometimes still wore his old black cassock in appearances at the St. John Vianney School. Other priests these days were called by their first names and so had become Father Al or Father Bob or Father Izzy, the latter in his opinion an unfortunate derivation if there ever was one. Nothing, though, did more to confirm his misgivings about the errors of informality than hearing Father James Spence to his face called Jimbo by an impertinent stripling and watching the priest fail to take the matter in hand. Meanwhile, Father Ulrich continued to be Father Ulrich, defending his formal terrain dressed in black, with a scowl and knitted brow at the ready.

He followed a determined schedule day by day to visit in the course of a year the home of every family in his parish. He even appeared from time to time in some of the Bell Harbor taverns, where a hush would settle in as he came through the front door. Men would pause in the middle of a story, and some—themselves of the old school—would get off their barstools and stand out of respect until he gestured for them to sit down again. He might even sip a glass of beer before leaving, and long after he was gone, the hush coming in with him would linger like an aroma from an older time and place.

He usually spent Friday mornings in his office unless a funeral intervened. Come the Friday after Independence Day, not a parishioner had succumbed, and Charlotte Hall was the only name on his appointment calendar. A fly buzzed in through his open office window, made a wide circle, and usherlike buzzed out just as Charlotte herself appeared. They soon got around to discussing Penelope.

"You mean to say she never knew he set fire to the church?"

"Yes, Father."

"How could that possibly be? Everybody knows. Are you sure?"

"She didn't know I was her godmother. She didn't even know her baptismal name was Philomena."

Father Ulrich cleared his throat, adjusted his glasses, and shifted his gaze from a composed Charlotte to his office window, trying to imagine such things. He often sought solutions outside while pacing along a section of sidewalk forming a square with a flagpole in its center between the church and the school. Breviary in hand, sometimes he read prayers, and sometimes he pretended to pray, using the breviary as a sort of prop so he would not be disturbed. He thought prayer a very good thing, but a value added was the reluctance of anyone other than a raving lunatic to disturb a priest at prayer. Since lunatics were in relatively short supply, this gave him time to think. Priests of the old school always kept their breviaries close by and survived on tricks like this. Since he was not outside and could not very well excuse himself to step out for a few minutes of prayer, he paced the rectangular walkway in his imagination, took note of his dog-eared breviary to his right under a lamp, and returned to Charlotte with a decision his chaplain uncle would have applauded.

"I haven't visited Star Island in a while", he said, after hearing her news from Shade Creek. "Let me help with this. Clearly the girl has to know how things stand with her father, the sooner the better, and clearly her family needs to support her. I will speak with Marvin."

Charlotte had arranged to meet Penelope at St. John Vianney afterward for a lesson on the church organ. She mentioned this.

"Right here? Any minute now?"

"Yes, Father."

"Then we can take care of part of this today. That much is certain."

He never expected to see the day Penelope and her aunt would traipse around together, either out of sight or in full view. Their almost daily meetings had lost their clandestine edge. They could not see it as others did, two very bright planets spinning into the same field of view after ages of traveling among separate constellations. Father Ulrich and Sister Serena were among the astonished stargazers.

At that point Penelope arrived in the school district driver's training car with another student behind the wheel and Mr. Stiller in the copilot seat, called by him the suicide seat, not facetiously. She ran into Sister Serena as she passed the front door of the grade school.

"I am going to have a lesson on the church organ", she said.

"I have just discovered a nidus", said Sister Serena. "Not nearly so exciting, but still exciting. Do you want to have a look after your lesson?"

"What's a nidus?"

"A hatching place for baby spiders."

This seeming too horrible either to contemplate or to ignore. Penelope said there might be time after her lesson. There would have been had she not gone first to the parish center and asked to see Father Ulrich just as Charlotte, having excused herself, had entered the church looking for her.

"Is there any chance, Father, that someday you could let me have a look at my baptismal record?"

"Today is as good as any", said the priest, who without the aid of a stool could reach several black volumes of the parish registry high on a shelf in his office. "This is quite surprising", he said, after locating her name in a large, leather-bound book, and in fact only a few minutes ago it *would* have been surprising.

She knew without being told what the surprise was.

"Here is a copy of a record from another parish. You were baptized Penelope Philomena Hall by Father Spence in Eveleth. I think there is not a St. Penelope, at least not yet." He smiled at her as if to say there's something to aim for. "Your patron is St. Philomena ... very interesting. Your aunt—just here a minute ago—was your sponsor. Your other sponsor's name, I'm afraid, is obscured in an ink smear."

What he decided not to mention was more interesting yet, a note attached amending the original to read Penelope Anne Hall, signed by Father Lyle, then parish priest of St. John Vianney. Father Ulrich was not sure such a change lay within the discretion of any priest. The name pronounced during a baptismal rite was the baptismal name, period. In this instance, though, he knew of a further complexity so absurd and confusing he decided not to mention it: The official Church no longer regarded Philomena as a historical saint and had excluded her from liturgical observance.

Perhaps this was the reason for the attempted amendment, possibly a dispute between priests: Father Spence, who had been happy to ignore it, and Father Lyle, who would not ignore it under any circumstances; or a dispute between priest and parishioner, in this instance between Warren Hall and Father Lyle. Father Spence had agreed to Philomena, saint or not. Father Lyle—among his fellow priests known to be obstinate, territorial, and in his later years given to temper tantrums—had possibly demanded the name change and a further hand in the baptism as well. Was this bit of silliness why the old church had burned? It would not have been the first time matters purely theological had led to fires, though usually a stake had been involved.

It was not, though, the only possible explanation, as Father at this point well knew. The easiest to put forward, it nevertheless was probably cockamamie, an evasion. Like everyone else in the picture, he had things he must keep to himself. He had been in contact with the bishop, who told him to stay out of matters beyond his pastoral concerns. "In other words," he said to Rex, "I was told it's none of my business."

Father Ulrich studied the baptismal certificate as if it might have been a hologram revealing different possibilities at different angles. He looked at it a bit too long, tilted it a bit too far, and saw something he would just as soon not think about. He closed the parish register and cleared his throat, though his head would take much longer to clear of this notion. If not his business, with the man's daughter standing before him, whose then?

"Egad", he said without bothering to go on from there.

St. Philomena had been swept away in the same massacre that finished off St. Christopher and along with it—in Father Ulrich's opinion—some of the Church's most appealing legends. Taking history too seriously led to such nonsense. Philomena was as good a name as any, and who knew or cared to know what saints or sinners had answered to it? The wonder was that Santa Claus was still sliding down chimneys given the official Church's mood back then. Priests, enmeshed as they were in matters of pragmatic significance, ought to have known better, and Vatican theologians with enough time on their hands to come up with something so ridiculous would have been put to better use dusting statuary.

"I guess that about settles it", said Father Ulrich, on his tiptoes again with the parish register in hand high overhead on its way back to the highest shelf. "One of these days I will have my secretary make you a copy if you like."

What it settled or what he thought it settled was not the point Penelope had in view: *Aunt Charlotte had been right.* She had remembered it the way it really was; Penelope's school records were wrong. If she was Philomena on her baptismal certificate, she would be the same on her birth certificate. Instead of having one unpronounceable name looking like antelope but sounding quite different, she now had two, and as Aunt Charlotte had said, pronouncing them together was like traveling over a series of tiny hills.

Father Ulrich walked with her to the church.

"When does Marvin usually get home from the sawmill, and your mother from Osgoode's?"

While awaiting Penelope, Charlotte had been organizing choir music in little stacks across the top of the organ. A sudden gust from an opening door undid her efforts. Something was in the wind. As if blown about by yet another gust, Penelope found herself suddenly in the middle of something unexpected. Father Ulrich pulled one of the choir chairs around for her and motioned to Charlotte, who took her seat on the organ bench with her back to the keyboard. He sat facing them in a front pew. He felt quite certain an old navy man was peering over his shoulder.

"Let us begin this with a prayer", he said. He led them in one of his favorites, sometimes called the Serenity Prayer, which Charlotte knew, but Penelope, bowing her head, had never before heard. At that moment Sister Serena came in, genuflected, and joined them. Father Ulrich had asked the parish secretary to call her.

"We have some things to tell you about your father ...", said Charlotte, looking at Father Ulrich, who then took over.

When it came to matters affecting his parishioners, he preferred to get over painful parts quickly and then let prayer and healing begin. However, with someone as young as Penelope—kept in the dark as long as she had been—praying first and letting her eyes adjust to the light had seemed a better approach: There would be time enough to see things more clearly. In the spiritual worlds of Father Ulrich and Sister Serena, with prayer came discernment, and with discernment came comfort.

Father spoke in the hushed tones unique to private moments in large empty spaces. His words seemed to echo regardless. From time to time he paused to gaze at Penelope's face for signs she understood. From his angle, the church's red vigil light flickered in the distance over her right shoulder. *Seriously ill* stood for dying, but dying nevertheless. An effort underway possibly leading to his parole was *good news. Compassionate leave* was not mentioned. Here was more ambiguity than he usually employed. Nonetheless she understood.

Not lost on her was sadness in the priest's eyes, with their almost liquid glow of tiny candle flames. Not lost was the presence of Sister Serena and Aunt Charlotte; nor was Father's promise to be sharing all this with Marvin and her mother, leaving it to her what she chose to say in the meantime; nor was Sister's firm hand on her shoulder as they left the church together; nor was Charlotte's silence for the ten minutes it took them to reach the parking lot of Lighthouse Consolidated School. The summer activity bus was already loading as she pulled into a parking space some distance away.

"Are you all right?" Charlotte's first words since they set out. "I'm sorry we didn't have your church organ lesson. . . . Another time."

"I'm all right." She swallowed. "Another time."

"I'll see you on Monday."

"On Monday", said Penelope, holding back tears and—whatever she did or did not do—determined not to cry, so her own voice sounded to her like a recorded voice.

"On Monday", she said again. "It's okay. It's really okay."

Another time sounded like far away and forever.

As the bus was rumbling over the wooden bridge onto Star Island, she remembered Sister Serena's nest of baby spiders. Perhaps on Sunday she would be brave enough to have a look.

Another time.

32

Tumbleweeds

Felix found himself in the same predicament as everyone else: Day by day, with more he needed to keep to himself or could not talk about even if he wanted to. Penelope's last letter, with its version of her life story, arriving two weeks ago, had yet to be answered. She had not written again, nor had he. The man having so much to say to everyone could think of nothing to say. If he told her he had been to Shade Creek and met her father, she would want to know more, mostly things he did not want to tell her or she should hear first from someone else. He could not reveal meeting her Aunt Charlotte, twice now, because much that had passed between them involved those same things, and word of that should come from her aunt.

Writing letters in the old way, full of memories, seemed not to work anymore and was like pretending nothing had happened in the meantime. The pen in his fingers quit moving beneath his large magnifying glass poised over a page remaining blank. Where to begin? He left his room and went downstairs just as Ralph came in and was about to come up. Ralph gestured in the direction of the tavern, where the aroma of Fred's fried chicken still lingered, and a few of the hotel residents sat at a table playing pinochle.

As tangles become especially tangled, it becomes ever harder to see what might have been there to begin with. Hesitation and misgiving are the usual results.

Felix brimmed with hesitations, an unfamiliar condition for a man who once drove into every farmyard within ten miles and made himself at home. What began as a simple exchange of letters between an old man imagining he was young and a young woman believing him had transformed itself into something complex and unwieldy like a tumbleweed rolling across prairies of western Clay County, raking up everything in its path until it became trapped in a corner, a gigantic skeletal tangle, with nowhere to go but in circles. Felix found himself in such a corner going in circles.

Ralph, not a man to move in circles when he could make a straight line, came right to his point. Actually, typical of Ralph, he flew right past it.

"Do you know how much a good lawyer charges per hour?"

"I know, and I don't care", said Felix, in this instance not the least hesitant.

Ralph pointed toward the ceiling in the general direction of Felix' room.

"More in one hour than your room up there in a month."

Felix seemed quite pleased to think of it that way, and the more pleased he seemed, the more Ralph's left fingers tapped, until he might have been doing a fair jazz improvisation if they had been planted on something like a clarinet. He and Esther worried that Felix had gotten in out of his depth and made financial commitments leading to his living on the street unless they offered him their guest room. He would have been welcome enough there, but Ed's seemed the better option all around. At this point Felix made a surprising suggestion: It being early Saturday evening of a pleasant summer day, would he and Esther mind taking him for a ride in the country?

"He's being mysterious", said Ralph.

"I love mysteries", said Esther. In fact, she had set one aside as Ralph came in.

They brought the car around to the front of Ed's. Fred, on whom none of this had been lost, was of course going out of his mind as they helped Felix into the backseat and drove off in the direction of Shade Creek with Esther behind the wheel. They drove about half the distance to the penitentiary before Felix directed them to turn left on a county road, and then right in a half mile on a gravel township road winding between fields of corn and soybeans on one side and on the other a reed canary grass slough where red-winged blackbirds perched on cattails.

Going uphill, they passed an abandoned farmhouse whose windmill—the surviving half of it—stood in a rock pile, onward toward a pine grove and a small cemetery with graves either side of a single lane through its middle. Neither of them had to ask where they were. At the far end of the cemetery, a doe and a spring fawn raised their heads, flicked their tails, and disappeared into rows of spruce planted as if a windbreak had been put there to prevent snow from obliterating memories. Felix led them on foot to a distant corner near a caretaker's tool shed. A killdeer danced among some grave markers, dragging a wing in its wounded bird routine.

"Must have some young nearby", said Ralph, immediately regretting it when he saw what Felix was up to.

On his knees he was wiping farmland dust and grass clippings from a tiny gray stone with his own young buried beneath it. He worked slowly and carefully, as if the thing he laid his fingers upon was not stone, the dirt was not dirt, the grass clippings and leaves were not leftovers from a recent lawn mowing, but something as tender and sensitive as the arm of a sleeping child. Esther took Ralph's hand with its dancing fingers. His other hand he laid on Felix' shoulder.

"Here she is", said Felix, with his fingers tracing the outlines of an inscription: "And also of their daughter, Penelope, 1947–1960".

One would have thought from the way he said it that she was actually there, and as far as he was concerned, she was there, waiting for him. He could see her still.

Ralph cast about for words, gave up, and looked away.

"There you have one side of it", said Felix, standing up and turning to face them with an expression somewhere between determined and resigned. He might have been returning from a war.

"You ask me if I know what attorneys cost", he said. "My answer is next to nothing if something good can come of it."

He pointed in the general direction of the penitentiary, out of sight from where they stood, so that he seemed to be directing their attention to a patch of sky above the windbreak where streaks of cirrus cloud were turning amber as the sun descended.

From the cemetery they drove another mile or two gradually downhill, with Ralph and Esther at first assuming they were taking another route back to the state highway. Occasionally they would catch a glimpse of the Shade Creek guard towers off in a distance hard to measure, before the winding road seemed to take them in a direction away from the prison. Then beyond a further bend they were closer to it than ever. Further downhill it disappeared from view as shadows deepened around them, and they crossed a narrow stream trickling through a culvert.

"The other Shade Creek," said Felix, "the better of the two." Then he added something about carp and suckers speared there in the spring-time years ago.

They drew near an abandoned railroad trestle and passed over the other Shade Creek again, this time on a single lane bridge, beyond which lay a field road Felix directed them to take, two dirt tracks with pigeon grass in the middle brushing the underside of their car.

"You sure you know where this goes?" said Ralph, glancing over his shoulder and immediately realizing how foolish the question was.

An instant later, the road ended in front of a large barn formed from sheet metal fastened to semicircular steel beams. Its wide front door was in fact several small doors hinged together and folding open from the middle toward each side, an expanse of some thirty feet float-ing on a steel track laid upon a concrete base. Felix took a key from his pocket and handed it to Ralph. The lock was harder to move than the door itself, which slid open smoothly with Esther manning one side and Ralph the other.

"Good Lord!" said Ralph, raising his head to stare directly into the enormous engine of Uncle Milton's biplane, which except for its flat tires reared its propeller above him as if prepared to take off.

"I used that tractor to pull her down here myself before the prison took the farm. In those days I could still see where I was going." He pointed to a small Allis Chalmers tractor parked against a wall to his left. "Same with the other."

Behind the biplane parked at an angle facing one side of the barn was Uncle Milton's other plane, a deep blue Stinson from the late 1930s.

"That Stinson baby was his pride and joy", said Felix, for whom the sights within reach seemed to be a youth-restoring tonic of the sort Ralph could have found in his drugstore, except none of them would have worked such magic. Felix seemed twenty years younger than he had been moments before.

"Made by the Cord people after young Stinson was killed in a plane crash. My uncle knew him, knew E. L. Cord, knew everybody, even Lindbergh himself. There never was such a man as my uncle."

Looking at him in amazement, Ralph thought there might have been one other, namely, Uncle Milton's nephew.

The barn entrance was in deep shadow by this time, with the sun sliding into an orange haze; what lay beyond the Stinson could not be seen except as a dark hulk under a large canvas of the sort used by farmers years ago in the threshing season. Felix led them in, past the biplane and around the tail end of the Stinson. He kicked a fieldstone off one corner of the canvas, pulling it back at an angle over what turned out to be the front bumper and fender of an automobile.

"My uncle's other pride and joy", said Felix, growing yet more breathless. "As good as new! I lost count of how many times I washed and shined up this baby for him!"

It was the Cord 810. Neither Ralph nor Esther knew that word of this had brought Marvin and Penelope to Clay Corners. Neither knew what Marvin would have told them had he been standing there agape: They were looking at the front end of a fortune in the antique collector's car world, one of the most sought-after vehicles on the planet, in about as good a condition as one could be after so many years. The Cord would have made a sensational cover story for any of his magazines, even had it not been hidden away in an old barn at the base of a forested hill, the romantic essence of the best of such stories. Better yet would have been the detail of the man looking for it, giving up any hope that it still existed until he discovered it in the care of a sentimental rural mail carrier. Antique car collector stories could not get better than that.

Ralph had his own reasons for being impressed, standing there in what amounted to a rural museum featuring the life of a legendary uncle. His head swam with intimations of E. L. Cord, Lindbergh, the Smith Brothers, Dr. Lyons, and gangsters with machine guns out open windows of iconic cars like this one.

They threaded their way back out of the barn in semidarkness, folded the doors shut, and with Felix leading the way in silence climbed the hill behind, through a grove of burr oaks growing progressively more ancient as they neared the brow, where a rubble of last year's broken acorns crackled underfoot and a vista awaited them as they stepped from the shadows. Without warning, below them in a valley sprawled the grim buildings and compounds of Shade Creek, just then bathed in the flaming gold-orange beams of a brilliant sunset.

"God forbid!" said Esther. "I had no idea we were so close."

"It looks like hell itself", said Ralph. "It seems to be ablaze."

"Uncle Milton's farm", said Felix, at least for the moment not sardonically.

For him, having just left the company of so many reminders, it was there still, just as it had been. He could see his uncle taxiing his planes, riding his cultivating tractor through rows of knee-high corn, and strolling his farmyard with his wolfhound at his heels. Esther only saw a disguised horror, the fleeting, sun-infused glitter that is not gold. Ralph saw what would have been in any light a great pragmatic failure. Any view of Shade Creek, even this one, was a sight revealing instantly all there was and would ever be to see. It both invited and defied reflection. It could not be elaborated because it was in itself a summary, complete with final punctuation.

From Esther came the last word: "If you had assembled a team of experts and asked them to think of the most expensive and least effective way of punishing criminals while serving the interests of society, this is what they would come up with."

They turned away, descending the hill to the barn and their car. By the time they had driven to the other end of the field road, a full moon had begun to rise.

The two of them had much to talk about after they left Felix back at Ed's, where Fred glanced at his watch and learned no more than what time it was. Felix went upstairs and did not appear again that evening. Esther and Ralph drove around to the back of the drugstore where they usually parked. Above, the darkened store lights came on. The long shadow of the village water tower lay diagonally across half the length of a Front Street hushed as only moonlight can accomplish, for at least as long as the black bus stayed away.

Auctioned off, there was probably more than enough stored in Uncle Milton's barn to keep young Crossman and his law firm going at high speed for months. Was that Felix' plan, to sell the "kit and caboodle", as Ralph put it? As much as they now knew, they did not suspect the half of it. A man full of determination in most respects had never been more determined.

"Stories and thoughts run through his mind on two tracks", said Esther. "He talks to himself, and he talks to us simultaneously. Sometimes the messages interweave. It can be confusing for those of us on the receiving end, but *he* knows what he is saying. It's often the case with people his age."

"I do a bit of that myself", said Ralph.

Esther smiled, but otherwise pretended she had not noticed.

"So what was he telling us?"

"He knows what he is doing," said Esther, "and we might as well sit back and enjoy the show. There is no stopping him even if we wanted to, which I don't."

33

How Many Ducks?

Instead of a letter from Felix, a note from Sister Hilaria had arrived in Star Island mail confirming Penelope's visit on Saturday in St. Cloud. Marvin was happy for once to have something he need not take to the pole barn. Instead he laid it in full view on the kitchen table. The next morning he and Penelope left for St. Cloud in the Chevy Bel-Air.

"Gentlemen, start your engines!"

Marvin drove the first hundred miles, taking the highway with its curves and bends along the North Shore and then from Duluth uphill away from the lake into more level terrain of forests and farmland beyond where several times in their journey south they crossed the winding course of the Mississippi River. With only small villages and a few stoplights between them and their destination, he let Penelope take over.

She drove till they reached the outskirts of St. Cloud with both hands on the wheel in the manner Mr. Stiller taught, the quarter of and quarter past the hour positions. Marvin had provided supplemental lessons in using a clutch and shifting during a series of short roundtrips summer evenings on the Star Island cut off, over the wooden bridge and back to the pole barn turnaround. The Star Island road had no other cars, so she had no experience shifting while making left turns against oncoming traffic. On their journey they went out of their way to avoid these, passing up gas stations until one appeared on the right. Marvin, even more easygoing that he usually was, brimmed with encouraging comments.

Nearing St. Cloud, they fell increasingly into something like a stream of other antique collectors' cars until it seemed like a parade with much honking and waving between vehicles. The *rally*, as it was called, would be held at a county fairgrounds in the course of which some vehicles would be offered for sale, in Marvin's opinion at prices only a moron would consider. His Bel-Air was not for sale. Next to the 1960 Desoto it was the pride of his collection. Before the day was out, he would be offered twice what it might have been worth. Turning down an offer like that made the whole trip worthwhile.

Penelope had all afternoon with Sister Hilaria, whose convent and school were near a city park on a bluff above the Mississippi River. It was a good place and a perfect day for trying out a box kite Sister had just constructed from newspapers and wire clothes hangers using instructions and a pattern found in a school library book.

Cartoonists and philosophical sorts have sometimes noted a resemblance between people and their pets, the more modest not knowing what to make of it and attempting no explanation beyond an occasional reference to the myth of Narcissus. Whether mysterious resemblance extended to people and their interests was equally beyond the reach of science or philosophy. Nor could one distinguish cause from effect, as resemblance seemed to accrete on both sides over time, with each looking more like the other: The baggy-eyed master with his basset hound, the skinny lady with her whippet, and Fred of Ed's resembling the pet crow whose tongue he had split in a failed attempt to have it repeat nonsense for the entertainment of his lodgers. Of yet more immediate interest were Sister Serena's spiderlike, watchful patience and her tiny fingers, which seemed designed for weaving fine threads. Tall and angular Sister Hilaria in her habit with a bit of breeze blowing could appear as a large kite about to be airborne.

Some ten years older than Sister Serena, she had recently celebrated the silver anniversary of her entrance into her religious order and was for the first time serving as a superior, in this instance of the small community associated with a St. Cloud primary school, six teaching sisters in all. She had entered the convent in France, taken her first vows there before coming to the United States to complete her university education, and then stayed on at the wishes of her Mother Superior.

If Sister Serena was an arachnologist of the amateur sort, Sister Hilaria was a philosopher of the same sort, more by disposition than from the formal training and education she also had. A Platonist as much by instinct as by having studied the *Dialogues*, and at heart a poet, she preferred to teach little children because she found them closer to what they already knew, her role being to remind them. She could see in kite flying an allegory of the Platonic sort: God creating the kite; Jesus holding the cord and providing gentle guidance; the Holy Spirit a dependable breeze; and her soul, inclined to be rambunctious, the kite lofting skyward.

It was an analogy worthy of her favorite French author, the aviator Antoine de Saint-Exupéry. No year passed without her reading *Le Petit Prince* to her grade school class, alternating between French and her own translation, and enchanting her young students as much by the sound of her voice as by the thought of baobab trees. As with Sister Serena, her religious training had imbued her with the unwavering perspective of a precisely established vanishing point, that being where the rational mind found its limits and faith took over. Thus both sisters, like ever so many of religious training, could seem to be simultaneously detached and involved, focused and yet circumspective. This made them both reliable observers and patient listeners.

Sister Hilaria had just returned from a "home visit" in France, her first in six years. Her parents were now quite old, and her father especially frail. She wondered if she would ever see him again. Still, what could one do but talk of a next visit that was sure to be? Where love was in the picture, no one could ever say goodbye forever. Perhaps for this reason she was more thoughtful and subdued than Penelope usually found her, and sometimes as they chatted she would slip into little French phrases, the meanings of which were evident more from their tone than from their similarity to anything in English.

"If anyone ever tells you to go fly a kite," said Sister, "be sure to thank them for the suggestion."

At this point her kite was at least three hundred feet in the air above the river bluff. Out of sight a further hundred feet in the river below, fishermen were craning their necks to have a look at it and discussing what it might be, since from where they stood it was a mere gray spot dancing in the sky. It seemed an unlikely moment for Sister Hilaria and Penelope to begin talking about St. John Vianney, the Curé d'Ars, unless one takes literally the meaning of something coming out of the blue, for above them the box kite occupied a sky swept clean of any cloud. Somewhere out of that uncluttered scene came tumbling toward them not only thoughts of the humble Curé, but also of Philomena, the saint he *especially* revered (Father Ulrich had not mentioned that remarkable coincidence yesterday).

Penelope's head swam with the serendipity of it, as if it always had been meant to be, and as if her life—with her new name—really had begun in the little French farm village named Ars near Lyon, described in the mostly French words of a nun who had been there.

"Of course St. Philomena is the reason I gave you the good Curé's biography", said Sister Hilaria, without explaining how she had *eventually* discovered Penelope's true—or at least her other—middle name.

Penelope had not forgotten the little book still in the Frazer's glove box. She had thought of it almost every day through the first half of summer vacation and managed to listen as if she *had* read it, all the while keeping her eyes on the kite and away from any chance look Sister might send her way. Since they were both gazing skyward, her revealing blush might have escaped detection.

Theirs was the sort of conversation attempted while preoccupied with something else, a dog, a cat, the antics of a small child, or in this case a dancing spot no larger than a gnat above them sending assurances about its continued existence by occasional tugs on a stick Sister held in hand with only a few dozen winds of kite cord left upon it. Even had Penelope read *St. Jean-Marie Baptiste Vianney* by Abbe Francois Trochu at the time it arrived in the mail, she would have missed the point of Sister's gift. Her middle name back then as far as she knew was still Anne.

"I only just learned my *real* middle name", said Penelope.

"*Ma chère*, how is this possible?" asked the astonished Sister. "In my homeland we would not say *only* the one name is real when they *both* are. French people have two and sometimes three of what here are called middle names. They are the names of saints and of family members and of sometimes famous people. This is *très français*. But it would be strange not to know one of them till now. So let's say from now on your full name is Penelope Philomena-Anne Lister. Insert a little dash between those two, and you become quite a French lady." She made all of it, even the very British Lister name, sound distinctly French.

"*Oui?*" She glanced at Penelope.

"*Oui.*"

"Perhaps it is time to reel this creature in", Sister said. "There seems to be more of a breeze up there, and I am not sure how strong it is. They don't make clothes hangers as they used to."

An instant later the time was too late. After several turns of cord on the stick, reassuring messages from the other end abruptly ceased, and the cord grew suddenly limp. The extra stress of drawing the kite to earth had brought it to its breaking point. Out of sight over the river, a shower of wire and drifting newsprint fell toward a sandbar. The cord, falling in loops, tangled out of sight in trees and draped over the bluff down toward the river. They walked toward it with Sister's rosary hung from her waist making a rhythmical clacking as she wound the cord onto the stick as far as the wooded edge of the bluff, where they could go no farther. Caught in branches, what remained of the cord would stay there.

"From which birds will fashion nests, but for us *la fin de l'histoire*", said Sister using melancholy intonations the French can manage so well and Nordic Minnesotans hardly at all. Like Felix on what happened to be the same Saturday afternoon, she seemed to be saying more than one thing at once.

Then they were suddenly at the end of one history and the beginning of another, talking not about St. John Vianney, but about Penelope's father, not Marvin but the *other* one. Without preface, but as if she had been awaiting the right moment, that seeming to be a moment after they could retrieve no more kite cord, Sister Hilaria mentioned him and glanced at her as if to say, *it's time at last we spoke of him, ma chère*. They had settled on a bench nearby under a tree facing an artificial stone pond in which a few ducks circled a central ornamental fountain spraying water.

Within a half hour Penelope had shared the story of her father almost as far as she knew it. Sister had maintained throughout the circumspection in which she had been so well trained. She let the tale unwind as cord in the fingers of an experienced kite flyer whose well-timed tugs kept the project airborne. She did not mention the parts of it she had previously known from occasional conversations with Charlotte, Father Ulrich, the recollections of sisters who had been stationed at the parish at the time of the fire, and most recently from something she herself had stumbled upon while preparing to leave St. John Vianney. Penelope's version had not yet advanced so far and had come from scattered sources. It depended heavily on the role of coincidence: Felix living near Shade Creek and having a deceased daughter Penelope, Charlotte assigned to the Hikers group at Pine Shadows, Marvin's love of old cars like the Cord 810, and of course the public library's microfiche reader.

"Some would say coincidence, *oui*", said Sister Hilaria. "Others would say, 'God is showing you the way.' That is what I think."

"Then there is the box you found with the broken weather vane in it. I think my father made it."

"So do I, and so I sent it to you. This is how God works, with little miracles."

"How did it happen to be in your classroom? How did Father Spence lose it? How did it get broken into so many pieces, and now I don't even know what's become of it."

"Not everything we will never know *cannot* be known", said Sister. "Some things are just never discovered."

She had been looking at the ducks swimming in the stone pond, in and out of view as they circled its central fountain. Here were three, then again four, and sometimes five.

"How many ducks are there?" she asked. "*Trois, quatre, cinq?* We cannot be sure sitting here, no matter how long. For all we know there is always one or more out of sight swimming on the other side."

This too might have come from Saint-Exupéry, though it did not, for Sister Hilaria herself could think of such things. They got up from the bench and walked across the park back to the little convent, a converted brick house with a chapel where its garage had once been, a cross on its roof. Penelope had run around to the other side of the stone pond as they set out.

"Five ducks for sure", she said. "*Cinq.*"

"*Cinq canards*," said Sister Hilaria, "but not everything can be made so clear. Do you know that the name Penelope is sometimes taken to mean *duck*?"

"No!" said Penelope, leaping and clapping her hands.

"*Oui*," said Sister, "and your name is also associated with weaving."

"I would rather be a duck", said Penelope, and then as suddenly as a kite falling apart from a single tug on a cord, she became instead Penelope, the legendary weaver undoing by night what she had fashioned by day. She took Sister Hilaria's hand.

"There's something I haven't yet told you about my father", Penelope said, and she spoke of his illness.

"So this, too, we have in common", Sister said. "I am afraid my father also might be leaving this world. Let's go into the chapel and pray together for both before Marvin comes—though I am sure he would pray with us given the chance—and then I have a little gift for you, *ma chère courageuse.*"

When Sister Hilaria and Penelope came from the chapel, they found Marvin waiting in the visitors' parlor among the religious pictures and bric-a-brac of countless Catholic homes that had been donated to the convent, where some might argue it was least needed for the inspiration it was intended to provide. He was drinking tea, eating oatmeal cookies, and basking in the sunlight of three laughing sisters, each of whom had a story to tell about an old car they remembered.

At the conclusion of each story, Marvin would say something they had not mentioned about that particular make and model of car: What its horn sounded like, or how it would not shut down right away when you turned off the ignition but coughed and rumbled instead, or the way it would leap forward when you shifted it, or how its glove box door flew open when you went over a bump, and so on, and the one who remembered it would say to the others, "Yes, now I remember that; it's just how it was!" Marvin had been talking about cars all day, but this was more fun than any of it. They all agreed he was a car encyclopedia. He beamed, finished off his tea, and ate yet another cookie.

Sister Hilaria brought out her gift for Penelope, a gray wool hooded cloak with a large silvery pin meant to fasten it just beneath the chin.

"My mother worries about cold weather in this other St. Cloud. I have told her too many stories about the North Shore. I tell her we have cloaks and coats for cold weather here, but still she insists, and then because she thinks of me yet as she remembers me from years ago, it is no bigger than this."

She put it over Penelope's shoulders. Its hem reached to just below her ankles.

"That is how it is supposed to look: Quite French", said Sister Hilaria.

Everyone said it seemed to have been made for Penelope, and Penelope, whose thoughts were still somewhere in the vicinity of Ars, could imagine herself wearing it while walking along a country road with haycocks either side among the shadows of poplar trees, just as Sister Hilaria had described it all. Something like that had to be in her future.

The sisters at last gathered around the Chevy Bel-Air and laughed when Marvin said, "Gentlemen, start your engines." With promises of prayers all around, the day was not quite ended.

They were driving along a boulevard past the park and the river when Penelope asked how far they were from Shade Creek.

"About thirty miles", said Marvin, caught completely by surprise that oatmeal cookies, laughter, and prayers could come to this.

"Will you take me there?"

For the next five minutes Marvin was silent while he tried to think of an answer other than the only one he could have said right away. He drove the length of the boulevard, crossed a highway, and stopped in the vacant parking lot of a small office building. He looked at his watch, he looked at the Bel-Air's gas gauge, he leaned forward to peer out his windshield to see where the sun was, he looked at Penelope, and he looked perfectly helpless. He was also suddenly miserable.

"I can't take you there", he said. "I don't see the point in it, and it would kill your mother if she found out."

"She *will* find out, Marvin. She *has* to find out pretty soon. My father is seriously ill. Father Ulrich's words, but I think it's worse than that. He just didn't want to say it. I know I can't visit Daddy today, but I have to at least get as close as I can. That's the point."

34

Following a Cross

A man of practical wisdom, Marvin weighed the probability of June versus the certainty of Penelope and chose the inevitable. Returning to a highway he had just crossed, he turned south toward Shade Creek and Clay Corners.

As they approached the prison, Marvin pulled into a small roadside rest area, where the highway curved along a ridge formed by a glacial moraine and overlooking what had once been a lake; then, as its waters receded, a swamp; then an ancient forest; and then a verdant valley whose irregular patchwork of fields had been dictated by natural contours of the hillsides north and south of it. The rest area itself was passing through its own stages of neglect. Its asphalt semicircle was crumbling into course gravel beneath. Mulleins and yellow goat's beard flowered in its patches of bare soil. Purple vetches crept along its edges. These days it would have been a good spot to watch an attempted prison escape, except that from Shade Creek no escape was possible, and none had ever been attempted. The once verdant valley had become the sprawling, barren compounds of the prison fortress far below them. Neither of them knew yet that this had once been Uncle Milton's farm. Remarkably, a vanished past has its own ways of persisting, in the minds of both those who long for its return and those happy to put it behind them, to slap its dust off their clothes and to knock its soil from their shoes. It is not so easily achieved either way, by those who want to keep it or by those who want to let go.

Somewhere there is always a reminder like an ancient footprint found in a glacier, a brass ring fashioned from the shell casing of a forgotten war, an old name reappearing through paint on a mailbox. The roadside rest area's very existence was such a reminder. Once from this vantage there had been a reason for stopping, a scene to inspire and to cherish, and perhaps long ago Uncle Milton and Felix had stood in this very place looking back like mountain climbers and reflecting upon the beauty at their feet.

Had June known where they were at this hour of this day, she might have recalled the story of Lot's wife turned to salt by looking back. For Penelope, though, this was a vision of what lay ahead, not behind her. By insisting so much to the contrary, June had flipped everything around. Life for Penelope had seemed like a shirt put on backward. She could never get used to it, and she could never stop thinking about it as long as it stayed that way. As awful as was the vision at her feet, at least it seemed to be made for her shoulders, whose size in this instance belied strength sometimes described as good for the long haul. A shudder passed over her; her hands clutched the wool cape. Sister Hilaria's words had been running through her mind on the way here: *Not everything we will never know is unknowable. Some things are just never discovered.*

Sister had seemed to be hinting at something Penelope did not yet know, but might someday discover. Learning about it would matter more than discovering the further duck on the other side of the fountain. Whatever it was, it was not as easy as that had been, Sister had said, an almost ominous tone in her words, almost a warning. Did it have anything to do with the spectacle upon which she now gazed, with her dying father somewhere there out of sight in the midst of it?

"You have always been okay, *really* okay, Marvin. I hope you know it. I cannot believe how lucky I've been. Sister herself said so today when your name came up—yes, and Mom loves me. Sister didn't have to remind me of that today."

Marvin, seldom at a loss for words, was at a loss for words. Had he ever had a *real* daughter, he would have known how unlikely such expressions are forthcoming even when as deserved as this one was. He attempted to say something, but the words went crosswise in his throat. Nevertheless she knew he understood: The journey to be with her father was *not* and would *never* be a journey away from him. She wanted him to know that, now at this moment of turning. Tears, not from a wellspring of sadness, but from a reservoir of resolve, ran down Penelope's cheeks as silently as trickles of rainwater on a window pane through which she could see what lay directly ahead.

"This has to end, Marvin. Daddy is down there in that horrible place, and I *have* to see him before anything more happens. We can go now."

And so they returned to the car. As they were heading back onto the highway, neither of them noticed another, on the other side of the valley making its way along a winding country road, circling in and out of sight as it moved toward a forested knoll a short distance from a railroad tracks. Even had they noticed, they were too far away to see the three people sitting in it: A woman driving, a man beside her, and another in the backseat leaning forward as if giving directions. They were not the *only* pilgrims on the road in what was becoming Saturday evening. Sunset flames were only beginning to ignite the hard edges of Shade Creek with long fingers of light extending toward its ramparts and equally long shadows extending the other way beyond them.

Nor did Penelope and Marvin notice the road sign placed long ago to mark where they had been. Not much larger than the Bel-Air's license plate, it bore the words "SCENIC OVERLOOK", half hidden now in brush long left to grow as ever it would. Once upon a time Uncle Milton's farm might have been viewed from there with his plane soaring and swooping above it.

Now, in the era of Shade Creek, it had been transmogrified into a reverse fairytale with a bright beginning and a grim, problematic ending where no one lived happily ever after. In those days the scenic overlook might have been seen as a promise fulfilled. Today it was no more than a cruel joke, sadly ambiguous and enigmatic, a suggestion about something to be overlooked rather than to be looked upon.

People stopping among its rampant undergrowth seldom intended it as a message sent to the Department of Corrections if they relieved themselves out of sight while gazing upon Shade Creek with nowhere else to look. You had to have a loved one there to feel that way about it. Nature, as the saying goes, abhors a vacuum.

35

The Parish Rounds

With one priest performing the tasks of three in days gone by, not many priests still made the "parish rounds" to visit families in their homes. Not wishing to be seen either as bragging or as being a fool, Father Ulrich had quit mentioning making his rounds when he met with diocesan colleagues already stretched beyond their limits.

On a day far from ordinary, but seeming like any other with parish rounds written in his appointment diary, Father drove across a rickety wooden bridge. Straight ahead was Marvin in his pole barn pacing among his car collection, awaiting the priest's arrival, and uncharacteristically engaged in rehearsing. As Father drove into the turn-around, Penelope, expecting him, as did Marvin, gazed out from her bedroom window. Marvin had asked her not to join them at first. Osgood barked and ran toward Father's car, where scents of Rex deflected him from paying any attention to the man following Marvin into the pole barn.

Their attention turned immediately to cars, with Marvin conducting a tour of his collection, from front to back and from one row to another. He would pause by each to describe how he came by it. He seemed to have forgotten that Father was not here for the first time. The priest was content not to remind him. Instead he mentioned how his chaplain uncle had once driven a Henry J. and hadn't much good to say about it and so on.

"Both ahead of its time in some ways and behind the times in others", said Marvin.

"Same with my uncle", said Father Ulrich, while drifting for the moment out of earshot beyond the 1960 Desoto. "After the war, it was easy to be both."

"The Studebaker—", said Marvin.

He was about to say he would sell his soul for a Studebaker Starlite, but on second thought—with a priest in the picture—changed that to selling the better part of his collection. Marvin opened the Desoto's door to display its swivel-out, red leather seat.

"Fit for the Pope himself", said Father. "Well, at any rate for a bishop."

He sat down for a moment and imagined himself a bishop until the thought became sufficiently disquieting that he stood up again. The last thing he wanted to be was a bishop.

"Father, we call this one the White Whale."

"I have tried reading *Moby Dick* at least a half dozen times," the priest said, "but could never get into it ... something about whales, even the one that swallowed Jonah, even white ones, I guess. My uncle loved the book, must have asked me twenty times when I was a boy if I had read it. Of course he was a navy man. I finally got so tired of disappointing him that I told him I read it even though I hadn't."

"You mean you lied?" Marvin was astonished.

"Of course I did, except he knew it straight off and asked me what I thought of Captain Hornblower. I said I really liked him. In fact he was my favorite character. Turned out Hornblower wasn't even in *Moby Dick*. My uncle knew how it was: People are forever telling priests things they think they want to hear. It's not so much lying as wishful thinking, I guess."

This was all heading in an especially sensitive direction for Marvin. If there was a car he hoped to avoid, it was the Frazer, which, as they approached it, had taken on the grim aspect of a confessional. He had slipped right past it when to his horror he discovered Father behind him settling into the Frazer, with its glove box in front of him. Marvin danced around to the other side, opened the door, and invited him to slide over behind the wheel. By that time Father Ulrich had done what people almost always do when getting into the front passenger seat of a car for the first time: He had opened the glove box and was staring at St. John Vianney's picture on a book's front cover.

"A most remarkable man", said Father, as if he wasn't surprised to see him there or most anywhere. "They say he sometimes heard confessions sixteen hours a day. I can't imagine it myself."

He glanced somewhat knowingly at Marvin as he closed the glove box lid.

"I would have fallen asleep before I got half that far. People think listening to sin must be exciting, but let me tell you, there's not much a priest does that turns out to be more boring than hearing confessions. Sin doesn't require a lot of imagination. Now virtue is another story. Feeding the hungry, giving drink to the thirsty, visiting the imprisoned: Such things take imagination."

Marvin sat down beside him in the Frazer's driver's seat. Had Warren Hall's weather vane been reassembled and mounted on the pole barn roof, it would have suddenly changed direction.

"Marvin, has Penelope told you about her father?"

"Saturday afternoon on our way back from a car show in St. Cloud."

"Yes, indeed", said Father Ulrich. "I wanted to give her the chance to do that before I stuck my nose in with my two cents' worth. And yesterday after Mass she told me about visiting Sister Hilaria."

"While I was at the car show", said Marvin.

"Penelope is a very special young woman. A lot of kids these days, if they had a father in prison would forget all about him, but she's not one to turn her back and walk away. One day she is flying a kite with Sister Hilaria. The next, after Mass, she is peering into a spider's nest with Sister Serena. She told me that someday she wants to make a pilgrimage to France to visit the little country church where St. John Vianney preached and heard confessions. She is made of a stronger alloy than most, and yet she takes things to heart, is full of love for you and her mother. Now she wants to visit her dad."

He put a hand on Marvin's shoulder.

"She knows he is seriously ill, probably has guessed he is dying. We have got to stand behind her, Marvin. Does June know?"

Marvin shook his head. "It hasn't gotten that far yet. We're working on it."

"I will hang around here till she gets home from work, and then I'll help you put that behind us if it's okay with you."

"We need to", said Marvin.

"Don't expect any miracles", said Father. "God works in inches, not feet, yards, and miles. He works in months and sometimes years, the way things happen in real life, not in seconds or minutes, the way they happen in a movie that cannot be longer than the time it takes to eat a bowl of popcorn."

"I hope you're right", said Marvin, who despite everything just said was feeling pretty hopeless.

"One more thing before I forget to mention it when June gets home: Penelope didn't find out about her father from Charlotte Hall. She read all about it in newspaper files at the public library three or so weeks ago when she was in some kind of summer reading program. That is how God works: Where and when you would least expect it."

Marvin knew who would have least expected this.

June arrived home from Osgoode Insurance. The other Osgood stayed behind dozing in front of the pole barn while the three of them and Penelope gathered around a table in the kitchen, visiting at first about Star Island, the Great Lake, and the cool summer so far while coffee brewed. No miracles occurred, but small steps were attempted. June looked at her hands a lot and smiled without looking up at Penelope, who blushed when Father praised her.

They all thanked him at the end and stood up when he did, as if at a church service. Though it was the wrong time of day, he led them in the Angelus, a prayer Penelope recalled from her days at St. John Vianney School.

"Pour forth we beseech Thee, O Lord, Thy grace into our hearts . . . "

He blessed them all; patted Osgood on the head on his way to his car; and waved to Penelope, who stepped outside as he was driving through the turnaround. Later on that evening, Rex heard all about it while sniffing Father's trouser cuffs.

Back on Star Island, frigid silence descended. Penelope in her bedroom attempted to decipher the other baptismal sponsor's name on the certificate copy Father had handed her in her mother's full view. The ink smear would not relinquish its secret. One of these days she would have to ask Aunt Charlotte about it.

Three days later, a Thursday afternoon, Father Ulrich was sitting at his desk in the parish study when his secretary brought in the day's mail with a certified letter on top for which she had just signed. Letters from attorney's offices have a look all their own, as many a person knows, having opened one with trembling fingers while expecting the worst. The black embossed return address on this envelope displayed five Irish names, as did the letterhead within. Father removed the top page of a packet and laid it on his desk. After reading the letter and flipping through its various attachments, he picked up the phone to call Charlotte Hall.

Twenty minutes later, Charlotte took a seat in front of his desk, and Father held up pages of watermarked paper, one by one, describing each in turn: A letter from Wayne Crossman Jr., enclosures, affidavits, releases, court procedures, sworn statements to be made, and so on. Last of all he held up a bank draft from the law firm's disbursement fund in the amount of five hundred thousand dollars plus interest for twelve years and 273 days, court-ordered restitution paid in full without prejudice for and in behalf of Warren Stephen Hall. Charlotte gasped and buried her face in her hands.

"If it lay within my power," said Father, "I would sign this entire payment over to you, after what you and your family have been put through."

"If it lay within your power, Father, I would not accept it", said Charlotte. "You can do some good with it for Warren's sake. Some good at last will have come from all this."

They both understood.

Part Five

The Journey Home

Because the Holy Ghost over the bent
World broods with warm breast and with ah! bright wings

—Gerard Manley Hopkins, "God's Grandeur"

36

The Righteous

A few days before Thanksgiving, and as if relishing the perversity of its timing, the Bell Harbor *Sentinel* announced Warren Hall's impending release on parole. Young Crossman and his legal team, anonymously fueled by money from Felix' sale of Uncle Milton's farm years before, had achieved the almost impossible.

Felix' role in this story remained unrevealed, which in turn encouraged suspicion and speculation when details surfaced in Bell Harbor. Who had come up with over a half million in restitution money, in the end counting for as much toward Warren's release as his terminal illness? Who had raised fifty thousand additional to guarantee all expenses, medical and law enforcement, associated with his release? Word of this had been greeted with a mixture of awe and indignation that a benefactor could be so misguided as to subvert justice. Not even Charlotte yet knew the source of Warren's rescue, if allowing a man at death's doorstep to go home and die in a bed he no longer remembered could be described as his rescue. At most he would end up serving just a few days short of a life sentence.

But as Esther Corrigan had said at the outset, the impediments to compassionate leave were as much political as bureaucratic. Crossman and his legal team could do what had to be done to maneuver Warren's way through the latter, and to a limited extent they could influence the political side of it with its foot dragging and delays. Most of these had resulted from local legislators posturing and responding to constituent concerns that justice was not being served when "dangerous criminals" were released to roam the streets and to terrorize neighborhoods. Every such call brought about further delay as preposterous safeguards to protect the public interest were worked into the picture, guaranteeing that a man who could barely take two steps would not

escape, and that should he arise like Lazarus from the grave he would
be immediately returned to Shade Creek. All this took more time and
was the reason most applicants for compassionate leave died behind
bars.

A local public outcry ensued and refused to abate among a few St.
John Vianney parishioners and townspeople as incendiary as any arsonist and not ready to forgive and forget. At the church, among parish
trustees, Father Ulrich met this as unflinching and head-on as his uncle
in a bombardment. He deviated from Christ's parables in the direction
of St. Paul at his most hard-nosed: There were moments to set aside
the appearance of sheep and adopt the ways of goats, head down,
obstinate, and ready to lock horns and butt a few heads. This was one
of those times.

"Warren has served his sentence in a place none of us would care to
spend a day. He is coming home to die. The debt we never expected
to be paid is paid in full. We will put the past behind us and move on.
It is what the Lord, the fountain of all forgiveness, expects of us. No
less than we should expect of ourselves."

In front of the courthouse a few demonstrators carried protest signs
the day after the *Sentinel's* announcement. Out of civic-minded concern for the public good, that responsible organ had recounted the
entire story from its pages years ago, last read by Penelope aboard the
public library's microfiche time machine. This time, though, she did
not have to journey into the past. It was all on the current front page,
along with a picture of her father—no longer as he looked—a picture
of the old church in flames, and, under the headline "Lest We Forget", a picture of Clarence, the church custodian. Gossip swirled like
snow in the approaching season. People at Lighthouse Consolidated
School were brimming with fake smiles, and Jackie Rae with knowing looks. Mr. Stiller dusted books between furtive glances Penelope's
way. Larry, the bus driver, wanted to invite a few *Sentinel* journalists
into a back alley somewhere and, as he thought of it, *punch their lights
out.* June was apoplectic and actually home sick from work. Marvin
spent a lot of time with Osgood in the pole barn. Sister Serena prayed;
Sister Hilaria prayed; Father Ulrich made Mass intentions and composed pointed homilies.

For the first time ever, he overheard a parishioner suggesting he
was full of pious platitudes. He knew many of them thought this, but

usually they kept their opinions at a distance. *Of course* he was full of platitudes, pious and otherwise. He had buckets of them, and where else might they be heard, and from whom would they hear them? He was not ordained a priest to act as parish comedian, master of ceremonies, and all-around "good times" guy.

"Not on my watch", his chaplain uncle used to say.

The very next *Sentinel* issue carried an account of local protests, with remarks from some of the protestors and pictures of demonstrations. Day after day, letters to the editor appeared on another page. Most were opposed to Warren's parole under any circumstances. "Let him die in prison as Clarence died in the church", more than one said, and many in the St. John Vianney congregation were quick to agree and to think Father Ulrich had somehow engineered the parole, a feat he would have been happy to have achieved but had no part in accomplishing. There was a saint in the picture somewhere, but he was not that saint.

Father Ulrich from time to time observed that if God were no more forgiving and merciful than most people, we would all wind up in hell. He was far from certain that the desire for revenge and retribution was stronger in this age than in any other, but it seemed to him to be more evident than in his youth, when he often heard adults say, "Let bygones be bygones" and "It's all water over the dam" and "To err is human and forgive divine"—sentiments he hardly ever heard expressed today.

Ten years after the war with Japan, he was playing sandlot baseball with a fielder's mitt shipped from Yokohama and fashioned from the hides of steers once grazing in Oklahoma. It was not that people back then had such short memories, but that they had better things to think about and wanted to look ahead and put the past behind them. God would sort it all out in the end anyway. Giving people a second chance and even a third seemed the better way to those who had read Dickens' *A Christmas Carol* and believed in personal redemption. Lock them up and throw the key away was the last thing tried, not the first.

It had seemed back then an altogether gentler, more considerate age in which every child knew by heart the Golden Rule, having heard adults say it so often. Pedestrians were less likely to be run over, and people attempting to make left turns did not have the impression that a truck heading their way was speeding up to cut them off or maybe kill them. Commenting on the gospel message for this year's feast of Christ the King, he had mentioned how during the Great Depression his grandmother had left cooked meals on her back porch for hoboes "riding the rails" on a train track near her house. He had gone through what were sometimes called the Corporal Works of Mercy, pausing after each to cite an example from personal experience.

The last Sunday of the Church's liturgical year arrived. It seemed as good a time as any for resolutions concerning duties toward even the least of Christ's brethren. Next Sunday, the first of Advent, a new year began. "Who are the least of Christ's brethren?" he had asked rhetorically, and then answered the question himself by running through a list: The hungry, the thirsty, the naked, the sick and infirm, the prisoner. He made a point of gazing out over his congregation as he finished. More than one angry face looked his way. Others preferred their shoes. Several parishioners stood up and walked out.

"Everyone without exception!" Father thundered at their backs. He too could stand up and be counted.

Disagreement was more palpable than it usually was when he reminded people not wishing to be reminded. As a rule they simply ignored him. He was after all just another priest out of touch with life in the real world, which he might have understood better while cutting them more slack if he had a wife, kids, and regular job instead of going around telling people what to think and living out of a wicker collection basket. Such was their charity. Outside after Mass, some who might have been expected to greet him looked away or made a point of involving themselves in conversations with other people. The time had come for him to stand on deck in the heat of battle alongside his uncle.

The First Sunday of Advent passed and then the Second, until when it seemed as if it would never happen in time, it finally happened; the date of Warren's release was conveyed to Charlotte, Monday after the Third Sunday, within ten days of Christmas.

The next day news of this appeared under the headline "Date Set for Release of Convicted Killer and Arsonist". Once again the old story was recounted. Two local legislators and Bell Harbor's mayor were quoted expressing their fears and opposition. Only the county sheriff, planning on retiring at the end of his term, seemed complacent. "The public's safety is as always our first concern", he said. "It's not my business to second guess courts and parole boards." A reporter had interviewed Father Ulrich, whose comments did not appear in the story.

Larry, the bus driver, glanced back at Penelope, the last student on the bus, as they drove over the wooden bridge. He spoke while look-ing straight ahead.

"I don't know if you ever heard this before," he said, "but I knew your dad, and believe me, they did not come any better. A lot of people running around loose these days did worse things and at the time *knew* they were doing them, which he didn't. I'm glad he's get-ting out. He would be really proud of you."

It was the only time he had ever spoken of her father. He honked three times going back over the wooden bridge as she made her way to the house. He assumed all along that Penelope knew he was her godfather.

37

A Soul with Blue Eyes in a Bottle

"Felix has made grandparents of us all", said Esther, words aimed at Ralph's feet, sticking out from a store window.

In there on his knees he still fiddled with a Christmas display he had been setting up since yesterday afternoon. He had arranged it, gone outside to have a look, rearranged it, and then after a cup of tea rearranged it again. Having spent so much time in the window, he might have been mistaken for a moving part of its decorations. Each time he climbed out was supposed to be the last time. Each time another trip inside followed. At the end of the most recent cycle, he uttered one of those human sounds best left to comic-strip artists. "They say having grandchildren before you have children is the best way to approach it", said Ralph, repeating an old joke.

Every Christmas season since they settled in Clay Corners, Ralph had decorated his storefront, each year elaborating and expanding on the previous until his Corner Drug glowed after dark like a map of the universe. It illuminated a broad swatch of Front Street and doubled his January electricity bill. It did little to bring in business: That was not the point. Tradition and the importance of spreading good cheer were the old-fashioned points with which he had begun. Small town decorated storefronts were as much a part of a valued lost past as neighborhood carolers moving from door to door, something else that hardly ever happened anymore.

For Ralph, though, this was only the beginning. In a subsequent stage his Christmas storefront became a psychological war for the spirit of the season with the hated black prison bus. Much as he might have resented it at other times, in this festive season it became a malicious repudiation of everything he most cherished. Advent, a time of preparation in the Christian tradition, had its own meaning for him. His simmering resentment flared into determined hatred. You did not have to be trained as Esther was to see this becoming an obsession, so she was happy that his thoughts seemed elsewhere when he stepped back from his efforts this Sunday morning.

"I hope it cheers that poor girl", he said.

The poor girl was Penelope, whom they would be meeting for the first time later today. She and her aunt Charlotte would be spending the night in their guestroom.

"I am sure she will be delighted with it", said Esther, "and equally sure she will need cheering."

In reality she was not quite so confident where Penelope's delight was anticipated. Having evolved well beyond Ralph's Norman Rockwell and *Our Gang* comedy notions of children, Esther's view of what they appreciated encompassed the likes of Marvin's nephews and the more extreme cases of kids in the back of Larry's school bus. Since Penelope was the rare sort who would write a pen pal and adopt a grandfather, Esther stepped back from that abyss, but not far enough back. She would be amazed when she discovered Ralph's nostalgia getting him closer to the true Penelope, who seemed to be from another, earlier era. However, even children in those days needed cheering now and then.

"She is in for a terrible shock, I'm afraid," said Esther, glancing at her watch just as the Clay Corners town siren announced the arrival of noon. "Her father is in dreadful shape."

Her intern had brought her up to date on Warren's condition just two days ago. Prison staff were wagering he would die before his scheduled release, even with that as close as Monday morning. His mental health medications had been replaced by sleep-inducing painkillers and antinausea drugs. As far as the intern could determine, he was aware of his impending release and his daughter's visit on Sunday. Infirmary staff had prepared for that to take place bedside, but in lucid moments Warren was insisting on being taken to a regular visiting room. Speculation all around was rampant.

Thanks to the intense legal maneuvering and the mountain of money whose source at this point was only known to Ralph, Esther, and Felix' attorneys, Warren's fate would not be the obscure passing from the scene of almost all terminally ill prisoners.

"When Penelope and Charlotte get here," said Esther, "let me have some time with them before you bring Felix over. They are both going to be making a tough transition, especially the girl, who is bound to have a head swimming in afterthoughts about how she wished it might have gone or how she would like to do it all over again some other way. It cannot be helped. Imagine it, seeing her father for the first time after all these years, and in these circumstances."

Ralph found it too painful to attempt imagining. He ducked back into his store window and fiddled some more. Esther addressed his feet again.

"Now and then I have worked with adults raised as adopted children who later come into contact with a natural parent. There is always a story in it, not always a good story, but *sometimes* it is."

"We can always hope", said Ralph, his words echoing in the enclosed space where he knelt again like one of the magi and with a stick in his hand shifted a distant star from one hook to another.

They were both worrying as sometimes grandparents do.

Meanwhile the lime green Volkswagen was completing its journey. Charlotte and Penelope had left well before sunrise, driving south from Bell Harbor toward Duluth. Turning west uphill from there, they headed toward St. Cloud, eventually crossing the Mississippi River and following its sometimes frozen course most of the rest of the way. South of that city they continued on toward Clay Corners and Shade Creek Penitentiary, descending past the scenic overlook, and arriving in the visitor's parking lot in the early afternoon with the mid-December sun already casting long shadows of its cement walls and guard towers, leaving half the parking lot in purplish twilight.

In the course of their journey they had passed through and beyond a snow-covered December landscape into one uniformly gray, ochre, and umber and yet wintry otherwise in terms of temperature, smoke rising straight skyward from chimneys, trees without leaves, and evergreens taking on the metallic look they acquire in cold weather. Signs of the Christmas season appeared everywhere in the early morning darkness. Spruce trees and house gables glowed with colored lights, some precisely arranged and others as if thrown in the air by a careless hand. They drove down village streets with strings of decorated pine boughs strung over intersections dancing in breezes. They passed rotund, inflated snowmen bouncing from tethers; herds of miniature reindeer; and crèches adjacent church entrances with their upright, oddly formal figures of recumbent farm animals, angels singing, and kings bearing gifts.

At times until the sun came up, Charlotte and Penelope too seemed to be following a bright star just above the horizon to a place as unlikely as a stable. In Bethlehem it had once been Christmas there, but nowhere else. At Shade Creek, it was Christmas *everywhere else*, but there. It was just another day at another time of the year, except for a chance ornament hanging from a rearview mirror in the car parked next to them. Here was a place perpetually barren and wintry in all seasons and never truly Christmas, even on the day itself, when anything passing for prison holiday observances seemed contrived to punish further. Esther once compared it to bringing in a juggler to entertain armless men.

Charlotte and Penelope had not spoken of Christmas all morning. Its very proximity at this moment in their lives made it seem out of place and all the further away. Ralph's festive preoccupation would have astounded them. They could think of nothing but the impending prison visit, the last for Charlotte of visits too numerous to count, the first ever for her niece, making this one so different from all the rest that it could have been the first for both of them. This might seem to matter more than it really did. Experience in this instance counted for nothing.

She knew better than her niece that there was no way of preparing without kidding yourself. A lot of times she kidded herself, or she would never have gotten on the road. Today she had been kidding both her niece and herself. Given Warren's condition, prediction was futile. It had almost never been the way she thought it might be. This could be either good or bad, wrenchingly painful or slaphappy, and sometimes both in the same visit. As Felix had discovered too late, it was best and safest to leave your expectations behind at the security gate and then avoid thinking about it afterward. Throw Penelope into the scene, and anything might happen, so it was best to stay with facts as unadorned as Shade Creek at Christmas: They would see him today, and then midmorning tomorrow, after spending the night in Clay Corners, follow his ambulance with a sheriff's escort north to Bell Harbor.

"After a while I lost count of how many times I had been here", said Charlotte as they paused in her car and glanced around, while she glanced back over the past thirteen years during which she had been Warren Hall's only visitor.

Arriving at the prison, no matter what the season or what the weather, was like falling out of bed in the middle of a pleasant dream: All you could do was sit up, look around, and wonder how you got there. Charlotte did not have to describe the feeling. She could see it in Penelope's face.

She had been speaking much less than her aunt, but in the silence of her thought, words had been traveling in an unbroken stream she could no more stop than quit breathing, unbroken ever since she had come before a judge in the Bell Harbor Courthouse and said simply, "Yes, your Honor", responding to a very long question: Was it her decision and hers alone, of her own free will, without pressure or persuasion from anyone, to have the previous order concerning this matter quashed. Yes, she wanted to see her natural father.

Young Crossman had guided her through it beforehand. She was to be sure to say "your Honor" and "quashed", a word silly-sounding enough to make her smile. She should repeat "quashed" without smiling and then say "natural father", words enough to make her cry. She could cry if she wanted to. That would be all right. Then it would be over, said Crossman, this part of it at any rate. He was so earnest and said this so sincerely, he must have truly believed it, yet it was far from over. It was just beginning.

The moment the judge's gavel came down with the single firm report of a gunshot at the beginning of a race, Penelope began rehearsing her part in a play for which no Crossman could prepare her. Nothing had happened to help her imagine her father more distinctly than she ever had. He remained an enigma in the remote reaches of her mother's interplanetary darkness. He did not become more visible just because in a certain sense it was over, as far as it concerned both the court and her mother, who had given up trying to stop her long before this day. June had become yet another remote enigma.

Penelope's father had always been something like a character in a story whose distinct features were left more to a reader's imagination than derived from any hint provided by a gray-toned newspaper photograph. Perhaps the reader would be told this particular character had blue eyes, but the rest would be left to a picture imagined as some nondescript, amorphous outline, the way a soul might look if you tried very hard to think about it after Sister Serena mentioned it in religion class.

She could almost see it as the afterimage of a blinding flash without there ever having been the blinding flash, suspended there in Sister

Serena's almost casual acknowledgment like a mysterious genie float-
ing in a translucent bottle. This was the soul. Attempting to think of
her father over the years was like imagining a soul with blue eyes in a
bottle.

"Not the color of our eyes", Aunt Charlotte had said.

She could not really prepare for seeing him the first time, what
amounted to the first time ever—unless a time she did not remember
counted—but she had to keep trying. Charlotte had cautioned her
more than once, "He might not be how you imagine." It was as far as
Charlotte could go. Meeting her father would be like going to a movie
based on a story she had read, seeing there the main character she had
imagined in some indistinct way, and never again being able to imagine him in the way she had before. Had anyone asked her how she
imagined her father, she might have said, "A soul with blue eyes." She
knew that her father would not be like this in the least, and that once
she met him for the first time, she would never be able to think of
him in the old way again. She was saying goodbye forever, quashing
one vision by coming here to exchange it for yet another. She could
never go back to the story after seeing the movie and find there again
the man she had imagined.

Nevertheless, "Yes, your Honor."

38

A Stream Called Time

Penelope had begun to think that the first moment with her father would be like the instant a curtain rolled up without warning, revealing a stage awaiting her and her father. She had been rehearsing her part in the coming play, first one way, and then another, as imagined scenes came into view. Some versions left her in tears while others made her laugh, yet there was little to distinguish those that were solemn from those that were ludicrous, those that were almost religious in their reverence from those that were informal. She had no way of predicting what the actual performance would be like.

Charlotte, having come around to Penelope's side of the car, held the door for her as she climbed out and put on the gray wool cloak Sister Hilaria had given her. Much of their conversation on the way here had concerned the routines of Shade Creek prisoner visitation, all too familiar to Charlotte and too shocking in its protocols, inspections, and not-so-veiled threats displayed everywhere for Penelope to face unprepared. Yet of the two of them, Charlotte herself seemed less prepared.

Doing her best to appear confident, she tightened a scarf round her neck and buttoned a coat she would soon unbutton, while fixing her eyes on the visitor's entrance. It was impossible to know what lay behind or ahead as they walked toward a security post. Penelope lifted her gaze over the massive central compound to the distant hillside viewpoint where she and Marvin had stood looking down this past summer on what had once been Uncle Milton's farm.

Charlotte glanced her way as they waited for a guard to examine their visiting permits. Penelope had grown in both stature and confidence from what had been the little girl at Pine Shadows Campground. She was now almost as tall as her aunt and, if not exactly at ease with thoughts of what lay immediately ahead, appeared serene and prepared as a well-trained soldier whose regimen had tapped a reservoir of inner strength previously unknown. It almost seemed as if Charlotte were now more dependent on Penelope than the other way around, one of several things turned inside out before this day ended.

"Pass through!" snapped the guard, who stared after them once they were by.

Recent events had lofted Warren Hall into general view. Formerly shrouded in derision, beaten, and as obscure and neglected as any prisoner, he was now shrouded in mystery and the closest thing Shade Creek had to a celebrity. Prison staff could talk about little else. First had come Felix, everyone's friend, suddenly a friend of the dying prisoner's family; then had come the Crossman legal team, like a colony of prairie dogs popping up everywhere; then had come word of the restitution payment and court actions; and now on the scene appeared a lovely young woman resembling a foreign princess in a gray hooded cloak. You did not have to be Fred of Ed's to be going crazy with speculation.

People visiting Shade Creek prisoners tended to be bedraggled and careworn, patched, scared, and sometimes themselves half crazy. They drove jalopies and showed signs of addiction. They seldom looked better than the prisoners themselves. They did not have friends like Felix. Had they a team of good attorneys looking after them in court, they would hardly have wound up here in the first place. A foreign princess coming to visit was the stuff of fairytales.

The girl in the cloak seemed to challenge Shade Creek's turgid processes as she appeared for clearance, inspection, scanning, and searches. When the cloak was folded and placed in a locker, the distraction of two women with the same extraordinary hair color took over. Prison staff stared and sometimes whispered after them as they moved from one point to the other, to a visiting room where a man appearing to be asleep waited slumped in a wheelchair.

Charlotte faltered and seemed about to retreat, while Penelope approached him as if she had been the one most recently there and had been doing this for years. Ignoring all instructions from Charlotte concerning greeting protocols, ignoring instruction sheets handed her, ignoring posted warning signs, ignoring everything she imagined doing, as if guided by a guardian angel, she knelt before him.

A guard jumped from his chair in a room beyond where visits were monitored on closed-circuit television screens. Since there were no regular visits permitted that day, all but one screen was blank.

"Hey, that's not going to work at all! Get a load of that!" he said to another guard sitting nearby. He reached for a microphone to shout a warning to Penelope. The other guard placed his hand on the microphone and pulled it out of reach.

"Stuff your protocol", he said. "It's the guy's daughter. She's never seen him before. He's half dead. Leave 'em be, for God's sake."

It was Matt, the mechanic who had once worked on Felix' mail delivery car and just ten minutes before had come in from Clay Corners on the prison bus.

"I'm not about to lose my job—"

"Then I'll lose mine", said Matt. "Let 'em be."

At that point, Penelope stood up anyway and bent over to touch her cheek against her father's. She kissed his forehead and retreated to a chair Charlotte had pushed in her direction, too close to the prisoner according to protocol, but with Matt in charge it would not matter from this point on. She sat there facing her father with her feet planted on the floor as she had been told to have them, and her hands in her lap as she had also been told. Belying all the dismal reasons for this, her formal pose might have been the studied aspect of her St. John Vianney teaching sisters, as serene and unafraid as the one named Serena, as cheerful and stoic as Hilaria. How could anyone have known—even Penelope—that all her life she had been preparing for this precise moment? Those two sisters had been praying, and now they might have said, "Prayer is the miracle itself." Indeed it seemed to be.

Warren lifted his head and looked around from the stupor into which he had fallen while awaiting them and into which he would fall again and again as the visit wore on, in the course of which he appeared to grow more alert when he did awaken. He even attempted to smile at times as she answered his half-mumbled questions of a sort so perfectly natural and spontaneous they might have come from a parent catching up with his daughter at what was simply the end of a school day for her and a tour of duty in some faraway place for him. Not often had Charlotte seen him more immediately aware of his surroundings and circumstances and more capable of making himself understood. She glanced back and forth from her brother to Penelope as the visit continued, not knowing on which side to rest disbelief. A visit she had expected to be leading as best she could had taken on a life of its own without her. When it was over, Penelope stepped forward, knelt again, kissed his forehead and cheek, and placed her hand on his shoulder as his head again lowered toward sleep.

"See you tomorrow, Daddy", she said simply and casually and without sign of strain, as if there had already been a thousand tomorrows. "I will be praying."

Charlotte, in stunned silence, tiptoed out behind her. In the room with the television screen, as if an afterimage remained, Matt stared long after there was anything to look at. Outside between there and the visitor's entrance others stared after the girl in the long gray cloak as she traversed an exit lane toward a steel door and the prison visitor's parking lot. More than ever she seemed to be an apparition. She settled into her seat beside Charlotte and fastened her seat belt.

"You never told me Felix gave him all my letters", she said.

"I didn't know how to do it", said Charlotte, who could now see what little cause for worry *that* had been.

For some reason they were both whispering.

"He's close to dying, isn't he?"

Charlotte had not known how to tell her that either, not in so many words. Her silence now was as a clear an answer as any. Penelope had already guessed. After a further mile or so, while this sank in, she had yet another question.

"He mentioned lawyers, Aunt Charlotte. The newspaper mentioned lawyers and restitution. I have met Crossman. Who is paying for all that?"

"I really do not know. It's like a miracle." Charlotte shook her head. Behind them Shade Creek had slipped out of sight beyond a broad highway curve through farmland now mostly brown stubble. Penelope lowered her face into loose folds of her cloak for a moment and then looked straight up the road ahead. For her everything, even what lay behind her, was always somewhere up ahead.

Like Felix, Penelope was someone whose sense of time had its own unique calibrations, not expressed by minutes, hours, and days. This trait, as much as anything, explained how they could be pen pals and how Penelope could meet her father as she had this day, defying all expectations, including her own. It explained how Uncle Milton's farm

could still be there somewhere. It explained how Felix' many friendships went on and on without apparent interruption as if a year or
two or five between meetings was the next instant. It explained how
June's efforts to deny Warren's existence had never worked for Penelope, and how despite this her father could seem to have been with
her a thousand mornings of her life: He had never really left her from
the day a sheriff's car took him away. It was as if Felix and Penelope
stood at the spot where a stream called *time* washed into an ocean
called *eternity*.

39

The Shoebox

Ralph's Christmas war pitting holiday tradition against the black prison bus had spun out of control, as wars are known to do, with the village itself a casualty looking all the more dismal by contrast. Darkness had descended upon Clay Corners, where the drugstore ablaze for the season could be seen from one end to the other of the two commercial blocks called Front Street. The rest of it had taken on the appearance of the homely bridesmaid every gussied-up bride would prefer to have alongside her.

All other attempts at Christmas decoration seemed so feeble and half-hearted that Fred of Ed's, regarding the spectacle across the street, thought it bad for his business. It was bound to discourage customers whose eyes next fell on his tavern windows, where he had hung a drab succession of artificial wreathes. The single colored bulb centered in each revealed telltale signs of its having spent the last eleven months in a closet under his stairway. Fred thought he would bring the matter of storefront Christmas decorations to the Clay Corners Chamber of Commerce, whose membership had dwindled to a few ragtag merchants pretending to have holiday business.

As he stood there surveying Ralph's starry cosmos, a familiar lime green car pulled up and parked in the center of it. Two women got out, one of them raising a hood over her head as they stepped toward Ralph's door. The drugstore had been closed since noon, but Ralph had come downstairs and was struggling to stay awake in the old wooden booth. Hand-processing prescription drug insurance claims forms was making him sleepy, as were the many aromas drifting downstairs from Esther's cooking.

Not to be outdone in the honorary grandparent category, especially with her college in holiday recess, Esther had spent the afternoon preparing a feast for ten instead of the three who would be joining them for dinner this evening.

"They will never be able to eat it all", said Ralph, who had been looking over her shoulder while inhaling deeply as two pies came out of the oven. He did not see leftover pie as a problem, but instead was looking ahead to the rest of the week, when eating what remained would fall to him.

"And they will never get around to tallying all the baubles in your store window", countered Esther.

Later on, at least an hour before Charlotte and Penelope were very likely to appear, Ralph had gone downstairs to keep watch, as he put it. The bell over his door announced the entrance of the girl whose voice he had heard six months ago from around a corner. He called to Esther upstairs and climbed out of the booth to meet the rest of her.

Awhile later, he and Penelope stepped outside, where they spent a few minutes in front of his store window admiring his Christmas display. Ralph gestured and pointed while her questions floated cloudlike above them in the cold air. Then they crossed the street to Ed's and, ignoring Fred's sign not allowing visitors, went upstairs to Felix' room.

At the top of the stairs, where a right turn would take them into a hallway, Ralph said, "Wait here till I make sure Felix is presentable."

He ducked around the corner and knocked on the first door to the left. Felix, seated on the edge of his bed still half asleep from an afternoon nap, was rumpled and looking for his glasses, but nonetheless presentable. Ralph called to Penelope as he located Felix' glasses. A moment later she stood in the doorway of a room where an old man, last seen as Grandpa Albert, struggled to stand up to greet her. The warmth and delight in his face, his grin both sheepish and impish, said more than words, for which he was temporarily at an uncharacteristic loss. She stepped forward as if it had only been yesterday and hugged him in the folds of her cloak.

Ralph headed downstairs carrying a shoebox under his good arm and then watched Penelope descending slowly with her arm under Felix' to steady him. It seemed so much as if they had always been doing this that Ralph found himself in the grip of a déjà vu feeling. Felix, who had fallen in the street while stepping off a curb a few days before, had been limping ever since. Upstairs across the street Esther and Charlotte were alone for the first time that evening.

"Esther, I don't know what to make of her. It's like she has grown up almost overnight. Sometimes I think she is more grownup and more prepared for all this than I am."

"I myself am rather surprised at how well she is handling all this so far," said Esther, "but I think she is drawing upon a reservoir that will in time need replenishing."

The evening ahead was also like nothing any of them had ever experienced. The sense of Penelope and Felix having always somehow known each other transformed itself into something similarly timeless for all of them.

After steaming dishes had been passed around and followed by pie and cups of tea, Ralph, Esther, and Charlotte grew subdued and almost solemn while they observed what passed between Penelope and Felix as he took his photographs one by one from the old shoebox.

First was one of Felix on the day of his release from the prisoner-of-war camp, emaciated and back in a uniform much too big, smiling the same smile that not long before had greeted Penelope in his room at Ed's. Then came a series from Uncle Milton's farm: Uncle Milton himself; Uncle Milton on his tractor; Uncle Milton with his Russian wolfhound; Uncle Milton and young Felix sitting in the biplane wearing leather aviator's helmets and goggles; and then sitting in the Cord 810, at which point Penelope gasped and asked to be able to show it to Marvin. Of course she could.

"Any of them you like", said Felix, sliding that one her way.

Next was a picture of the old barn with Felix standing in its doorway sans the gigantic spider and instead holding his pet guinea pig. His whole life came tumbling out of the shoebox.

With each photograph he would invite her to look through his magnifying glass, shifting it her way as if she could only then see it as he did. She would look through it and seem to be astonished at the difference it made. Sometimes from there the pictures would be passed around to the others, making their way around a circle until they joined a shifting, top-heavy pile near Felix' arm. Last of all, from deep within the box, came pictures of Felix' wife and parents, including one of his father in his World War One doughboy's uniform, at which point he pointed to the brass cartridge ring on his father's finger, now on his own.

"Those were the days", Ralph observed dreamily, attempting to complete a thought that included the Smith Brothers, Dr. Lyon's, and fountain Coke.

Esther nudged him.

Out of the shoebox at last came a picture of Felix' daughter, Penelope. Ralph put his fingers either side of his nose as that went around. Esther and Charlotte were both teary eyed. Penelope laid a trembling hand on Felix' shoulder. Felix simply smiled because for him she was sitting there beside him.

When it was all over, Ralph and Penelope guided Felix back to his room. Penelope hugged him once again and stood around the corner while Ralph helped him into bed. Downstairs on an evening so close to Christmas, the tavern was especially noisy, with nearly every table full. Ralph's cosmic holiday storefront had not been bad for business after all. Someone was attempting to sing a Christmas carol. Someone else was complaining to Fred that it sounded like a hog-calling contest. Laughter and loud talk echoed from every corner as beer glasses were filled and refilled while plates of pickled herring went around. Then all became silent as if a signal switch had been thrown. All eyes turned to the young woman descending from above behind Ralph, going out the door and crossing the street.

"That's Warren Hall's daughter", said one named Matt, who had risen unsteadily from his table too late to greet her. "She was out at the pen this morning visiting him."

Ralph and Penelope once more stopped to view his Christmas display. A few snowflakes cartwheeled though the air over their heads. A cold wind tore at a canvas awning folded over above the storefront, making rippling sounds, and the wind seem all the windier.

Upstairs Esther was echoing Ralph's thoughts down below. "I was saying to him just this morning," she said, "Felix has made grandparents of us all."

The next day dawned clear and frigid. After a warming breakfast with Felix, Charlotte and Penelope left for Shade Creek. Promises to stay in touch and to keep each other informed were made all around; thanks were sent from all directions and received from all directions; and Christmas greetings, necessarily subdued by awareness of the interval immediately ahead, were now shared by all of them in a fashion not possible before the past two days. Everyone received hugs from both Charlotte and Penelope. Penelope's where Felix was concerned lasted longer than before and with something whispered in his ear. With further goodbyes, with waves from windows and storefront and a honking of the Volkswagen's horn, they headed out of the village on the highway to Shade Creek.

"I think it was Felix' money", said Penelope. "He never said it was, but when I whispered it just now, he didn't say anything. He *knew* that I knew somehow."

Charlotte slowed down and seemed as though she might pull the car off the road. "How do you know it's his money? How can it be, when he's so poor?"

It was not exactly a guess.

"There was an envelope on his desk in his room upstairs," Penelope said. "It was under the shoebox of pictures when Ralph picked that up to bring with us. It had the name Crossman scribbled diagonally across it in Felix' handwriting. When he caught me looking at it, he slid it under his writing tablet."

Charlotte swallowed hard, resumed her speed on the highway, and more than ever felt herself involved in a miracle.

40

He's Gone!

Prison staff wagering against Warren's "making it" to his parole would not lose by much. He was loaded unconscious into an ambulance. With a sheriff's patrol car following and Charlotte and Penelope behind that, he traveled through the snow-covered landscape on his return to Bell Harbor. For Warren it had been a roundtrip of almost fourteen years.

The ambulance with its escort moved cautiously along highways made slippery by traffic on light snow overnight, but not so slowly that Charlotte in her little car could keep up except by traveling more quickly than she cared to. At times the official entourage seemed hopelessly ahead around bends and the other side of hills obscured in wintry haze. Vehicles passed and came between them; when the patrol car could be seen somewhere in front, these inevitably slowed and stayed in place. Over time, between villages, something resembling a procession developed. Charlotte at the tail end of this seemed to be losing her brother again. She gripped her steering wheel the tighter and leaned forward as if a few inches made a difference. The same Christmas displays she and Penelope had hardly noticed the day before in their drive south beckoned from front yards and village crossings, still unnoticed and seeming as irrelevant as if January were already upon them.

Aunt and niece both felt themselves caught up in a dream whose conclusion, while predictable, lay out of sight up ahead somewhere. Sooner or later they would have to catch up with it. Yesterday it had been Shade Creek; today it was Bell Harbor, with whatever that might bring. With Warren free, the prison fortress dissolved behind them, leaving intact images of Uncle Milton's farm. Felix had achieved much of what he had hoped for. In the end, memory and nostalgia had won the war. When the procession paused for a few minutes midway at a truck stop near Grand Rapids, Charlotte called Father Ulrich, who would be waiting in his car parked near her house when they arrived. Alone there but briefly, he soon found himself in something passing for bedlam.

The sun had slipped behind distant forest ridges, leaving a sky yet brightly lit, while darkness settled into depths nearer the lake, where Bell Harbor blazed all the brighter and hummed with Christmas shopping. Inexplicably, the escorting patrol car had its lights flashing as it approached the city. Then the ambulance lights began to flash. Then a Lighthouse County Sheriff's car appeared behind Charlotte and Penelope with its lights flashing, joining what was becoming a contagion. Though they might have taken a less conspicuous and more direct route to Charlotte's house, something like a parade route was followed as if to maximize public awareness. A chance visitor might have thought it the beginning of a holiday evening festival. Shoppers passing from store to store peered over the tops of bags and boxes. Some paused, looking back in doorways half open. Warren's return to Bell Harbor would not have been much more sensational if the ambulance had been led by the high school band marching behind a banner stretching the width of the street. It could not have proceeded with much more fanfare if he had been a returning war hero.

"I cannot believe this!" said Charlotte.

Penelope closed her eyes. It was the sort of scene to elicit a child's instinct that things unseen will go away.

The aunt and niece with carrot red hair anywhere near each other had always stirred memories and speculation. For a reason of another color, Charlotte's Volkswagen was among the most familiar of Bell Harbor's vehicles. Everyone of course had read the *Sentinel*'s stories, including today's front page headline: "Arsonist Home for Christmas". Throw it all together, and Warren's arrival looked planned to draw attention to itself.

Gawkers lined sidewalks on both sides of the street. Fingers pointed in their direction and followed after them. Cell phones were raised overhead to snap pictures. Congested intersections in the middle of the Christmas shopping season became even more congested, while cars yielded right of way, and drivers unaware of the cause honked from behind. Charlotte was already close to despair even before she encountered a crowd gathering beyond a police barrier in the vicinity

of her house. As opposed to the casual onlookers and chance witnesses they had passed in the shopping district, these were people deliberately on hand. Many wore disdainful faces, and a few carried signs
protesting her brother's release.

Father would say long afterward when he reflected upon this time,
"They could not possibly have known what they were doing." He
thought of Peter once raising his sword and cutting off an ear. He had
felt like doing the same.

Across the street a news reporter with a camera and a cell phone
was perched in a tree. Either side of him, strings of holiday lights
blinked from porch railings as if nothing out of the ordinary was happening. Beneath him a television news crew had set up large cameras
on tripods with floodlights illuminating every paint flake on the front
of Charlotte's house. Before one of the cameras stood a reporter with
a microphone held toward a local legislator at the forefront of efforts
to block Warren's parole. The legislator was claiming his release would
encourage the local criminal element and set a bad example for Bell
Harbor children.

"I have been opposed to it from the very beginning", he said. He
promised a further legislature inquiry.

Given the sword of St. Peter in hand, Father Ulrich would have
seen him as his preferred target. Another reporter approaching Father's
car had the impudence to ask what he was doing on the scene and
then the utter insolence to question whether a priest's presence was
violating the seal of confession.

"No more than if I were here balancing a red ball on the end of my
nose", said the enraged priest, putting the reporter's own nose at risk
as he rolled up his window. "Seal of confession indeed!" he snorted
under his breath. "Where do they get this theological poppycock?"

The ambulance stopped in front of Charlotte's house, parking in
the middle of the street, since nowhere else could be found. With
Charlotte's driveway just then blocked by a police car, she and Penelope were forced to continue uphill toward the school, where they
parked on a side street and ran back on foot. Marvin saw television
footage that evening of the two of them pushing their way through
deep snow across neighbors' yards to Charlotte's back door. When
Warren's stretcher was lifted out of the ambulance, a crescendo of cat-
calls and boos swept behind it up the driveway and into the house,

where it could still be heard. June, unable to witness such a sight, had long ago gone to bed.

Among law enforcement officers, something like a changing of the guard took place as local deputies with flashlights took over from the Clay County patrol. Despite all the mayhem around them, this led to grins, handshakes, and an occasional pat on the back amid new rounds of jeering and booing and the ringing of a cowbell otherwise only heard at local football games. One of the deputies raised a bullhorn as if to make an announcement and then lowered it without saying anything. Perhaps he had Father Ulrich in mind as the priest in plain view left his car. He ducked under a police tape and strode forward through the glare of television cameras. He carried a small briefcase containing the tools of his priestly trade, everything he needed to give Warren Hall the healing and strengthening sacraments of the Church.

Not even the throng that had chosen Barabbas could have been more noisy and irrational than those all around him. There had come days now and then in his life, as inevitably arrive in the lives of most priests and religious, when he had wondered what it meant to be a priest and whether he made any more difference in the lives of people than if he had been an electrician or a plumber or a cab driver. Contrary to what many people might have thought, it was not the easiest question to answer. He had sometimes prayed alone in church with this question on his lips, arisen, and continued in his priestly rounds without a response any firmer than he might have gotten from Rex' reassuring tail.

Like all people of prayerful habits, he had grown accustomed to God's taciturn ways. Answers could be forthcoming, but not in so many words, God seeming to prefer nudges and hints to voices from burning bushes. Perhaps God had grown tired of shouting. Yet here directly ahead was an answer that could not be clearer. Here was the day no shadow of uncertainty could fall across the memory of his ordination. Here at last was his battleship moment. The louder and more belligerent the crowd behind him and down the street on both sides, the more confident he was of the role he had embraced. He knew what he must do and why from the very beginning his priesthood had been called a *calling*.

Minutes later he was anointing Warren, who had come sufficiently out of his coma to receive Communion. Sister Serena, having walked there from the convent, assisted him. Charlotte and Penelope, without even having removed their winter garments, stood alongside responding to prayers and receiving Communion, with snow yet melting from their trouser legs and shoes. It was all happening so quickly that none of them had time to think about it. No one even had time to call a physician.

Outside on the street, as the crowd dwindled, police presence shrank with it. The barricade was left in place, but the television crew folded its tripods, and the reporter climbed out of the tree. Meantime a deputy sheriff stationed himself on a folding chair in Charlotte's living room. He had been instructed to call for reinforcements should the parolee revive or drop what might be simply a pretense and attempt to escape. He glanced at his watch: His four-hour shift had barely begun. Meanwhile the talkative legislator, taking due credit for insisting a guard be posted within sight of the criminal, bantered with a few stragglers.

Attorney Crossman had fought this stipulation to a point where it seemed about to upend everything else and then gave in, having at least won the language for a reasonable time. This had not been the first time that negotiations in the Warren Hall Compassionate Leave Matter reminded him of a story his attorney father often repeated, there being no end of occasions for it.

"Is this the law, or is it preposterous?" a frustrated client had asked.

"It is *both* the law and preposterous", the elder Crossman had said. "So let us get on with it."

In the end, his son got on with it: There would be a sheriff's deputy in Charlotte's house for a few days at least.

As it turned out, an escape was attempted and accomplished within a few minutes, though far from the way this stipulation envisioned. Warren opened his eyes, glanced lovingly at his daughter, and extended a trembling hand toward her. She took it in hers, holding it firmly long after he escaped to a world from which there would never be a need to escape and to which no pursuit was possible by any authority this side of heaven. Sister Serena and Charlotte knelt by the bedside praying. Father Ulrich made a Sign of the Cross with a sweeping gesture of a blessing that seemed to include both Warren and Penelope, who wept silently into her father's outstretched palm. It was over.

The deputy in a position to observe this sad drama unfolding in a living room mirror was much more prepared for the other sort of escape. Whether from embarrassment, shame, or grasping the sheer ridiculousness of his presence, he stood up and walked outside just as a Bell Harbor police car approached.

"How is it going in there?" an officer shouted from a rolled down window.

"He's gone!" the deputy shouted back in a voice sufficiently stressed that the resulting misinterpretation in the state of heightened alert was perhaps inevitable.

Thinking Warren had physically fled, the officer hit a button on his car's dash and called for reinforcements. Within five minutes, sirens wailed all around. A further half dozen squad cars had raced in from every direction, with some blocking the street, and teams of armed officers approaching. Spotlights swept back and forth over Charlotte's house front and rear. Police shouted through bullhorns for onlookers to leave the vicinity for their own safety. Cell phones seemed to be in every hand.

"You left too soon!" someone shouted into one. "He's gone!"

Within minutes these words reverberated through the city from cell phone to cell phone. From harbor to the overhanging cliffs, everything else seemed to halt with time suspended. Only law enforcement moved forward.

Esther Corrigan had her own way of viewing similar instances brought to her attention in the course of her career.

"The law never sleeps," she said, "but justice often dozes."

While justice dozed, the preposterous stood watch. Neighbors were instructed to lock their doors. Sister Serena confronted an officer with a drawn gun at a bedroom window. She slowly raised the sash and steadied her hand in front of a barrel briefly pointed directly at her heart. The astonished officer was the parent of one of her fifth-grade students.

"I'm sorry, Sister", he said, backing away into a privet hedge.

"So am I", said Sister Serena.

She gestured toward the still figures behind her, one stretched out on a bed, the other in a gray cloak bent over him. She lowered the sash and drew a curtain over the window. Meanwhile Father Ulrich had stepped out onto Charlotte's front porch, where a dozen more guns had been drawn, and snipers had taken up positions across the street. He seemed to face a firing squad.

"The man you are seeking has left this world!" he shouted. "He has taken to the Lord both his guilt and his innocence. Warren Hall is dead."

For all their eloquence, sincerity, and passionate belief, uttered this way in the open air as the Apostles themselves might have preached to the throngs, these words struck him as strange and unfamiliar. He was sure he had said things like this before, and yet he seemed to be saying them for the first time ever. After a pause, he struggled to find other words and came up empty-handed. At least guns were back in their holsters. Then, without thinking about it, more out of habit than from any conscious decision, since all this seemed so much like an ending, Father Ulrich raised his right hand and blessed the gathering. Among the police, the sheriff's deputies, and some of the bystanders, Catholics from long habit crossed themselves and said, "Thanks be to God." Whatever they meant by that at this moment in these circumstances, they alone and the God they thanked could have known.

Father stepped back into Charlotte's house. The remaining crowd slowly dispersed. Squad cars drove away with their lights still flashing. The reporter climbed back down from the tree. The television crew again folded its tripods and slid its large cameras into plastic shell cases. Soon the street outside of Charlotte's house had returned to some semblance of its usual self except for all the footprints in snow, a cap lying on a sidewalk, a single Bell Harbor police car with two patrolmen parked nearby, and a few neighbors furtively peering out now and then.

Early evening was turning into night. Long after a hearse had come for Warren's body, Father Ulrich and Sister Serena sat with Charlotte and Penelope, who cried with her head on Charlotte's shoulder.

"I almost never saw him", she sobbed.

"Yet you did see him in time," said Father, "and *he* saw you."

A Rosary was said, not as might be supposed with purely prayerful intent. Old technician that he was, Father Ulrich had discovered the sedative effects of that peculiarly Catholic devotion, with its many repetitions. Irreverent sorts could call it mind-numbing without perceiving this was precisely the point of it: When minds needed to seek shelter for a while, there was nothing like it. Twenty minutes and fifty some beads later, a calm of the sort associated with moonrise in the silent stillness of midwinter had settled in place. Penelope dozed on a sofa alongside Charlotte. A clock could be once again heard ticking from a shelf above Charlotte's reed organ, as if time itself had resumed its movement. Sister Serena appeared to be contemplating the intricacies of an imagined spiderweb, and Father thought of something to say to Penelope, who sat up and glanced around the room.

"The Lord will be kind to your father", the priest said. "He will find more kindness and mercy than he ever found here. You can depend on it. But of this I am also sure: His last moments here with you and your aunt were among the happiest of his life. And the two of you made that possible."

And Felix, said Penelope in the silence of her thoughts as she pictured the old man when last she saw him, just this morning, though it seemed not to belong to any time.

"And now I think it time we all called it a day." Father Ulrich fumbled for his scarf and found it not where he left it. It had slipped to the floor from the back of his chair.

Knowing when to leave was not a lesson taught by the seminary, though it was one he first learned when his chaplain uncle visited him there and said:

"Life can't get back to normal with the likes of us hanging around. People are never themselves in the company of a priest. Learn to make your exit, my boy. It's a sometimes lonely path we've chosen."

Thus Father Ulrich made his exit, promising to be back in touch tomorrow.

When Sister Serena reached for her coat, Charlotte offered a ride back to the convent.

"I feel like walking", she said, and with that she took her leave.

Rumor of the prisoner's attempted escape could not be quelled as easily as Father's words had quelled the crowd. Long afterward it leaped from table to table, from bar stool to bar stool, and from front seat to back all over Bell Harbor. Some even said he had been shot and killed in the attempt. Many looked in vain for the story on the front page of the next day's edition of the *Sentinel*. Instead, an article announced the death of the paroled arsonist with a scattering of mostly churlish comments from those at the scene. Justice as far as they were concerned had *almost* been served.

Penelope called Marvin to say she would be staying with her aunt till after the funeral.

"I hope you are all right", said Marvin. He sounded far away.

"I'm all right", said Penelope. She felt far away.

"How is Mom doing?" she asked.

"She is going to need time", said Marvin.

They all would need time.

Star Island seemed far away. Having left her mother to get to her father, she now needed to travel back the other way. For Penelope one long odyssey was ending and another only just beginning.

Epilogue

Finally, brothers and sisters, whatever is true, whatever is noble, whatever is right, whatever is pure, whatever is lovely, whatever is admirable—if anything is excellent or praiseworthy—think about such things.

—St. Paul, *Philippians 4:8*

After her graduation from Lighthouse Consolidated School, Penelope enrolled in a Catholic college for women prior to joining the Sisters of St. Genevieve, the French religious order of teachers to which Sisters Serena and Hilaria belonged. Her years as a postulant and novice were spent in Paris, where she took her vows and became Sister Felicity. She remained in France teaching English for a few years before her transfer to the United States and a location nearer her mother, then terminally ill.

While yet a postulant, she received a letter from her Aunt Charlotte about lawsuits resulting from activities of Father Lyle, long since deceased. Many of these involved altar boys, one or two during the priest's first assignment at St. John Vianney. Warren Hall's name never surfaced, he being deceased and there being no witnesses. Still, in view of everything else, it seemed likely he might have been a further victim. The puzzle pieces Esther Corrigan had first cautiously noted fell into place. Others who had wondered, Charlotte among them, could almost quit wondering.

"Does this news make you feel differently about your vocation?" Charlotte had written her niece.

Penelope herself did not at first know, but over time an answer came in the form of her memories of Father Ulrich and her admiration for Sisters Serena and Hilaria. Her letter to Charlotte arrived in an envelope with red-and-blue-striped piping, by coincidence the last of Marvin's. It said:

Long before your news arrived, I had chosen to stay and keep going.

I knew of Father Lyle before it ever became public. Father Ulrich informed me when I stopped by the parish office one afternoon to tell him of my vocation plans. He thought I should know in case it would make a difference. "Better now than later", he said. He said he wasn't supposed to talk about such things, but he was going to do it regardless of what the bishop might say.

He had learned about Father Lyle from a letter discovered by Sister Hilaria, in the box with the broken weather vane. It was from Daddy to Father Lyle accusing him of horrible things. Father Ulrich passed the letter on to the bishop. He said this was the last he heard of it, and then he apologized "for a brother priest and for a flawed Church in a broken world". That was how he put it.

He quoted from a poem he had first heard from Sister Serena and had thought about from time to time ever since, something about "wood that wasn't heartwood" and "would that wasn't heart would". He wrote it out for me on a slip of paper, so I could see how it went. It was the only time I ever saw tears in the eyes of a priest. When I was a little girl I used to wonder if priests and sisters ever cried. Now I have seen both.

So I decided to go ahead.

You cannot find your life's true direction from people who failed. You follow pathways of those who succeed. When Judas betrayed Christ, the other apostles did not pack up and go home.

As Sister Hilaria used to say, "You don't quit flying kites because you can't control the wind." I have a few kites to fly, dear Aunt Charlotte. I hope this makes sense.

Charlotte herself still had kites in the air, so of course it made sense. Besides, she would not have expected anything else: The Penelope she knew was still Penelope. She could close her eyes and still hear her niece saying, as she so often did, "It's okay. It's really okay."

Acknowledgments

This story would never have been written without foremost the support and encouragement of my wife, Katherine.

It draws its inspiration from several sources:

From the teaching sisters and priests of my childhood and youth whose dedicated service in their vocations contributed to the lives of so many in countless ways. They were there when we needed them, whether we knew we needed them or not, whether we knew they were there or not, whether we were grateful or not, whether they would be remembered or not;

From Frank Pakenham (Lord Longford), the inspiring example of his lifelong efforts on behalf of prisoners and the cause of prison reform and his conviction that all true charity is rooted in the actions of individuals helping individuals;

From Mark Twain, the posthumous advice implicit in his novels and followed as best one can in the path of a story-telling genius.

I also wish to thank my cousin Karen Hilgers, CSJ, who read an early version of the manuscript and provided valuable insight and encouragement.